AB(SOLUTELY) NORMAL

NORMAL

SHORT STORIES THAT
SMASH MENTAL HEALTH STEREOTYPES

EDITED BY

Nora Shalaway Carpenter

AND **Rocky Callen**

* * * * * * * * * *

CANDLEWICK PRESS

First edition 2023

Library of Congress Catalog Card Number 2022915220
ISBN 978-1-5362-2414-6

23 24 25 26 27 28 SHD 10 9 8 7 6 5 4 3 2 1

Printed in Chelsea, MI, USA

This book was typeset in Warnock Pro, Museo Slab, and Palmer Lake Print. The illustrations in "My Sister Rafaela Is a Good Person" were created digitally.

Candlewick Press
99 Dover Street
Somerville, Massachusetts 02144

www.candlewick.com

To G
NSC

For the ab(solutely) normal ones who are
learning to hold their own messy beautiful
stories with tender hands and open hearts
RC

CONTENTS

INTRODUCTION

* * * * * * * * *

Dear Reader,

When we first envisioned this anthology, we had no idea that in the not-too-distant future, the US surgeon general would issue a warning about a national youth mental health crisis. Unfortunately, the need for this warning didn't shock us. Both of our debut novels explore mental health themes, and because of this, we've each had numerous readers reach out to us to share their own (often silent) struggles with mental health. The more we talked about our own experiences, it seemed, the more others felt empowered to share theirs.

We weren't always so comfortable sharing our stories, however. Like many characters in this anthology, because of prevailing stigmas surrounding mental health conditions, we felt isolated, othered, and deeply ashamed that our mental wellness didn't appear to be as stable as other people's.

But after each of us found the strength to seek help, we realized we weren't alone at all. In fact, recent statistics detailing the pervasiveness of mental health struggles are staggering:

- The National Institute of Mental Health reports that an estimated **49.5 percent of adolescents** have had a mental health disorder at some point in their lives.
- According to the National Alliance on Mental Illness, suicide

was the second-leading cause of death for people between the ages of ten and thirty-four in the United States in 2019. Furthermore, the risk of suicide quadruples for youth who identify as gay, lesbian, or bisexual—and the risk is even more significant for transgender teens.

• Even *before* the pandemic and its tremendous negative impacts on mental health, a study conducted by the Pew Research Center revealed that seven in ten teenagers surveyed saw anxiety and depression as "major problems among their peers."

• The World Health Organization asserts that half of mental health disorders appear by the age of fourteen. Unfortunately, most of them remain undiagnosed and therefore untreated, "impairing both physical and mental health and limiting opportunities to lead fulfilling lives as adults."

The number of books featuring characters with mental health conditions is growing, but there remain a plethora of books and popular media stories in which mental health disorders are stereotyped, idealized, trivialized, or incorporated primarily to give a character a funny or memorable "quirk." These pop culture and media portrayals too often cast people with mental health conditions as caricatures that serve a story's plotline. We want to disrupt that trend with this collection.

For these reasons, all contributors to this anthology have *lived experiences of the mental health conditions with which their protagonists struggle.* They may not have an official diagnosis, but they all identify as members of the mental health community.

Limiting contributors to those who meet this criterion was a difficult decision to make. We want to be clear that lived-experience-adjacent stories (for example, stories from the point of view of a family member of someone struggling with mental health) are important.

There are places in the world for those stories. But the reason this collection features only stories written by people who possess that lived experience extends beyond authentic representation. This anthology creates space for these unique experiences while honoring the characters and the authors who write them. We wanted readers to receive the unstated message this representation sends: you can struggle daily with a serious mental health condition and still live a good and full life. Still be happy. Still be creative and successful, just like the authors in this book. If our mission is to break the silence and stigma around mental health care, then this is a step in raising our collective voice.

Many stories that come to mind when people think of YA books with mental health representation focus almost exclusively on a character's identity as having a mental health condition—either realizing it or finally accepting it or learning how to get help. And those stories are powerful and necessary. But this collection isn't about characters reconciling with their conditions, at least not exclusively. These contributions are simply stories—varying in form (fictional prose, graphic, verse, epistolary, transcript, one-act play) and genre (contemporary, fantasy, science fiction)—whose protagonists just so happen to struggle with mental health.

Furthermore, because so many conversations surrounding mental health come at the topic from a white, male, suburban, middle-class, cisgender perspective, this collection aims to show the importance of intersectionality to an individual's conception of mental health and that person's access to resources. We have often discussed on panels how necessary it is to curate collections that show that mental health conditions exist within all communities, and so the authors in this book are diverse in ethnic and cultural background, gender identity, sexual orientation, religious background, age, and socioeconomic status.

The sixteen stories you're about to read are as diverse as their creators, and run the gamut from whimsical and romantic to speculative and philosophical to raw and gritty with a deep emotional punch.

As much as we hope this anthology provides a mirror for members of the mental health community, this book is as much for people who do *not* struggle with mental health as it is for those who do. As the Pew study revealed, even if you don't have personal experience with a mental health condition, you absolutely know someone who does. And more likely than not, it's someone close to you.

One of the many incredible things about this anthology is that every single story includes some kind of relationship that makes a crucial difference to the main character. As the COVID-19 pandemic has made abundantly clear, connection matters. Relationships—of all kinds—matter. They can, quite literally, save lives.

In a call to action in December 2021, US surgeon general Vivek Murthy stated: "We're asking for individuals to take action to change how we think and talk about mental health so people with mental health struggles know that they have nothing to be ashamed of, and it's okay to ask for help. That stigma is so powerful still around mental health. . . . But we're also calling for expanded access to mental health care, for increases in mental health counselors in schools and investments in social-emotional learning curricula in schools."

We hope this book can be a step toward meeting this call. After each story, you'll find a note from the contributor, and at the end of the book, a detailed resource section. Additionally, you can find professionally produced guides—a Guide for Educators, a Guide for Parents, and a Guide for Mental Health Professionals—on our websites, noracarpenterwrites.com and rockycallen.com. Resources are also available on our publisher's site, candlewick.com.

Ab(solutely) Normal aims to inspire readers to let go of stigma, seek help if they need it, and live their truths proudly. These stories will uplift and empower you, break your heart and heal it so it's stronger than before.

We hope you live your truth, dear reader, and that you recognize and honor others who are living theirs.

Thank you for reading,
Nora Shalaway Carpenter & Rocky Callen

SOURCE NOTES

p. ix: **49.5 percent of adolescents have had a mental health disorder at some point in their lives:** National Institute of Mental Health, "Mental Illness," updated January 2022, https://www.nimh.nih.gov /health/statistics/mental-illness.

p. x: **suicide was the second-leading cause of death for people between the ages of ten and thirty-four:** National Alliance on Mental Illness, "It's Okay to Talk About Suicide," https://nami.org /NAMI/media/NAMI-Media/Infographics/NAMI_Suicide_2020 _FINAL.pdf.

p. x: **seven in ten teenagers surveyed saw anxiety and depression as "major problems among their peers":** Pew Research Center, "Most U.S. Teens See Anxiety and Depression as a Major Problem Among Their Peers," https://www.pewresearch.org /social-trends/2019/02/20/most-u-s-teens-see-anxiety-and -depression-as-a-major-problem-among-their-peers/.

p. x: **most of them remain undiagnosed and therefore untreated:** World Health Organization, "Adolescent and Young Adult Health," January 18, 2021, https://www.who.int/news-room/fact-sheets /detail/adolescents-health-risks-and-solutions.

THEY CALL ME HURRICANE

ROCKY CALLEN

Content Note: This story references suicidal ideation.

1. AIDA

I was born during a hurricane in the back of my parents' faded blue 1997 Camry on the shoulder of the road. Papi had taken the wrong exit, and I feel like I have been taking wrong turns ever since. I was born in the midst of floods and endless gray and winds that howled past the car that held my mamá howling inside.

Mamá once told me that the rain was the sky's tears of sorrow, regret, and pain. When I was little, I often sat by the window and watched as the clouds turned dark and wondered why the sky was sad that day. I would curl up and read it happy stories. I would go out on the front stoop and let it soak me through just so it knew that it wasn't alone. I would sit by the window for hours because I wanted to wait and watch for the moment when the clouds cleared and a stray beam of sunlight would reach for the earth and graze its finger across it.

I wanted the sky to be happy.

Just like I wanted Mamá to be happy.

Just like, soon after I turned ten, I wished I could be happy, too.

Mamá later told me that the sky soaked us through to our bones with its tears the day I was born. Me dio luz when the world was dark and violent. And when the sun finally appeared, we kept the sky's tears inside our sinew and marrow. Deep, deep inside, where no one could see.

But Mamá didn't tell me about when I was born until later.

Until it was too late.

Until it made absolute sense.

And that day, I ran out of my house and I screamed at the sky for the curse of its tears. I yelled until my voice strained and my throat ached. I cursed the sky right back until I fell to my knees and begged it to take the sorrow, pain, and regret away.

It didn't listen.

Instead, when the rain pounded my back and bruised me with its anguish, it whispered for me to *be still*, to *give up* and *give in* to the mud and misery.

I didn't listen, either.

2. AIDA

Aida "the Hurricane" Maya.

That's me. Complete with an apodo that I didn't choose for myself. It was a fighter's name from years ago, whose story was rife with pain and tragedy and strength. Papi talked about him all the time. But I wasn't named after him. Coach said the name chose me the day I was born. I cringed when Coach gave it to me a few years ago, and the team hollered with appreciation when they found out that I came screaming into the world during the biggest storm to hit Baltimore in the last two decades. They didn't know that wasn't why Coach named me the Hurricane. They didn't have to know. I have bruises on my knuckles. Calluses on my palms. Cuts that itch. And a left hook that can knock any one of them out even though I am the only girl on the crew. That's all they need to know.

I don't open my eyes when the alarm goes off. I'm thinking about what my name would sound like on a loudspeaker before my first big fight. I am thinking if I want to keep it. I fidget with the bracelet of threads around my wrist. Breathe in. *I'm here. I'm strong. I got this.* Breathe out. *Get the fuck out of bed.*

I throw the blankets off me, snap my eyes open, and land my feet on the floor.

It's raining. Of course it is raining.

I shove a middle finger toward the window so that the rain knows I am not here to mess around with its company. I follow my routine. My doc says that routines help on the bad days, and she's right. It is so annoying when adults in pin-striped skirts, penny loafers, and big, sweet smiles are right. I take the meds on the bathroom counter. Mamá's pill bottle is still full, but I can't think about that right now. I count the seconds as I brush my teeth. I stare at the mirror and I remember my best run times, my favorite things about the week before. I dig to find anything that makes me feel solid and steady. *Here.*

This is part of the routine. It didn't start smoothly. There's a hole behind the painting above the light switch to prove it. But over the years, I have carefully constructed a dam inside. A place for all those unshed tears to live, beating against the cement and bone of the barrier. I always feel them, like a levee just one rainfall away from overflowing, but I do what I need to do to stay sure-footed, to be certain my reflexes are quick enough to redirect my thoughts whenever the cruel ones spill over.

I touch my thread bracelet again. It has been 397 days since I have thought about it, 397 days since I added a thread.

I grab my gym bag and head toward the door. I light the candle sitting on the side table with the keys and wilting flowers and leave the quiet house behind me.

* * *

The gym is all noise. It smells like leather and sweat and dreams. My dreams. Beaten into every heavy bag and bled out on the boxing ring's mat. I've been in this gym nearly every day since they took Papi. Since his gloves became mine. They didn't fit me until last year.

Jesé is sweeping when I walk in. He's only a year older than me. His black hair spills over his forehead and the scar that I know cuts through his left eyebrow. He must have a bachata song playing in his mind because his feet move in step with the rhythm. When he looks up and spots me, he raises the broom in salute. I walk over to him, soaked from the rain, and fake a high five, then wrap him up in a hug instead.

"No manches, vieja. Get off me."

"What? You don't want a hug?"

"No! You are getting me all wet!" He's annoyed. I love him annoyed. "And look at the floor!" He gestures wildly at the water I tracked all over the ground.

I squeeze him three times. Too tight. It's like I am trying to fit all his bones into the circle of my arms. He relents, frustration defused, relaxes, rolls his eyes, and hugs me back twice. I am about to respond when Coach sees me and waves me over.

"Huracán! Come here, I've got news!"

"'Kay, Coach." I let go of Jesé and whip around fast, making sure my long braid slaps him square in the jaw. He curses as I practically skip away toward the office.

Coach is behind his desk, looking down at a stack of papers. "You did it, mija."

I raise my eyebrows, waiting for an explanation.

He comes around the desk and grasps my shoulders. "You got the fight."

Four words. That's all it takes to snatch the air right out of my lungs. "*The* fight?"

Coach smiles and nods. "*The* fight."

I flop back into the chair. "I can't believe it." I look up at Papi's portrait on the wall with his gloved hand raised after an eleventh-round KO with Coach right behind him. "The Golden Gloves fight." I was undefeated in my last five matches, but Golden Gloves is the big time. If I won, I could go to Nationals, and if I won there, then international opportunities could open up to me. Those opportunities could lead to glory. To money. To being able to help Mamá. "I can't believe it!" I jump out of the chair and hug Coach. "I won't let you down."

He hugs me back. "I know, mija."

"She get you wet, too, Pops?" Jesé is by the door.

Coach's laugh is a rumble in his chest. "Yes, she did!"

"Jes, I got the fight! I'm going to compete in the Golden Gloves tournament!"

His smile takes up almost as many zip codes as my ass, and he cranks up his deep announcer's voice and uses the broom like a microphone before joining in on the hug. "Ha! The storm is about to hit the GG!"

He is saying something else, but I don't hear it. Because as I hug them both, I feel it. I feel something sloshing inside me, threatening to spill over. I squeeze my eyes shut and try to ignore it.

But as the day goes on, doubt creeps in. The ugly thoughts start to seep through the tiniest cracks. I make rookie mistakes. I slip and feel unsteady. *Please, please, please take these thoughts away.* But they only get louder and so does the rain outside, hitting the tin roof like bullets.

Coach is on the phone getting my paperwork set up for the tournament. "Ready for this?" He smiles. He knows I am ready for this. To him, I am going places and going to take the gym's name with me. He believes in me.

But I don't. Not now.

I start to jump rope. *Breathe. Breathe. BREATHE.* But my breathing is unsteady and I start to feel a cramp in my side.

I am not ready for this fight. There is no way I am going to step into the ring in front of those judges. Gear is sanctioned by the organizers. I won't even be able to wear Papi's gloves. I envision how I am going to get out of it. The lies I will tell. I am too anxious to tell my coach that I am too afraid, that I am too weak, that he should have never taken a chance on me, that . . .

Stop.

Breathe in.

I feel the pressure building and the way my words are turning into violence against me, trying to shove my face down in the mud.

Breathe out.

I got this.

I'm not sure if I believe that. The jump rope skitters to a stop.

Coach slaps me on my back. "That's right! This storm is about to strike." Coach was a badass striker himself, but he is also cheesy as hell, just like his son.

He shoves me toward the training ring. "Go run drills with Trent."

I make my way to the center of the gym. You can only fight one fight at a time. That's what Coach always says. Usually the focus helps me calm the ragged storm within me. But right now, I feel the fight in front of me and inside me colliding, picking up speed, and I can't find my footing. Mamá never calls what we have "depression." She says, "La lluvia vino fuerte hoy, ¿verdad mija?" Like our depression, our brains, have their own weather system. And they did. The winds and rain could change direction at any moment and hit us with a downpour.

I know that the medication helps, the gym helps, the support from my team helps. But there are days when I am not sure it is enough. I run my thumb over my bracelet of threads before shoving my hands into my gloves and stepping through the ropes.

* * *

3. COACH

Coach Suarez remembered when he saw the little girl swing the door open and charge in from the rain all those years ago. Aida. Jesé's best friend and Pepe's daughter. She didn't come to him as she usually did; she went straight to her papi's training bag, dripping rainwater in her wake, and started slamming her fists against it. She was hitting the heavy bag with every bit of strength in her tiny biceps, like she didn't want to just punch the bag—she wanted to hit straight through the leather and puncture it with her fist. Like she wanted its sandy innards to spill out and make a mess at her feet. Like she wanted to break something. He watched as her arms, erratic and desperate, wailed on the bag until all of a sudden, her high thin voice was wailing, too. He looked around and saw the boxers stopping midstrike or midexercise to crane their necks toward the girl. He snapped at them to focus on their routines, and reluctantly, they all did. He walked over, quiet and steady, to Aida. She was a fierce, crying thing. All fists and fury.

"Mija . . ."

She didn't listen. Her cries turned into a growling roar.

"Mija . . ." He reached out to touch her, and when he did, she swung at him. He grasped her shoulders to stop the attack, and in a whoosh, her pinched face streaked with tears, she collapsed onto him, hugging him tight like if she let go, he'd float away. "Shhh, you are okay. You are . . ."

"I'm not okay," she said. "I'm not okay. I feel this storm inside me." She looked up at him, afraid. "And I can't control it."

Coach Suarez knew that Aida and her mother could slip into days, weeks, months of melancholy. He didn't understand it, but Pepe had said that they felt like there were too many tears inside them and sometimes they just needed to spill out everywhere and make a mess. Pepe said he would always be there to pull them out of it, to help clean up, to let the light in. Pepe loved his family more than he loved the ring, but then he was gone, and the little girl and her mother had to face the lluvia—that's what the mother called it—alone. Aida shook in his arms, and on that day, he gave the girl her papi's gloves and said, "Then let me teach you to *be* the storm."

And he did. She was the most devoted, talented, and passionate fighter he had ever seen. She was focused and disciplined and every strike was calculated. But today she reminded him of that girl who was all heartache. She was there, but not. She was up against the ropes, but it looked like she was fighting some other fight that he couldn't see. Every time her fist lashed out in a punch, it looked more like a desperate attempt to hang on to something.

He should have stopped the sparring match when he saw her eyes go faraway and glassy, but by then it was too late.

4. AIDA

Coach shouts from the floor, and the sparring match is on. Trent is moving fast, footwork like a dance. Everything feels slow, as if I am unattached from my body. I'm trying to breathe and bob and weave and shift my weight between my feet, but it all feels disjointed, like every part of me is a dead weight that I have to shove into position. Trent throws out a combo, and I barely block it.

"Hands up, Aida!" Coach yells, and him saying my real name throws me off even more. Like I have to think about who he is talking to. I drag my hands up to guard my face. Trent's next punch lands right on my ribs and knocks the wind out of me. I stumble.

"Eh, you okay?" Trent whispers, still bursting with rambunctious energy. He's here to win.

Usually I am too.

But with every circle around the ring, I just hear a torrent of words spilling over.

You-will-never-be-enough-you-are-so-stupid-you-are-weak-why-can't-you-do-anything-right-you-are-pathetic-you-are-ridiculous-no-one-wants-you-you-are-a-failure-why-do-you-keep-trying-give-up-give-in-let-go.

Breathe. Breathe. BREATHE. I shake, angry and overwhelmed. *Get into the eye of the storm, get into the calm, look out and see clearly. These words aren't real. They are lies. They are things I don't need to hold too close. Let them go.* But I can't and I just hear them getting louder and louder and I feel the resolve of the dam inside me chipping away.

And now I am not anxious about getting hit but about the feeling of an inner shift in my weather system, like the rains are coming, like the dam is full and overflowing and the rest of me is getting the flood warning too late to evacuate. I shut my eyes and grit my teeth. *Stop, please stop, please, please stop.* And I am a little girl again in the mud, screaming at the rain to take its curse back. A little girl who didn't have her papi anymore—her papi, who was like the earth and could turn any shower into something that bloomed beautiful. But he was gone. Immigration had taken him two years before that, and then our green phone in the living room had stopped ringing. He died in Ecuador. A heart attack. Doctors said it was from stress. Mamá said it was from heartbreak. His ashes are by the side table next to the door with the wilting flowers and flaming candle.

And so the little girl had no one to lean on when the rain came.

Depression and grief and my papi's red gloves on my hands all slam into me at once. The dam is breaking. Coach is yelling something, but I can't process it. I just feel the strike that clips my jaw, then the ones that slam into my ribs and my stomach. A final hook that turns the world black as I fall.

Give in to the mud and misery, I hear before I open my eyes. *Stay down.*

I don't stay down, but I am not free of the mud and misery. I'm crying. I'm crying in front of everyone. I am doubling over and I vaguely see people hovering above me, touching me, asking if I am okay. Trent apologizing.

They think I am crying because of a cracked bone or my bloody nose. They don't see the broken dam or the flooding or the rubble still falling everywhere.

I run.

Off the mat. Out of the room. Into the closet.

I'm hyperventilating and I silent-scream into the dark. I almost forgot how this feels. How it hurts to have to make the scream quiet, like the sharp-edged sound cuts you on the way back down your throat. It has been over a year since I have felt the ache of it.

How could the best news of my life be eclipsed by this? Because that's how it always is: the depression sneaking in and taking over out of nowhere. Like Mamá says, the lágrimas run deep, where no one can see, and not even we know when they will want out.

I don't turn the lights on. I am hiccuping breaths and sniffling through a snotty, bloody nose. In the dark I can pretend that I am not an indelicate mess of a crier. I hear the knob of the door click open and I almost pull it shut again, but then I see Jesé's body illuminated in the doorframe for a split second before he steps inside and shuts the door behind him. He doesn't turn the lights on, either. He just sits down next to me.

"Five threads, huh." Only Jesé knows what the bracelet means. He also is the only one who knows about the tattoo on my hip because he's the one who put it there, when I was fourteen, with a makeshift tattoo gun made out of the motor from his dad's beard trimmer and a hollowed-out Bic pen. That was the second time I wanted to die. That was the day I added the second thread to my bracelet. That was the day he tattooed WARR;OR into my skin. The semicolon in place of the *I* as a reminder that my fight isn't over yet.

"Which is the last one?" he asks, and I point to the fading orange thread that I tied there 397 days ago. He takes a deep breath, leans back, and says, "Now tell me, what has happened since then?"

This is why I have my bracelet. As a reminder that there was a day I felt like I wanted to die, but I lived on anyway and am still here. That I have made memories and lived as best I could since that day, even if I made a mess, turned the wrong way, or felt lost. I'm still here. And that is enough. I list the things that made me feel good, proud, or happy in the past year. I list memories of when I laughed and when I won. I list my doc and new meds. I list fitting into Papi's gloves.

We sit there in the silence with my memories.

He squeezes my hand. This is something we've done since we were children. He taught it to me.

"Why are you squeezing my hand?" I had said.

"It's code."

"For what?"

Squeeze. Squeeze. Squeeze.

I blinked at our clasped hands, and then I blinked at his eleven-year-old face, barely able to see either of them. We were sitting in the dark in my closet, because I always run to a closet to hide my tears from the world.

Squeeze. "I." Squeeze. "Love." Squeeze. "You."

I giggled, because that's what I always did when I was excited or nervous and I had been both in that closet in the dark.

"Now you squeeze my hand two times."

As I did, he whispered what that meant: "How. Much?"

Then he said, "This much." And he clamped my hand so tight that I thought he might break my tiny bones.

"That's too much!" I shoved him and he was laughing and we played the game back and forth, trying to see who loved the other more.

And for years, that's what we always did. When my days faded to numbness or when his father yelled at him or when we failed a class, we tangled our fingers where no one could see, and we squeezed our hands together until we could squeeze out the world. Two palms and a promise.

He's holding my hand now in the dark. There's snot on my face again, just like that day when he saw my tears for the first time, only now it's mixed with blood.

"Why did you start fighting?" he asks, and I am startled by the question. I have been in the gym so long now that it feels like home. But I remember that first day when I came here.

Because I wanted to fight my tears back.

Because I could pretend the punching bag was all the terrible things I ever said to myself and I could beat the air out of them and I could still be breathing, standing on my own two feet.

Because with every punch, strike, push-up, and personal best, I felt like maybe I could do anything.

"Because I wanted to feel strong."

"Like a hurricane."

I hear the smile in his voice. I cock my head to the side, considering. Coach wanted to teach me to be the hurricane instead of being beaten by it, and for the first time, the name doesn't sound like a jab. It sounds right.

"Do you feel strong?" Jesé asks in the dark.

I don't say anything.

But then he says, "Because you are the strongest person I know."

And then he squeezes my hand so tight that I feel like it might just break, but it doesn't. Instead, it feels like all the tear-soaked pieces of me are being squeezed back together.

5. AIDA

There is something about my days and the way they bob and weave together, like a fighter avoiding a well-placed strike. Some days are lightning fast, playful, and ready for every win. But some days are never fast enough. They are sluggish on the pivot, and on those days I wake up feeling like life has punched me in the face even before I open my goddamn eyes.

Luckily, I have learned to punch back.

I was born during a hurricane in the back seat of my parents' faded blue 1997 Camry on the shoulder of the road. Papi had taken the wrong exit, and while I used to feel like I have been taking wrong turns ever since, the one that brought me here was right.

I am where I belong. I have five threads on my bracelet because I didn't need another one that day in the gym closet. I walked out of it and back into the ring for the next round, ready. That was months ago. And now we are here.

The crowd is bigger than I expected. Louder. I shake out my arms as I stare around at the Golden Gloves tournament. My papi's gloves in the seat he should have been in, my mamá, Jesé, and Coach right beside it.

"Aida *the Hurricane* Maya!" My name booms out of the speakers. They call me Hurricane.

I roll back my shoulders and smile. I am the storm. And I am ready to strike.

A NOTE FROM ROCKY CALLEN

* * * * * * * * * * * *

I have struggled with suicidal ideation since I was eleven years old. On the outside, I am a confident, ambitious, happy woman. On the inside, sitting beside those very real parts of me, is my depression. It can feel like a sudden hollowing out, an emptiness, and other times it feels like I am being beaten into submission by torrents of thoughts that try to make me feel unworthy and unlovable. The storm gets worse when colliding with grief and trauma, and my life has been full of both. For me, mental and behavioral techniques have helped me manage my mental health. There are days when I feel like I am winning and days when I feel like I am up against the ropes and in a fight for my life. Luckily, those bad days have become far fewer over the last several years. With Aida's story, I wanted to show what so many don't see—the invisible inner fight that leaves its own bruises. But Aida, even stumbling and aching, is strong. She knows deep down that she is worth that fight. I want readers to remember that whatever storms they are facing, their lives are worth that fight, too.

A BODY WITH WHOLES

EBONY STEWART

BODIED

My body requires too much while reminding me that I am not
   enough.
My body finds mirrors and laughs at me, all awkward and
   asymmetrical.
My body works out faithfully, but doesn't know how to keep up with
   what other bodies are supposed to look like.
My body should definitely pay closer attention to what other bodies
   are

supposed to look like.
'Cause I really want one of those Teyana Taylor, Tina Turner, Nicki,
   Badu, Megan Thee Stallion hybrid bodies. But
all the body doctors I've talked to don't really see my body's vision.
Why can't my body be one of those bodies that looks good while
   naked,

walking in slow motion or doing nothing?
My body be so regular and unimpressive.
I think my body definitely looks better in clothing.
It's a catch-22, though, 'cause I can't always find clothes that look
    good on my body.
And still, my body just wants to fit in, but poke out.

Be wanted by some body that my body wants.
My body is in a complicated relationship with numbers.
My body gathers and collects guilt in large amounts.
My body doesn't get what it deserves, it gets what it can negotiate.
My body and its trauma responses,

counting, cutting, curves.
My body cries, hides, and gets sunk.
My body is slowly unraveling
into coping mechanisms after being triggered.
My body is low-key exhausted.

My body and its lack of discipline always ready to give up.
My body can turn wounds to wisdom but somehow still has poor
    body image.
Because what is a body if not a shape-shifter?
My body is not a temple, it's a chandelier of strange fruit,
a museum of memories.

I don't always listen to my body.
And it's funny 'cause how can you say *body* without also calling
    home?
This body I belong and come home to never leaves me.
My body wants approval first from me, then from everybody.
My body wants to be a wonder but only with the lights off so

you won't see my body and wonder.
My body wakes up early in the morning only to disappoint me
by being a body without a filter or an airbrush.
Why can't my body be Barbie and Bad Bitch?
I wish my body was slim thick.

And my body be so dramatic, making rolls in my stomach when I sit.
My body and its elaborate stretch marks like spirit fingers
and random weird body acne.
And I know that every body is different, but sometimes
my body really overdoes it by comparing itself to

others.
My body is low-key passive-aggressive.
Sometimes I wish my body weren't so annoying,
always wanting to be thought of.
When somebody tells me that my body is beautiful,

my body has a hard time believing it.
One thing about my body: it's not for everybody.
But I wish my body was perfect.
My body is not perfect.
My body is perfectly imperfect and

I kinda love it.

BREATHE

This is for the ones who went unnoticed, unexpected, left out, out-casted, and judged. The ones whose inhale and exhale sometimes get confused.

This is for the bastards out of wedlock. For those who have a mother and father in jail. This is for that nine-year-old who carried a Glock to the playground for the bully whose words do break bones and those whose spirits and lives feel like hell.

For the vegetarians, meat lovers, and truest vegans. For the anorexic girl who doesn't know what to eat, for the skinny girl who can't gain weight, and for the heavyset beauty who society calls fat. This is for the high school adolescent with face acne. The gay and nonbinary. And the ones who feel like they're never enough.

This is for the little girl in me who kept the nightmares of her mother's beaten bruises, sobs, and screams embedded in the room down the hallway, and kept the secrets. Or for those who've had to hold their breath while receiving unwanted touches. Or those of us who cried, kicked, and screamed.

For those of us who have ever hid under a desk, in the closet next to the broom. For the ones who heard the gunshots, gasps, and survived death but have the mind of a grave site or tomb. For those who have bullet holes for hands, so they write with their tongues. For those who give it everything they've got and get nothing in return. This is for the nerds, disabled, emos, punks, and the first to lose.

This is for the Black kids exhausted and surviving.
The dancer, the scientist, and fashion guru.
The oppressed, depressed, anxious with suicidal ideations.
For the ones who didn't think they'd make it but resiliently keep
    going.
I see you deserving to take a breath.

(Breathe)

NOTE TO SELF

Dear Universe,
I'm still standing here.
I'm still loving here, in this body, with this heart.
Peace be,
love be,
forgiveness be,
and I dare you to try and stop me.
I love you because you're worth it,
because you're a good thing,
because I can.
There,
take that!

Note to self: take chances, on purpose.

When the voices turn on you.
When you're soggy and soiled.
When something is telling you, "You can't do it."
Your insecurities are showing, stop it!
You have permission to fight back.
You have permission to love you first.
Where you gone get another one?
Those eyes.
These hands.
That laugh match the way you walk, who told you you had time to be
    sad?
Never mind those tears.
Them, like all the others, don't stand a chance.
Wipe them
like this,
let them see you

like that.
This is me loving hard, with both hands.

Note to self: forgive yourself, heart included.

Sometimes you're in your own way.
Move.
Like time,
like worry.
Sprinkle courage.
Pour confidence.
Mix
   here you go,
   be brave.
Now believe it.
Go the distance.
Move from hoping
      to making it happen.
Change your mind.
Go with your first mind.
Love.
Even when you don't want to,
even when they don't deserve it.
When I love,
I love on purpose.
What's love got to do with it?
Everything!
Your life is depending on it.

Make rhythm.
Make clarity.
Make lists.

It only takes five fingers to push on:
1. Be positive.   2. Stay positive.
3. Love.   4. Pray.
5. Grind on.

Get out of your own head.
Breathe.
Pay attention.
Be slow to speak, listen.

*Note to self and keep reminding yourself: Don't attract negative
thoughts or people. Their egos don't belong here.*

Dear Depression,
        You can leave now.
I am aware of the energy I bring into a room.
I gotta French kiss for fear with this mouth.
        Now is a good time to say I was here.
        That's permanent,
                like hugging yourself.
                Hug yourself.
                        Mmmm, that feels good.
                        Mmm-mmmm,
                        nobody does it better.

Misplacing yourself is equivalent to losing your mind,
take that back.
Forget where you put people and things that don't love you back.
Trust yourself.
Believe in self.
Take what you need,
but give everything.

And you might not have much,
but fight for the little bit you have.
When a poem finds you, you have no choice but to believe in God.
This thing is bigger than you.
I choose me.
I choose me.
I choose to love life to the fullest.

And when I love,
the way I love,
I love on purpose.
And you
can't stop me.

A NOTE FROM EBONY STEWART

* * * * * * * * * * * * * *

I've never felt completely enough. My mother was a single parent, so I never wanted to ask for too much; I'd suppress my wants and ask for less because I didn't believe I deserved more. When I was younger, sometimes I'd get really sad and then feel guilty about being sad—I knew my mother was doing the best she could. I also knew my life wasn't as bad as it could be, and still, it just didn't feel as good as I was hoping for. I'd compare myself with other people who were more beautiful than me and got the attention I wanted. A lot of times I felt overlooked. I felt small and so many things were out of my control. My self-esteem was low, but I'd pretend that every-thing was fine. Sometimes my idea of resilience was to suffer in silence. I'd put a lot of effort into making sure everyone else felt good; meanwhile, I was hurting. I didn't know or under-stand that post-traumatic stress disorder (PTSD) was not just a term veterans reserved the right to use, but that a person-in-environment enduring the mental gymnastics of adversity from day-to-day stressors could also contribute to PTSD. I don't know why some of us go through such turmoil. I don't know why some of us struggle mentally the way we do. I'm still learning how to ask for what I need. I still have to convince myself, every day, that I am enough. Because sometimes, you have to be your own cheerleader and first love. I hope these poems hold you and help you feel seen. Oh, and your exis-tence is necessary, you're not asking for too much, and you deserve good things.

SPIDEY SENSE

NORA SHALAWAY CARPENTER

Content Note: This story references obsessive-compulsive disorder.

Sometimes, in the mountains, the rain snuck up on the world and sliced through the bright, piercing sunlight. It lasted only a breath. Everything was surprised—the trees and the grass, even the sky, which couldn't decide if it should stay light or give in to darkness.

Flor pushed up from her spot on the cliffside, not wanting to miss the brief shimmer of the world. It was the best thing about the rains, how the light changed just after. How, for a split second, everything gleamed brighter.

"What is it?" Jax asked from where he lay on his back beside her. Her best friend was still sort of dozing and hadn't even bothered opening his eyes.

"Nothing, really," she said. Or everything. She couldn't be sure.

Flor inhaled the honeysuckle-tinged breeze, savoring the way it rippled against her clothes and hair, cooling her sun-soaked skin. There were birds singing, but their distinct trills and caws sounded more like one melody than many, a pleasing song that hooked into Flor and made her notice. *Seven*, she thought suddenly, though she didn't know why that number came to her; they were all voicing together and there was no way she could separate them out so quickly. But if someone had asked her in that moment how many birds were singing, she'd have staked her life on the number. It was as though she could feel the essence of each one, as if each one were connected to her by an invisible thread and all she had to do was count the lines.

That was . . . different.

She rolled onto her stomach and crawled carefully to the edge of the cliff, looking down at the expansive forest below. There was always birdsong in the mountains, but usually it was background noise, nothing more. But not now. Now each song felt magnified. Now *everything* felt magnified.

Even as she thought it, the feeling blurred and dissipated.

Flor rubbed her forehead, wondering, as she often did, what sorts of thoughts regular people had. Why was she—and specifically her brain—so strange?

"Flor?" Jax's eyes were open now, and he glanced at her sideways. "Hey." He rolled over and grabbed her ankle. "Careful."

She scooted back from the cliff's edge. "Do you believe there's magic in the world?" she asked.

"What? Like, fairies and stuff?"

"No. Like, I don't know . . . real magic?" Flor tried to put into words what she'd felt just now, with the rain and the shimmering. The connection with the birds. Like something in the earth or the universe had opened for a moment and let her in. "Forces that we can't explain? But they're there, if we just know where to look."

Jax's dark eyebrows rose. "Whoa. That question got real deep real fast."

She side-eyed him with an air of feigned indignity. "You know," she said, "for someone who loves superhero movies, all of which rely on some kind of magic and pretty high suspensions of disbelief, I'd think you wouldn't be so quick to dismiss the question."

Jax tilted his head, studying her. "Wait, you serious, Florie?"

Flor gave a noncommittal shrug, smiling to herself. The nickname was a remnant of their childhood, and she would never let anyone else use it. But in Jax's mouth, she didn't mind it. More and more, in fact, she found herself not only not minding but actively liking it, and what would Jax think if he knew?

The thought unsettled her, and Flor felt a familiar twitchiness building beneath her skin. Before she could stop herself, she bit the minuscule hairs below her knuckles. She yanked one out, then had to pull it from between her teeth.

Damn it.

Her prescription was supposed to help with stuff like this, and usually it did. She stole a glance at Jax, but he was looking away, thank goodness, so at least he hadn't seen. She still remembered the disgusted "Ewww!" that Cynthia Tresbin had let out in seventh grade when she'd noticed Flor's biting in the library. How Cynthia had actually moved seats when Flor pulled a tiny hair from her mouth.

"There's this quote my chem teacher uses," Jax said, bringing Flor back to the present. *"Magic's just science that we don't understand."*

Flor turned the words around in her mind. There was so much in her own brain she didn't understand, so much that, according to her doctor, science simply didn't know yet about the way minds function and why. She curled her fingers around the browning grass, flecks of leftover rain moistening her palms. A foot ahead of them, where the grass gave way to the solid rock at the cliff's edge, Flor noticed a dandelion sprouting from a crack. She'd never understood why people classified them as weeds. They were beautiful, really. Brilliant and persistent in ways few flowers were.

"Dig's playing the Orange Peel tomorrow night," Jax said. "Opening for some small indie band. It's a shitty time slot, especially on a Sunday, but tickets are cheap. You wanna go?"

Flor reached out and touched the tiny petals, and she swore, *she swore*, the breath of a heartbeat whispered against her finger pads. Except that was impossible.

Wasn't it?

She pulled her hand back. "I would, but I'm babysitting the Meyer kids tomorrow."

"The twins? On the lower loop?"

"Uh-huh. Across from the park. They have a two-year-old, too. Zane." Flor's eyes strayed back to the dandelion, unsure if touching it again would make things better or worse. Had her brain just invented a pulse for a flower?

Flor closed her eyes. She knew all too well that she couldn't always trust her brain, that sometimes it sent thoughts disguised as truths: *If you touch that, you'll hurt someone. If you don't keep flipping the light switch, there might be a fire. If you don't wash your hands one more time, you'll spread a disease that will kill someone. If you pull out one more hair, just one, the anxiety slowly crushing you will disappear forever.*

Her eyes opened, hardening, because she could recognize the untruths now, ever since therapy and meds had given her back control of her own mind.

But the flower—

She pressed her fingers into the ground, away from her mouth, and sensations exploded along her nerves. Lines, reaching—so many lines! She heard them pulsing, connecting everything and linking it all to her. Images burst through her, sudden as firefly flickers and just as fleeting: the tributary below their neighborhood; the forest above it; the trails curving along the mountainside, all the way up to this cliff; the river, far below them now and across the main road from their houses. All the places she and Jax had been adventuring together since they were ten years old.

"Do you want me to help?"

"What?" She blinked, trying to orient herself. Earth, cliff, Jax. *Here.* She sat up, shifty with energy, and pulled her knees to her chest.

"Tomorrow." Jax swung his legs around to sit cross-legged beside her. "I could meet you at the park, if you want. Help you entertain them."

Flor's thinking felt slow, half her neurons still trying to understand what had just happened. What she had felt beneath the earth. "I thought you were going to Connor's concert?" she said. "And I thought you didn't like babysitting?"

Jax stared at her, one breath, then two. His eyes were the same shade as the forest, a startling mix of green and brown flecks. "Yeah," he said, then turned his gaze to the valley. "I guess. He's worried about people not showing up."

The afternoon sun just brushed the treetops, thin clouds softening it to a rich ocher yellow, warm and kind and comforting. Jax's color, Flor thought suddenly, if he had one. Her fingers itched. *Just one hair. One will calm you.*

"You know," Jax said, still looking out over the trees, "I can't say that I believe magic exists. But I guess . . . I also won't say it doesn't."

Flor's pulse quickened. He couldn't have felt what she had, right? That the world had opened briefly and revealed a secret part of itself. Her hand strayed to her mouth. She balled it into a fist.

"We should go," she said, standing. "It might rain more." It wouldn't, she could tell. But she was anxious now, and it was a good excuse to get home before the tic got worse and Jax saw.

"I thought you wanted to go to the river?"

"Maybe later." She adjusted her thick black ponytail into a bun just to give her hands something to do.

"Hey, you okay?" Jax's arm was out; she realized she was swaying. Something was pulling her, physically, first one way, then another. She felt like a compass needle, gently turning back and forth, unable to locate true north.

She forced herself to still, but resisting the pull made her head throb. A sharp tug to her left jerked her in that direction, and the headache dulled as soon as she took a step. She tested the reaction several more times. Each time, the headache returned when she resisted the pull, then eased when she followed it.

Whatishappeningwhatishappeningwhatishappening?

"Actually," Flor said, walking as steadily as she could, "maybe we will go to the riv—whoa." She stumbled. "Or maybe . . . just hike a bit."

Jax watched her. "If you're sure you're feeling up to it."

She nodded, because there was no question. She had to see where it would take her.

The pull led them down a deer trail, then back the way they'd come and into a grove of rhododendron.

"Um, weren't we just here?" Jax asked.

Flor stopped, but the headache returned immediately, so she kept going. "I just changed my mind," she said. "Come on."

Sometimes the pull jerked her so violently that she tripped. After her third stumble, Jax caught her elbow.

"Seriously, you're worrying me a little." He was so close, holding on to her even after she was steady. "Maybe we should head back."

Flor focused on the tiny freckles dusting his brown cheekbones, because if she met his eyes, she'd leak the truth and sound like she was losing it. She inhaled a sweet scent, like the cinnamon applesauce his mom made. Jax must have eaten some for breakfast.

"Flor?"

"I'm okay, really." And it was true, sort of. More than true even. With every step, her senses bloomed more, and she didn't think she'd ever understood what it meant to taste or smell or touch until this second, when the world was realigning itself. It was impossible, but just like with the dandelion, she swore she could hear the soft patter of Jax's heart.

Then the pull jerked her again, and she shuffled away from him. "Come on," she said.

Uncertainty radiated off him, but he followed her deeper and deeper into the forest. The more they walked, the sharper the pull became, and Flor had the distinct impression that their destination was close. Like with the birds earlier, she felt joined to whatever waited for them at the end. At one point she held up her hand, as if an invisible thread might exist there, but of course there was only air. She brought her knuckles to her teeth. Forced them down.

"Where are we going, exactly?" Jax asked finally, his cross-trainers snapping a twig. "I don't recognize where we are anymore."

Flor pushed aside a tangle of wild grapevines. "There's something over there, I think. I want to see."

"But how—" Before he could finish, they heard thrashing in the nearby brush. Flor surged ahead, forcing her way through a patch of thorns, because something was wrong, wrong, wrong. She felt it deep in her marrow. Jax followed, cursing as briars snagged his shorts and hair.

They emerged in time to see the final flailing of a gray fox. Flor darted toward it, but the link between them had snapped, and she knew it was too late.

"Shit," Jax said. "Do you think . . . rabies?"

Flor shook her head, squatting to investigate the reflective slivers she'd noticed on the ground. "Plastic." She pointed. Close to the fox's still head were larger slivers, one containing a white blob. "A cheese stick or something like that." She swallowed the sorrow threatening to close her throat. "It choked, I think. If we'd just been a couple minutes earlier . . ."

"It wouldn't have let us get close," Jax said. "How would we have helped?"

Flor knew the answer: they could have picked up the trash and stopped the fox from eating the plastic in the first place. And they would have, too, if the pull hadn't led her in circles so many times.

The urge to bite the tiny hairs near her knuckles was so strong that she curled her nails into her palms, jabbing the soft pads of her skin for distraction.

The pull was real.

It had led her to an animal that needed help. Only it hadn't worked right, or she'd messed up and not understood, and those missteps, those pulls in the wrong direction, had cost her the ability to help.

That was not normal. That was very much not normal.

"Let's go home," she whispered.

Jax looked around. "I'm not sure which way home is. Are you?"

She wasn't, Flor realized, and shook her head.

"Okay," Jax said. "I'll pull up Maps."

Service was slow in the woods, so while they waited, Flor did a test, because why the hell not? She turned, pretending to examine the bark of a large oak, and closed her eyes, imagining her beige-sided house. She drew it in as much detail as she could—the small perennial garden of native plants out front, the stone porch, the vines along the side that needed cutting. Then she remembered the feeling of the pull that had guided her here, the hook of it inside her gut.

She breathed out deeply, sending all her rational doubts away, and whispered, "Where?"

One second passed. Two.

Nothing happened.

Flor snuck a peek at Jax, but he was still focused on his phone, waiting for the app to load.

She rested her forehead against the trunk. She was so damn tired of things happening *to* her mind. If she'd somehow gained magical connection powers, she should at least be able to control them.

The rough bark felt good against her skin, so she pressed harder and was suddenly flooded with impressions: *A black bear, no, two, small ones, scampering up the tree. A buck sharpening his antlers. Squirrels running the length of the trunk, climbing in spiral patterns.*

Flor staggered back. The impressions were so visceral, she'd heard the pattering of the squirrels' paws and tiny pieces of bark breaking off as the buck scraped against them. She'd felt the bear cubs' breath and their rambunctious, playful energy.

What the actual hell was happening?

"Finally," Jax muttered. "It's locating now."

Flor had the fleeting thought that she was losing her mind, but she knew that wasn't true. She'd been feeling great since starting therapy. More confident. More in control. More . . . *her*. She pressed her palm into the bark and the sensations returned, exactly as before. This time she smiled. Because yeah, it was strange as shit what was happening, but she'd be a liar if she denied that it was also kind of thrilling.

Whatever was going on, it felt *right* somehow. Like a puzzle piece in her brain that had been slightly askew her whole life had finally clicked, deliciously, into place.

She'd always known she could feel energy, that it clung to and soaked into her in ways it didn't with most people. Her therapist had said that was just part of being an empath. But this . . . this wasn't anywhere close to that kind of energy reading. This was in a whole different universe.

Flor imagined her senses reaching out, trying to connect to whatever had pulled her in earlier and tethered her to the fox. Because if it could lead her places, why couldn't she control and initiate it? Why couldn't she use it to find her home?

And then a thought struck. A fox was a living, breathing creature. This time when she closed her eyes, she imagined her family terrier, Salt. "Where?" she whispered.

Almost immediately, Flor felt spun and firmly rooted simultaneously. For a horrible moment she wondered if she was going to be torn apart. But then a surer tug jerked behind her navel, swaying her to the left, and her eyes opened as her hand came up to point.

"That way," she and Jax said together. His finger pointed the same direction.

"How . . ." His forehead crinkled. "Can you see my phone from there?"

Holy. Shit.

Flor forced herself to speak. "A guess."

"A pretty spot-on guess."

Her heart beat fiercely, anxiety spring-loaded beneath her bones, a small trigger away from exploding.

"Flor?" Jax took a step toward her, his mouth quirking just the tiniest bit at the edge. "Is something . . . I mean . . ." He rubbed the back of his neck. "Today's been a little weird, right?"

It was such an understatement that Flor wanted to laugh, except she wasn't feeling so well anymore. Today was absurd. And magic was real. She popped two of her knuckles, desperate to bite their hairs, but she'd turn to stone before she let Jax see that. "Just a little," she said. "Let's go."

By the time Flor arrived at her house, she felt like a blister rubbed raw. The lights shone too bright, the usual pleasant temperature of her home too cold. Maybe she'd used too much of the magic for too long, or maybe she just wasn't used to it. Either way, it wasn't a lie when she told her parents she needed to rest. She added two quilts onto her weighted blanket, creating a heavy cocoon that anchored her firmly to the mattress.

It was such a relief, the pressure, because she felt unmoored. The blankets held her, reminding her she was in a body, that she was *there*, and not just a spinning ball of energy.

Just a little rest, she thought. *I only need a little rest and then I'll figure things out.* But a little rest bled into hours, and when she woke early the next morning, she had a vague memory of her mom bringing her a grilled cheese. She turned and found it, half-eaten, next to her water bottle on the nightstand.

She sat up. The extra sleep had definitely helped her recover from yesterday's . . . whatever it was. Her mind leapt back to the woods, to the pull and her own use of it. Today, though, it didn't trigger anxiety or compulsions. Today all she felt was exhilaration.

Flor swallowed her prescription pill from the bottle on the

nightstand, her morning routine, before remembering to take an additional half pill. Last week she'd started a new dose, the one she and her doc had agreed made the most sense when she had to switch from the old meds that gave her heartburn.

She dressed quickly, eager to check if the power was still there. She closed her eyes and pictured her father. This time she thought the word. *Where?*

Unlike the disorienting swirl yesterday, there was no spinning at all. Instead, it felt like something shot out of her, an invisible thread she could track by feeling alone. She followed it out of her room and down the stairs to the kitchen, where her dad busied himself preparing blueberry pancakes.

"Not quite ready, kiddo," he said, flipping a sizzling oval of batter. "You feeling better? Mom said you passed right out."

Flor stared at him, thoughts racing. "Yeah. Overtired, I guess."

Dad nodded. "Pancakes will be done in a few."

She rushed back upstairs. *It had worked.* Or had it? She paced the small space between her bedroom door and closet, her fingers tapping her cheeks lightly as she ran things through her mind. That test wasn't exactly conclusive; her subconscious knew where her dad would most likely be on a Sunday morning. Same for her mom, who'd still be sleeping. Salt would be on the couch. And she supposed yesterday could really have been a lucky guess. She walked the length of the room again.

I can't say that I believe magic exists, Jax had said. *But I also won't say it doesn't.*

She grabbed her phone. Three texts waited for her, all sent in the space of two hours last night and all from Jax.

J: **Feeling better?**

J: **Are you okay?**

J: **Text me.**

Her thumbs hovered over the keyboard, something inside her

twisting at how thoughtful seven little words could be. She typed a quick **I'm good**. Then added, **u up?**

Sunday was the only day Jax didn't get up at 5:00 a.m. to swim at the Y, but that meant that even 7:30 was sleeping in for him. After a few seconds, her phone pinged.

J: Yeah just showered. What's up?

Flor's brain briefly short-circuited, but she pushed away the image of Jax showering and pressed his number.

"You're alive." His voice was smiling but also relieved.

"Sorry. I fell asleep. Listen, I need to talk to you. But first, can you do something for me?"

"What is it? Are you all right?"

"Yeah, I'm okay. Listen, this is gonna sound strange, but yesterday, when I knew the way home? It wasn't a guess. And I think . . . I think I should show you something. So can you just, like, hide somewhere in the neighborhood? Somewhere I'd never think to look. And then I'll find you, okay?" She glanced at her wall clock. "Would twenty minutes give you enough time? I'll find you at seven fifty-five."

There was a long pause.

"Jax? Hello? I know this sounds weird . . ."

"It does sound weird, Flor. Really weird."

"Yeah, well, will you do it?"

"I mean . . . you're asking me to play hide-and-seek with you?"

"No! Well, I guess. Sort of. Jax, *come on*. Please. I need your help."

That last part got him. She knew it would.

"How do I know you won't just track my phone?"

"Leave your phone at home."

"What if you don't find me?"

"I'll find you."

"Ooh." His tone lightened. "That sounds very dramatic. If you come after me with some kind of dog . . ."

"Jax! Stop it. This is serious. It will just be me. But I guess if I don't show by five past eight, then meet me back at my house, all right?"

He sighed. "If you're pranking me, I'm gonna be seriously pissed."

"Jax!"

"Fine. See you at five past eight."

"Seven fifty-five! I'm finding you, remember?"

"Uh-huh. We'll see."

Flor found Jax in the community park storage shed at exactly 7:56.

"What the hell?" he said when he opened the shed's door to her knock. "How could you possibly know I'd be here? I had to go borrow the key from Mrs. Gold!"

"Told you," Flor said.

"You cheated, didn't you? You followed me."

"I didn't!"

His eyes narrowed, then he burst out of the shed at a run. "Find me again!" he called over his shoulder. And then he was gone, his long legs already carrying him around the bend at the edge of the park.

"Honestly," Flor muttered. But if he needed another go to believe her, she didn't mind. She worried that it might take too much out of her, like yesterday, but so far she didn't feel fatigued at all.

She hopped onto one of the playground swings, giving Jax a little extra time. Across the road, the seven-year-old Meyer twins and their adorable chipmunk-cheeked baby brother were intermittently chalking designs on their driveway and sprinting through their neighbor's yard for no discernable reason. They waved as soon as they saw her, giggling and shouting her name. She waved back before closing her eyes and focusing on Jax.

Five minutes later she found herself nearing his home, several houses down from her own. "Are you kidding me, Jax?" she muttered. "Your own house?" But the tugging led her away from the front door and around the side. She paused, checking the pull, but it was definitely leading to the three-foot-high crawl space near the back fence.

She dropped to her knees and knocked on the small door. "Jax? You can come out of the crawl space now."

There was muffled movement and a sound that Flor was pretty sure was Jax banging his head.

"Wow." Flor smirked as he opened the door and crawled out onto the lawn beside her. "You look . . . fantastic."

He pulled a stringy cobweb off his arm, eyes wide. "I know you couldn't have caught up with me. How did you do that?"

"Believe me yet?" she asked.

"You swear you're not doing anything? No secret tricks?"

"I swear."

"Shit," he whispered. "How, though?"

Flor sat back on her heels. "I'm worried you won't believe me."

Jax's eyebrows lifted. "We're talking about some kind of supernatural power you suddenly possess, so I think we should maybe widen our limits of what we believe in right now. Try me."

So she did.

"Wow," Jax said when Flor finished. "That's . . . wow." He spread his legs out in front of him, his shin accidentally brushing Flor's knee. "Why yesterday, though? Like, what caused this . . . power . . . to start yesterday instead of today? Or tomorrow? And you said it's working perfectly today, but yesterday it was sending you in circles and stuff."

Flor shook her head slowly, dragging her focus away from the fractional space where her skin touched his. "Maybe I was just getting used to it," she said. "Unless . . ." Her brain snagged on the blurred edge of an idea.

"Unless?" Jax prompted.

It was her serotonin levels. It had to be. But Jax didn't know . . .

"What is it?" Jax scooted toward her, like he could read her mind. "What aren't you telling me?" He was so close to her. She smelled the musty scent of the crawl space mixed with the tanginess of his freshly shampooed hair.

Jax bumped his shoulder against hers, and she found herself leaning into him, bumping back. "Okay," she said, and sat straighter. "But first you have to know . . ."

What if her words changed everything? What if he looked at her the way Cynthia Tresbin had and their friendship dissolved? She exhaled a deep, determined breath.

"So I have OCD." She waited for him to grimace or ask what that meant exactly, but Jax only nodded.

"Yeah, I know."

It took Flor several seconds to find her voice. "What do you mean you know? How could you know?"

"Well, I didn't *officially* know." Jax shrugged. "But I kinda thought so. My cousin has mild OCD, so I notice it in other people." He nodded toward her hands. "Like, you have some tics and stuff when you get stressed."

Flor fought a tremendous urge to bite her knuckles. This was the stuff of nightmares.

"You're telling me that you've seen . . ." She couldn't quite spell it out. "My hands . . ."

"That you bite them when you're nervous? Yeah."

Flor groaned.

"It's not that bad."

"Not that bad! Jax, I don't just bite my hands. I bite *the hairs* on them. I yank them out with my teeth. It's freakin' gross! People have told me."

Jax frowned. "Maybe. But I mean, I'm in a guys' locker room every day. I've seen grosser."

"Ugh." Flor dropped her head to her knees. She'd thought she'd done such a good job of hiding it.

Her heart ached, literally—there were actual pains. But then . . . Jax had known the whole time and it hadn't bothered him at all. He'd never even brought it up.

She fought the urge to throw her arms around him. She should have trusted him. She should have known he wasn't a bit like Cynthia Tresbin.

Flor met Jax's kind eyes, the ones she realized were always watching out for her. The ones that, sometime between when they were ten and now, had turned kind of beautiful.

As she stared at him, another realization clicked into place.

"I started a new OCD medication!"

Jax nodded. "Okay."

"No, listen. Last week was my first time at the higher dose, and it usually takes a week for my body to feel the adjustment in serotonin levels. I think the powers started because my serotonin levels are optimized now!"

"Wait. So that means . . ." Jax's eyes brightened as he understood. "You have this power because of your brain chemistry?"

"It makes sense! It even fits with why the pull didn't work as well yesterday. My body hadn't fully acclimated to the new dose."

"So you're finally on the right dosage of the right medicine for you." Jax shook his head. "Wow. My cousin said he felt like a new person when he got on medicine, but I'm pretty sure he didn't have a latent superpower."

"It's not a *super*power," Flor said. "It's just, you know . . ."

"What? A regular power? Magic? Because that's what a superpower is, technically."

"Or it's science," Flor said. "It has to be some kind of science, right?"

"Just science we don't understand yet?"

"Exactly."

"So, magic."

Flor rolled her eyes before closing them. There was so much energy, everywhere, and she suspected that with some practice, she could open herself to all of it. She reached out with her senses—she was already getting better at controlling them—and new vibrations, soft and rippling, pulsed into her consciousness. *Plants.* There: a tree two houses over, its huge roots entwining eighteen feet underground. There: two streets up from them, a whole garden of flowers and shrubs, each with its own unique flicker. The grass beneath her, buried bulbs, weeds—all of them she could separate out and feel if she wanted to, and the way they connected. The way they connected to her.

She *had* felt a pulse in the dandelion.

She opened her eyes, slowly letting her senses dull back to normal. It was a lot to take in, but she knew she was barely scratching the surface of what might be possible. "Okay," she said, eyes sliding to Jax. "Maybe magic."

He was watching her, staring at her the way she sometimes stared at the sky after the rains.

"You were using it just now, weren't you?" he asked.

She nodded.

"What's it like?"

"I guess . . . it's like I'm expanding. Like I can feel the heartbeat of everything around me, even plants and stuff."

Jax straightened. "Could you feel my heartbeat? From there?"

Flor felt her face flush. "I mean, probably. If I concentrated."

"Try," he said.

She gave him a questioning look before closing her eyes and homing in on him. It took a few moments since she was nervous, but then she had it. She tapped its rhythm against her knee, a quick *da-dah, da-dah, da-dah.*

"Shit," Jax said.

Flor opened her eyes. "Is that it?"

"Keep tapping." Jax's fingers were on the pulse point of his neck. He reached out and took the wrist of Flor's nontapping hand and placed her fingers on the other side of his neck. She felt the soft beat there, pulsing in perfect time to her own rhythm.

"This is amazing, Flor," he said. "And maybe just a tiny bit scary."

Flor barely breathed as she took in how close they were, his hand on her wrist, her fingers on his neck, her knees on either side of his leg so she could reach him. Jax's eyes strayed to her mouth.

And then something jerked her, tugged at her gut so sharply it made her gasp.

"Is it happening?" Jax asked. "You feel something?"

"Yes. Something's wrong." She jumped up. "Really wrong."

"What can I do?" he said, but Flor was already running.

The pull was furious, twice as hard as the fox's had been, and Flor felt a pulse flickering, trying to keep steady. "Shit," she breathed, and pushed herself harder. She ran down the bottom loop of the neighborhood and past the park, then vaulted over the wooden fence that separated the houses from a small tributary, which ran parallel to the main road and disappeared underneath it before spilling into the river on the other side. It was wooded down here, too. The neighborhood kids would often come to catch salamanders or look for crawfish. Sometimes she took the Meyers—

Oh no. Oh no, no, no.

The pull intensified, and Flor knew it wasn't an animal this time. She crashed through a patch of brush, following the laser-straight thread in her mind. She was close, so close now. She jumped a fallen tree and landed right on the bank. At first she didn't see anything. Then the pull tugged her down, and she saw a small head bobbing, a hand splashing frantically at the water's surface.

"Zane!" she screamed, and barreled into the water. Most of the tributary was shallow, but Zane was so little, and his foot had lodged between the rocks. Flor heaved him free just as Jax met them on the bank.

"It's okay, Zane," Flor said, holding him tight against her chest. "You're okay now. You're okay."

Water streamed out of Zane's mouth in coughs and gags, finally giving him enough air to cry. "It's okay," Flor repeated. "You're safe now, you're safe." She bounced him gently and he wrapped his small arms tight around her neck, sobbing. "Let's take you home."

Flor slipped away from Zane's parents, whom they'd found frantically searching the park, as soon as possible. Zane's mom had burst into tears when Jax explained where Flor had found Zane, and she kept squeezing Flor and thanking her. Flor wasn't as light-headed as the day before, but she still couldn't handle the commotion. Plus, she was desperately hungry. Which was how, fifteen minutes later, she and Jax ended up on the bench swing beneath her back deck, eating leftover blueberry pancakes like nothing significant had happened.

"You okay?" Jax asked after Flor had devoured her third pancake without a word. He gently rocked the swing with one foot, his other leg curled underneath him.

"Yeah," she said. "That was just . . ."

"Intense?"

She nodded.

"Tell me about it." He paused before adding, "You have your own spidey sense, Flor. It's amazing. You're basically Spider-Man."

She laughed, grateful for Jax for the millionth time that day. "If I'm Spider-Man," she teased, "what does that make you? Mary Jane?"

Jax's smile vanished, the easy energy between them suddenly taut and tense, and Flor realized immediately she'd made a mistake. Both of them knew exactly what MJ was to Spider-Man: everything.

"I didn't mean—" she tried, but Jax shook his head, mortification plain on his face, and the words died on her tongue. He put both feet solidly on the ground, stopping the swing. Any moment he was going to leave, explain that she was a great person but he didn't feel that way about her, that they could still be friends although of course their friendship would never be the same and why couldn't her power have been to rewind time?

"Actually," Jax said slowly, "in that analogy, I think I might be Spider-Man."

Flor's brain ran rapid-fire through all the possible meanings of his statement. "What do you mean?"

Jax worked his jaw. "Spider-Man is the one too afraid to tell MJ what she means to him." He glanced sidelong at her. "At least at first."

She wasn't even trying to sense Jax's heartbeat when it came to her, pounding fierce and fast and perfect. She reached out and touched the soft spot beneath his jaw. He let her, watching her every movement.

"In this scenario," she said quietly, "I'm okay being MJ."

Jax's pulse intensified, and he turned his cheek toward her hand, the edge of his lips catching her fingertip.

"Can I kiss you?" he asked. "I've wanted to kiss you for, like, two years."

Flor wished he could feel the joy explode out of her, the way she felt their energy entwining, tangling, and strengthening into something bigger than both of them.

She'd just have to show him. Her hand slipped behind his neck, and she brought his beautiful mouth to hers.

A NOTE FROM NORA SHALAWAY CARPENTER
✻ ✻ ✻ ✻ ✻ ✻ ✻ ✻ ✻ ✻ ✻ ✻ ✻ ✻ ✻ ✻ ✻ ✻ ✻

The use of medicine to assist with mental health struggles is a personal decision for everyone. For me, combining medicine with cognitive behavioral therapy quite literally saved my life. At one point in time, the combination of trauma, undiagnosed PTSD, and severe OCD rendered me almost nonfunctional, and I thought—no, I was certain—that I would never resurface from the whirlpool of despair in which I found myself drowning. For months I resisted medicine. Then I became pregnant.

Despite the assurances of several doctors that the prescription and dose of medication offered me the safest and best path forward for both me and my son, I couldn't stand the thought of potentially endangering my baby because I wasn't "strong" enough to endure what was happening to me. Finally, I realized I couldn't go on as things were, and I started medication. I wrote "Spidey Sense" to reflect the euphoric sensation of finding the correct dose of the correct medicine. I had my life back, my self back, and that was magic in itself. For information on OCD, visit the Resources section at the end of this book.

NOTHING FEELS NO PAIN

SONIA PATEL

*Content Note: This story references cutting
and post-traumatic stress disorder.*

My name is Vijali Shah-Nielsen and I hate the sun, which sucks since I live in Hawai'i. If only I had the luxury of being a teenage vampire dormant in her coffin until nightfall, then things would be easier. But it's all good. This half-Indian, half-white girl with short henna-red matted hair, which everyone calls locs but are actually jaṭā, has forged another existence as a reggae cave dweller. The reggae: the thick and heavy Bob Marley bass lines me and my Fender J create. The cave: my dimly lit room.

There are only two reasons I *choose* to emerge from the refuge of my cave. First, to chill with my girlfriend, Nari. Second, for the band. Over the summer, a bunch of Polynesian guys, all recent grads from my high school, asked me to join their Bob Marley cover band. I couldn't say yes fast enough—not to the big brown brothers who promised to "hold it down for their lil sistah" but to the only man I really trust, Bob, even though he's dead. His brilliant lyrics of peace, love, and freedom shine down onto my tortured soul like safe sunbeams. I feel bad for the band's previous bass player, who "went schizo" after vaping some potent THC oil, punched his neighbor, and got locked up in OCCC. I get that he assaulted someone, but since when is going mental a crime? Shouldn't the cops have taken him to Kekela, the adult psych ward, instead of prison? But what do I know?

Anyway, every other time I emerge from my cave it's because I *have* to. Like for school. Or to run boring errands for my mom. Or, the worst, to meet one of her new boyfriends. Obviously those horndogs are only after one thing from my Indian immigrant mom, who presents herself to the online dating community not with mythical model minority ostentation but rather with the username KamaSutraQueen atop a seductive profile photo.

I'm not supposed to know about Mom's online man hunting. But then she shouldn't leave her phone to charge overnight in the kitchen. I mean, come on, she knows I've got a chronic case of late-night munchies, and it's not because I'm stoned. So obviously I'll have first eyes on the wee-hour meetup notifications blowing up her screen like illegal New Year's Eve fireworks—

Hold up. Speaking of Mom and the phone, she just texted me.

Mom: Lunch with us. 12. Waikele food trucks.

I groan at *us*. No doubt *us* is Mom and a new boyfriend.

Fuck.

For the millionth time, I wonder why Mom insists on me meeting her new boy toys. Even though she talks more to them than she talks to me, it's not as if they're ever around that long. And the thought of having lunch with one of them feels about as logical as a sheep purposefully straying from the flock to hang out with a ravenous wolf.

I'm not a sheep. But I'm also not a bastard who'll flake out on Mom.

The one time I didn't show up to meet the him-of-the-month, because Nari and I had missed the bus home from town, Mom gave me an earful later. *I don't ask for much, Vij. After all I've done for you, why do you break my heart like this?*

My Indian mom's guilt trip isn't about me becoming a doctor or engineer or marrying a suitable Indian boy and having perfect babies; it's to parade around for her latest simp like a circus act.

Pissed off, I stuff my tank-topped self into a hoodie, grab my backpack, then emerge. Take the bus to Waikele, the open-air premium outlet shopper's paradise. Arrive at noon.

As I stand on the curb behind Saks Off 5th, the sun pelts me with rays like hot hail. The healed cuts on my arms sizzle under my long sleeves. My shadow seems to melt into an oily stain on the burning asphalt.

Some might say today's sun is a perfect yolk in the ultramarine Oʻahu sky. I say it's the flaming Eye of Sauron. And the parking lot leading to the food trucks might as well be the fiery Mount Doom.

Hands in my pockets, I schlep toward Mom and the bald white guy who's cupping her ass.

Gross.

My scars tingle in a not-good way. I wish I were back in the lovely dark of my cave.

I force myself to keep going. Heat rises from the blacktop. It's hot. So hot. The sun morphs into an anaconda, and its golden body slithers down from its sky lair to coil around me. Squeezing, it whispers, *There's no escape.*

Sweat runs down my back. "Crazy Baldhead" blares from my AirPods. It gets itchy under my jaṭā. My fingers wiggle and stretch, jonesing to fall behind the beat on some flatwound strings.

When I'm finally standing in front of them, Mom asks, "Where's your other half?" She speaks in English with an Indian accent as if I don't understand Gujarati. All for Baldie's sake.

I double tap my AirPods to pause Bob. "She's not mine or a half," I say, moving a little to the right so that a telephone pole blocks out the harsh sun. The shade emboldens me. I cross my arms, making sure my long sleeves don't pull away from my wrists, then add, "You're the one with other halves."

Facts.

I'm pretty sure that Mom's revolving door of other halves commenced twelve years ago, when a judge approved the permanent restraining order on Dad "for being a danger to his child." I found the paperwork one night a few years ago.

How was Dad a danger to me? Paperwork in hand, I asked Mom. "Neglect" was all she said, and still says.

Sometimes I stare at Dad's photo, the only one I have of him, which I keep tucked away in my bass guitar bag. Can't look at his face for too long, though, because otherwise it feels like his lapis eyes are Bunsen burners on full blast, scorching me.

Back in the parking lot, Mom puts her hands up. "Well, excuse me." She tucks her long wavy hair behind her ears. She elbows Baldie as she leans into him. "Nari is my daughter's first girlfriend," she loud-whispers, moving her eyebrows up and down.

Baldie chuckles.

I frown.

I don't appreciate when Mom talks about Nari, or anything else about me, to these guys.

I slip my hand under my long sleeve and move my fingertips over a keloid left to right as if I'm reading braille, a memory etched in skin. This raised scar is from six months ago, when I cut a little too deep. Had to after Nari's two-timing Instagram story. There for everyone to see was Nari kissing Kimi at Makaha.

I had DM'd Nari right away.

Me: Why?

N: It's not a big deal.

Me: It's cuz I won't go to the beach, right?

Nari didn't respond until the next day. And it wasn't with an answer—it was with an invite to get boba.

But in the witching hours before boba, it felt like I was on the banks of the Ganges being forced to throw myself onto a burning funeral pyre. I didn't want to burn to death in a lesbian sati, so I stood under the air conditioner. But the adrenaline kept pumping through my veins. The pressure kept building. Something had to give or I'd explode like Mom's pressure cooker flinging lentils and veggies everywhere.

That was when a sliver of the remaining virgin skin on my arm prickled with crazed bloodlust, not for the sake of being murdered or maimed but for the guarantee of calm and relief . . .

Mom clears her throat. "Vijali, I'd like you to meet Jake," she says.

It takes everything in me not to arch my back, hiss, and claw at him when he smiles and thrusts out a hand.

The sneaky sun shifts and finds me.

I fan my hoodie with one hand and force my other hand up for the obligatory shake.

"Nice to meet you, Vij," Jake says. His moist, fleshy palm squishes against mine.

I yank my hand away, staring at him. Only Mom and Nari are allowed to call me Vij. "It's Vijali," I say, leaving out *until you prove yourself, which you never will because Mom will replace you by next week.*

Jake's smile vanishes.

Mom touches his arm and says, "Vijali means electricity in Gujarati, and aakash vijali means sky electricity or lightning. She's proud of her name."

I exhale a frustrated breath.

The sun burrows into my gut and begins reverse-melting me. I don't want to go out like that—a pool of sludge—in front of this unworthy dude. So I take cover behind the near future I invent that instant—skip lunch with these fools and meet up with Nari instead.

Beautiful Nari.

Ever since boba, we've been good. She didn't exactly apologize—I just let it go. I didn't want to fight. I didn't want to lose her.

The first time I saw Nari was at Kawaii Kon in the spring as she was being awarded first place in the cosplay contest. The shape-shifting headhunter in barely-there metallic armor stepped off the stage, grabbed my hand, and together we began trying to slay our demons. Turns out we both had dad demons. Hers: the spawn of her slick, cheater dad. Mine: the ghost of a vanished dad.

Nari's full name, Kaminari, means thunder in Japanese . . .

"Vijali it is," Jake mutters, his expression smug.

I smile to myself, picturing aakash vijali forking down to smite him, and then a couple of seconds later, kaminari cracking up in delight.

Jake unfolds the glossy Godiva paper bag he's holding. He plucks out a gigantic chocolate-covered strawberry. "Want one, *Prem?*" he asks Mom, but he's squinting at me. The right corner of his mouth lifts to gloat.

I remain unaffected. *So what if Mom lets you chop her magnificent Indian name that means "full of love"? Wait and see—Premila's full love will always elude you, the way it eludes everyone.*

Mom's shaking her head. "I told you already in the store, Jake," she says.

"What?" he asks.

"Nothing with added sugar," she says.

I smirk at Jake. *Not so easy, is it, dating an addict whose sobriety also includes the sweet white stuff that makes food fun?*

Jake shrugs. "Suit yourself," he says. He offers the decadent treat to me.

I don't want to want it, but there's something about a strawberry almost the size of half a human heart that's irresistible. "Thanks," I say, accepting it.

I bite into it. There's an initial crunch followed by a burst of juicy sweetness in my mouth.

While Mom and Jake debate over lunch options—pancit, tacos, or laulau—I slowly chew on the luscious strawberry. How can it possibly taste this perfect?

Something stirs inside me.

Strawberry sweet turns sour.

My hand drifts to my throat, which suddenly feels swollen. I don't eat strawberries often, but I'm not allergic to them. Why is this happening?

Then my chest tightens—beyond that of the binder I'm wearing.

Can't get enough air.

Am I dying?

I don't want to die.

Why aren't Mom and Jake noticing my desperate attempts to gulp air?

I blink.

Everything goes back to normal. My breath slides in and out.

But I spit out the mouthful of mashed-up strawberry, totally freaked.

"I gotta go," I say, tossing the rest of the poisonous treat into a nearby trash can. I pivot on my heels before Mom and Jake can react, my thumbs already pounding out a text to Nari: **Can you meet?**

The bus is a jumbo cradle and the wheels bumping over Kamehameha Highway gently rock me. AirPods in my ears, Bob Marley croons one of his final gifts to the world before he died—"Redemption Song."

A soft breath frees itself from between my cracked lips.

I'm okay. I can get myself to okay all by myself.

I stare out the window at the trees and houses that sail by. At the passing shops and restaurants and people . . .

All the people.

But I don't need people.

I don't need anyone, I shouldn't need anyone, though sometimes I don't want to be alone. Sometimes being alone is scary. Even physically painful. It's a burning pain, like someone has poured kerosene on my nerves, then tossed a lighter . . .

I look at my empty hands—they begin aching, this time not with the desire to play bass but with an urgent longing to be held.

Lucky for me, Nari will be holding my hands soon.

Bob keeps prophesying.

I reach into my backpack, bring out my sketchbook. The tattered cover between my fingers is a balm. The spine makes a sound like a bone being broken when I open to the first page—Nari drawn in thin black lines and curves, shadows and light. Her merciless eyes take me in and don't let go.

I turn the page. Jerky strokes of our shady picnic at Kapiʻolani Park. My own matted hair, dangling like the hanging banyan roots behind us, covers my face. Nari's looking at me, her expression deliberate. *I still see you.*

My eyes shift to the adjacent page. Thick outlines in the shape of Oʻahu and Kauaʻi on the canvas of Nari's décolletage—the hickeys I gave her the first time we made out.

That afternoon, the mellow groove of "Sun Is Shining" floated out of my Bluetooth speaker while Nari and I stirred it up in the shade of a lush tree.

Only when the awful sun sent its ray piercing through the branches did I unsuction my mouth from Nari and look. "Oh, shit, sorry," I said as soon as I noticed the second hickey to the right of the first.

Nari opened her eyes, her fingers emerging from my jaṭā. "What?" she asked, breathy, leaning on her elbows.

I pointed to the pair of reddish marks on the pale skin above and between her cleavage.

She looked. She raised an eyebrow and a corner of her lips. "Such passion, Vij," she said, the gold flecks in her green eyes flashing like streaks of brilliant light on a stormy evening.

I smiled. When Nari slashed my name, it sounded so BOOM. "Your ex–boy toys should take notes," I said with a wink.

Then Nari traced the outlines of the love bites. "Those boys were my mistake, but you . . ." she whispered, twirling a lock of her long red hair.

The sun tiptoed to the left and pounced on us.

Nari glared at the sky. "Damn you, sun," she said. "Vij hates you, so leave her alone!"

I basked in her understanding, and in the cool trade winds . . .

I turn the page. In the corner, I'm melting into a puddle while a larger-than-life Nari attempts to block out the sun, her owl eyes all-seeing.

My phone chimes.

I blink, then check the text.

Mom: Are you ok?

Me: Yes.

Mom: What happened?

Me: Nothing. Had plans with Nari so I left.

Mom: Sure you don't have a fever? You looked flushed.

My thumbs flail for a second. So what if Mom's a nurse and it's her job to check on people when they're sick? I don't want her to check on me. Not anymore.

Me: No fever.

Mom: That's good. BTW, Jake

She sent her reply without finishing, and an ellipsis bubble tells me that she's typing the rest.

Before she can finish it, my thumbs smash and send: **GTG**

My preemptive strike against any possible guilt trip. And, fuck Jake.

An hour with Nari at Central Oʻahu Regional Park roars by like the motorcycle clubs sometimes do on the nearby highway.

We slide over to a shadier spot against the thick tree trunk.

Nari leans in, kisses me softly. She pulls her lips away. "Are you okay?" she asks.

Our foreheads are touching.

"With you, always," I say. Then I lick my lips. The lingering taste of her guava lip gloss is a natural upper. The only drug for me. I don't even vape or smoke cigarettes or pakalolo like my bandmates. Not because I walk on some moral high ground, but because I don't want to be anything like my addict parents. Yup, my dad was one as well. Found out a few months ago when I walked in on Mom and her then-boyfriend cuddling on the sofa.

Mom was whispering, "My ex-husband and I used to get high together. Booze, weed, and pills. Sometimes coke. But then he started using batu. It got bad. And then it got worse. He did something unimaginable."

"What did he do?" I asked, guessing maybe Dad started selling drugs or had a bad trip or got arrested or something like that.

Mom and her boyfriend looked up.

I waited.

All Mom did was drop her eyes and mumble, "He changed . . ."

A hand on my shoulder. "Vij?"

I look.

Nari's gazing at me, concern etched on her face.

The wind tosses and then spreads her wispy bangs across her freckled cheeks.

I gently sweep them away. "Please don't ever change," I say, starting to smile, but then my lips dive in the opposite direction.

"What happened?" she asks.

I keep looking at her, but my vision is blurry. I shrug.

She lifts my hands.

I stare at her hands hugging mine.

"You're shaking," she says. She lets go of my hands to cradle my face. "Look at me."

I do.

"I love you, Vijali Shah-Nielsen," she whispers.

My heart swells.

"I love you, too, Kaminari Murphy," I say.

Clouds cloak the sun. Bless us with a drizzle.

I kiss a few raindrops off her cheek. When she does the same for me, it feels like she's drawing me in the sketchbook of her life. *I'm not alone.*

All my troubles scatter like fluffy dandelion seeds in the brisk trades. It doesn't even matter anymore that there was once another Nari on the Gram who might've said, *I love you, Kimi.* At least Nari and her affection are here now . . .

Is this the salvation my parents used to feel when they'd down their first shot or swallow their first pill of the day? If it is, there's no denying that I'm addicted to Nari.

Her lips settle on mine as she slides her hands under my hoodie and tank top. She fiddles with my binder, but it's impenetrable. So her fingers find other flesh . . .

Minutes pass. Maybe ten? Twenty? Who knows, who cares.

Only when a dog barks and a siren wails somewhere in different distances do we pry our mouths apart.

Nari drops her eyes to my arms and pushes up one of the long sleeves. Her forehead wrinkles. Light as a feather, she traces a scar. "No matter how bad it gets, don't kill yourself," she says in a delicate voice. "Please."

"I won't," I say, touching Nari's fingers that are still on my scar. "I promised you I wouldn't cut anymore, and I'd never break that promise."

Nari lifts my hand and clutches it against her heart. "Good," she says. "Because I don't know what I'd do if you became a suicide statistic."

I wish I could tell Nari that cutting was never about killing myself. It's the opposite—it's always about living. Cutting is like cold water and ice when it feels like the sun is drowning me in a sea of fire. But that sounds crazy, so instead I say, "I'm not going anywhere you're not."

She kisses a scar.

Does Kimi have scars? Has Nari kissed them?

"I'm glad," Nari says. She kisses my neck.

My eyes drift closed.

Nari's here, with me.

Brilliant zigzags pierce the graphite sky behind my eyelids. Then thunder cracks.

Aakash vijali and kaminari. Flash and boom. Inseparable. Forever.

I blink my eyes open. Dig around in my backpack for a pen. Find one. Then I lift Nari's hand and hold it on my lap with the pen poised. "May I?" I ask, looking at her with an eyebrow raised.

"You may," she says.

I draw the outline of jagged aakash vijali streaks, then shade dark clouds—one with the word *BOOM* outlined—and black sky behind. When I'm done, I say, "You and I, always together."

Nari takes a second to admire the ink on the back of her hand. The lightning brightens the tempestuous night between her knuckles and wrist. "It's terrifying. It's beautiful," she says.

I half smile. Touching the letters of *BOOM* on her hand, I say, "You're my muse."

Nari's eyes get shinier. "I *need* you, Vij," she says.

I attempt to say it back to her, but my lips feel sewn shut. My scars ignite. A thin layer of perspiration varnishes my body. Blurry images of Nari and Kimi kissing and strawberries appear before me like a mirage. I try to ignore all of it. I try to ground myself.

When I finally get my mouth open, what I want to say—*I need you, too* and *don't leave me*—refuses to come out. Only a tear crawls down my cheek.

"It's okay, I gotchu," Nari says, embracing me.

I wrap my arms around her, and we hold on until the clouds stop crying.

The next morning, Mom catches me in the hallway as I'm heading back to my cave.

"There's a hospital staff party at six," she says in Gujarati, studying her interlaced hands. "I was wondering . . ." Her voice trails off as she glances at me. "If you want to go with me." Then light dances in her eyes like diya flames as she adds, "It's Greek food. Your favorite."

I pull my long sleeves down farther so they cover my hands before I cross my arms high and tight like chest armor. "What, Jake can't go?" I ask in English, my tone sarcastic.

A pitiful expression consumes Mom's face, but she forces her lips into a neutral smile. "I didn't ask him. I was hoping you'd want to go. I know I haven't—" She cuts off her soft Gujarati words and swallows her lips.

So many things you "haven't," Mom. Haven't been to one of my gigs. Haven't bothered to listen to me. Haven't noticed my cuts even though I don't want you to . . .

I can't muster any sympathy for her.

But then, despite myself, her "haves" echo in my head. *Home-cooked meals. Buying me all my bass guitar equipment, no questions asked. Making me that midnight mango lassi last week. Trying to start a conversation about college with me the other day . . .*

"Fine," I blurt. "I'll go."

That afternoon, I syncopate the set list for the gig tomorrow night. Head nodding, jaṭā brushing my cheeks, time has ceased to exist and so have the chronic burning emotions in my head.

There comes a point when I'm ready to surface from the depths of the reggae trance. I remove my headphones, unplug, and gently place my bass on its stand. Everything feels right and good. My mind is clear. My heart is the pitter-patter of soft rain. I sink to the floor. Pick up my phone. Check my Instagram.

Literally two seconds before, Nari posted one of those fake AF pics of herself and some girl I don't recognize, a first since her story with Kimi. I stare, then glare at the two of them posing outside the

Starbucks in Waikele with their matching duck lips, peace signs, and venti drinks. The entire filtered scene makes me nauseous, but it's the caption that makes me gag: *But first, chai tea lattes.*

Chai means "tea." Tea tea latte, really, Starbucks? That's some lazy-ass appropriation. Like when people say naan bread. Naan *is* bread. I lift my head and catch my reflection in the full-length mirror. I swear my image arches a sly brow back at me and says, *Look who's talking, you fake-ass Rasta.*

My face falls. I'm not trying to be Rasta. I'm trying to find peace in dark reggae bass grooves because I can't find it in the Indian yoga and meditation my mom swears by. As for my jaṭā, I'm not copying the locs of the Rastafarian movement. Jaṭā are an ancient Hindu tradition, and one of the only ways I feel Indian.

I shift my attention back to Nari in the photo. The fingers of her non-peace-sign hand are resting on the unmutilated brown flesh of the other girl's upper arm.

Is this like Kimi all over again?

But this morning, Nari texted: **Love you, need you, Vijali Shah-Nielsen.**

Did she tell Starbucks Girl that she loves her, needs her?

I check the post again to see if Nari tagged the girl. She did. Chloe Sato.

Is Nari kissing Chloe while I'm here . . . ?

It feels like my scars open up. Then a strange question occurs to me: Is this the moment before the worst moment?

Light-headed, frantic, I text Nari.

Me: Hello?

N: Hey.

Me: You busy?

N: Kind of.

Me: What are you doing?

N: Hanging out with a friend.

Me: Who?

N: No one you know.

A frigid tsunami pummels my inner shores, but at the same time, I'm sweating like I'm forty-five minutes into a ninety-minute hot yoga class.

Chloe-the-new-Kimi.

I glance at my scarred arms sticking out of my tank top. Then I read Nari's caption again. This time, her words seem to mutate into *Hanging out with undamaged goods.*

I bite on a hangnail, drawing blood as I tear it off. Can I muster up the courage to tell Nari that it makes me jealous when I see her like this with another girl?

But being jealous after an incredible yesterday together seems so petty. I decide to steer the conversation to what's kind of always really nagging me—when will I get my next Nari hit? And if it's not right away, can I at least get the reassurance that the candy man is just around the corner, waiting to slip me a baggie full of Nari?

Nari is, after all, a healthy drug, like a daily multivitamin. Right?

Me: Wanna Netflix later?

N: Can't tonight.

Me: Tomorrow, then?

N: Maybe.

My hands skip the earthquake and go straight to a magnitude 9.5 aftershock. I stare at her ellipsis bubble until it's replaced with words.

N: Don't you have to practice tonight anyway?

Me: Already did.

Then, before I can talk myself out of it, I add: **Please, a teleparty later? I really need you.**

I hold my breath, blinking back tears as I wait for her reply.

N: Codependent much? Not healthy.

My heart turns to stone.

Me: What? How am I codependent?

N: Do I really have to explain it to you?

I'm alternating between gulping air and puking it back up.

Me: No, but yesterday was so awesome.

I consider reminding Nari that I was there for her last week when she was having a hard time with her dad and his latest side chick. But throwing that in her face is petty, too.

My gut twists.

Or maybe this isn't my Nari. Maybe this is her evil twin who hooks up with random girls and displays them like trophies on her Instagram. Maybe the evil twin is holding my sweet Nari hostage in some dark, dank basement . . .

N: It was, and we'll have more, but not today.

I feel my boo slipping through my fingers like angel dust from a broken vial. All my thumbs can do is beg.

Me: Come on! Please!

Ellipsis bubble. On pins and needles that feel like swords and daggers, I wait.

N: Maybe we need a break.

Crushing pain in my chest like an orc has shoved its hand into my rib cage, grabbed my beating heart, and is about to rip it out. Two more orcs close in, grab ahold of my lungs and my windpipe.

Why didn't I see it before? Maybe there's always been only one Nari—the smooth-talking cheater daughter of her smooth-talking cheater dad.

I can barely breathe. I can barely type.

Me: Wait, what?

Or maybe I'm not enough? My thumbs mistranslate.

Me: Did I do something?

N: It's not always about you.

Skipping vinyl in my head. *Not always about you. Not always about you.*

Fuck.

I didn't ask her again how she was doing with her dad stuff. Is that why she turned to Chloe?

I'm sorry, Nari! I'm so sorry!

I panic-call her. It goes straight to voice mail. I don't leave a message. Instead I panic-text her: **Please call me.** No *Read* appears under the text bubble this time. I go to DM her on Instagram, but it won't let me.

Holy shit, Nari blocked me everywhere.

The phone slips out of my hand, lands on my foot. *This* is the worst moment. I shut my eyes, hoping that maybe then I don't have to see it.

But the red-hot truth doesn't need to be seen, only heard. It taunts, *Ghosted by the girl who was supposed to have your back the most.*

Thunder always has lightning's back. Who will have mine now?

The cave conditions in my room are adequate—curtains drawn and the AC cranked—but I become a slab of dough stuck against the side of a clay tandoor, getting charred and blistered in the heat. My scars cry sweat, but my eyes remain dry.

"Nari doesn't need me, but I need her," I mumble under my breath.

There. I said it.

But admitting it only reminds me that sometimes when I need someone, they leave. Like Mom with her boyfriends. Now Nari with Chloe. And I'm alone. In the end, I'm always alone.

Hazy. Everything grows hazy.

I'm about to burn to death.

I'm about to die.

But I don't want to die.

My heart is pounding. I'm pacing.

I blink and it's happening. It has to happen or . . .

X-Acto knife in my hand.

Blink.

Not enough room on my arms. Angle the blade against my thigh.

Blink.

Doesn't hurt.

The knife falls from my hand.

My eyelids fuse. My head tilts back. I'm a floating lotus on the Byodo-In Temple pond.

I open my eyes. Inspect the surgical site. Five letters carved into my flesh, spelling the one word that is my truth.

Warm, healing blood.

It slows. Drips. Dives off my thigh. *Plink, plink.* A few drops on the floor like crimson bindis. Whatever blood is left near the cuts I smear around into a holy Hindu om sign. Unblinking, I stare at it until I'm staring at nothing.

I'm nothing.

Somewhere in my skull, "Trenchtown Rock" echoes. The lyrics transform . . .

Nothing feels no pain.

I'm drowsy. I grab some tissues, lie down on my bed, only to remember that I haven't locked the—

Too late.

Quick knock before the cave door creaks open. Mom steps in, smiling. Then her gaze crashes into my thigh. In the pin-drop silence that follows, she brings her hands to her mouth in what seems like slow motion. Three seconds later, she screams.

I bolt up, my post-cutting stupor replaced by the alarm of being found out by her for the first time.

In a flash, Mom's conjoined to my hip. "Betta," she whispers, hardly breathing.

Until today, never once have I forgotten to lock my door if I was about to cut, and never once have I forgotten to cover up my scars if there was a chance I'd be around other people.

Mom's fingers bump over some keloids on my arms, but her eyes return to the bloody scene of today's crime. "Why?" she asks, straining to keep her voice even.

I hear her, but the memory of my "So Much Trouble in the World" bass cover from earlier reverberates between my ears. It draws me and my words inward.

"Why didn't you come to me?" Mom asks, sounding far away because Bob's voice has joined the lunar bass solo in my head, poking and prodding me.

Mom's finger hovers over the five gory letters on my thigh, her eyes swampy with tears and her forehead puckered like the folds of a shruti box.

Does she finally realize I'm not always okay?

Meanwhile, Bob shrinks me with his song's bridge.

Mom shudders. Then she clenches her fists. Her lips part. "Alone," she says, her voice cracking.

My carved truth hangs in our shared air, but only I'm privy to Bob's sagacious second verse.

Maybe he's right.

I lift my eyes to meet Mom's.

We hold each other's gaze for a minute.

"But I'm right—" Mom starts, then cuts herself off, her upper lip trembling. She kisses my hand.

Hot tears begin to blur my vision.

Mom scoops up the knife and says, "I'll be right back." She runs out of the room with it.

Will she be right back? Something deep inside me warns that it's a lie. A sense of déjà vu brings almost everything in my body to a screeching halt. My heart cowers in my rib cage. My lungs hold their breath. My gut ties itself into a tight knot. Only my tears rush down my cheeks like lava.

I count to get a grip. At forty-one, Mom comes back.

A tiny cry, puppylike, escapes from between my lips.

"Let's go," Mom says, offering her empty hands to me.

I watch my own hands rise and tuck themselves into Mom's. Only two thin layers of flesh exist between our pumping blood. It's almost as if our hearts are connected . . .

Mom pulls me up, tows me to the bathroom.

"Sit, feet in," she says, pointing to the tub.

I do.

First, Mom washes her own hands. Then she gets the removable showerhead and drops to her knees next to me. She turns on the water, lets it spill over her inner wrist. When the temperature is just right, she brings the gentle stream of warm water and some antibacterial soap to my slashed-up thigh.

The blood, the soap disappear down the drain. Maybe some of my pain, too?

Water off. Clean wound patted dry with a fresh towel. Neosporin. A soft bandage taped at all four edges.

Mom stands up. "Chaal, betta," she says. "There's something I want to show you." She holds out her empty hands again.

Pretty yellow canaries—three of them—perch on a branch in my brain, tweeting the way they did for Bob on Hope Road in Kingston, Jamaica.

Maybe, everything will be okay.

Maybe, everything is *okay.*

For the second time, I let Mom's hands embrace mine.

Mom and I sit side by side at the dining table, our knees touching. In front of me is a newspaper clipping from twelve years ago that she'd planned on showing me when I turned eighteen.

It's quiet except for my thrashing heart and Mom's soft breath.

It dawns on me that the reason I never found this article online all those times I googled "Axel Nielsen" was because it leaves out Dad's name. And Mom's. And mine.

Mom taps the edge of the clipping. "I'm sorry I didn't tell you," she says. "I couldn't. My guilt wouldn't let me. I convinced myself that you'd be okay as long as I kept you safe going forward. You were so young. I didn't think you'd remember."

"I didn't," I say. "I don't."

"But your body does," Mom says, her palm a blanket on the scars of my left forearm.

I blink, then decide to read the article again, my index fingers flanking the headline—"HPD Officer Rescues Three-Year-Old Left in Locked, Hot Vehicle at Ala Moana Beach Park."

The third time, my eyes play hopscotch with the words.

left alone

sweating

covered in vomit

clutching a pint of strawberries

police

shattered a window

Child Protective Services

Honolulu grand jury

The fourth time, I stare at two words.

left alone

The fifth time, one word.

alone

That word ricochets in my skull for a while. Finally, it rolls away and settles into a corner. My heart simmers down. My thoughts become a distant plink of water on a stone. I count the soft splats. *One, two, three . . .*

When I get to twenty-one, I remember that I brought out my sketchbook. "There's something I want to show you, too," I say, lifting my right arm off it. I open it to the back third, then slide it over to Mom.

She smooths the pages. She takes a deep breath, then lowers her eyes to the first drawing on the left page: my X-Acto knife gleaming against my arm.

Right page: Dad's eyes shooting flames, burning me.

I peek at her. *What is she thinking?* I wonder.

She turns the page.

Left: the fright in my eyes as the sun blowtorches me and my bass guitar on an outdoor stage.

Right: the sun in the form of a clear golden vulture, pecking at my face the way a real one would peck at carrion.

A storm rolls across Mom's face as she turns the page again. The fifth drawing demands too much from her senses, and she cries out like a wounded animal. She looks away for a second. When she looks back, she's biting her knuckles.

My torso, naked except for a binder, is on a rotating spit, being grilled over flaming mesquite wood, the smoke rising. My scarred arms and smooth legs, neatly stacked, are waiting to become huli-huli. My head is under a splintered table, leaking blood that's coagulated into the words *DIED ALONE.*

Mom blinks hard to fight back tears.

A text ding on her phone.

We both look.

Jake: ANSWER ME!

Mom scowls as she shoves the phone across the table. Then she sucks in her snot and rubs her eyes with the heels of her palms.

My eyebrows lift. "Aren't you going to reply?" I ask, wishing Nari would text me the same thing because the deep ache of loss suddenly turns into a stabbing sensation.

Mom breaks down. Her hands become leeches sucking on her face. Her chest heaves in quiet sobs as she shakes her head.

"It's okay, Mom," I say. "You can answer."

Mom drops her hands, whips her head up. "No, it's not okay, and no, I won't answer," she says. "He's not important." She draws an invisible line from her to me. "You're important."

She pushes her chair back, stands up. She grabs her cell phone, turns it off, then pitches it across the room. It lands on the sofa. She exhales a long, slow breath. She moves behind me, bends over, and hugs me. "I'm here," she says.

I feel my hand rise to touch hers.

We stay like that. Connected. Our hearts are beating in sync.

"You're not alone," she whispers.

Her words are a giant excavator at the burial site of me.

"It's fuzzy, but I think Dad said, 'I'll be right back,'" I mumble. I look over my shoulder at Mom. "Why didn't he come back?"

"He was long gone," she says. "I'm so sorry. I wish I hadn't been at work that day. You could've died." Fresh tears cascade down her tortured face. She touches the bandage on my thigh, then a few keloids on my arms. "Please don't kill yourself."

"It's never about killing myself, Mom. It's always been about surviving," I say.

"Why didn't you ask me for help?" Mom asks, tracing a scar.

"Ask you for help with what? How could I explain that sometimes it felt like the sun was out to get only me? Or that I was being burned alive at the stake? Or that I was melting? Or that I was so afraid of being alone even when you were right down the hall?" I ask.

Mom squats next to me. She tilts her head, her eyes attempting to capture mine, which are downturned. She begins to stroke the back of my hand.

After a while, she says, "Maybe from now on, *we* can figure out how to help *you*."

I remain silent. My head's quiet, too.

"Together," Mom adds.

I drape my fingers on her hand.

"Hey Alexa," she says. "Shuffle songs by Bob Marley."

The first song starts—"I'm Hurting Inside." Bob's voice fills the room and speaks to me about pain and hope.

"Together?" Mom asks.

I shift my eyes to hers. "I'm down to try."

A NOTE FROM SONIA PATEL

* * * * * * * * * * * * *

*Adverse experiences and invalidation in my youth left perma-
nent marks on my developing brain. I didn't understand that
my shame, unconscious repetition of being a sexual object,
and thoughts of self-injury and suicide were scientifically
proven symptoms of my traumatized brain. Those symptoms
developed as counterintuitive ways of self-soothing, control,
and survival in the midst of the adversity that had prevented
the healthy development of emotional regulation and personal decision-making skills. As I later figured out, my self-
injurious and suicidal thoughts were a complex code that,
when decoded, spelled out:* Stop using and hurting me, and
don't ignore or minimize reality. *In "Nothing Feels No Pain,"
Vij's self-inflicted scars are a gruesome reflection of the trau-
matic scars on her brain. Vij wants to live and she wants to feel
better, but her brain hasn't been wired to allow her to cope in
healthy ways. So she survives by releasing intolerable emotional pain through seemingly more tolerable physical pain. If
only Vij had viewed her cutting symptom as code for something that, if determined, would help her to find healthy release
and to heal. How would you decode Vij's cutting symptom?*

PECULIAR FALLS

JONATHAN LENORE KASTIN

Content Note: This story references anxiety.

Max had been undead for seventeen years and he still couldn't figure out how to talk to people. It wasn't like he didn't have things to say. It was just that people were terrifying. He couldn't keep his brain from going staticky with panic whenever someone approached him. When he tried to talk, the words jumbled up in his mouth like he had an extra pair of fangs, his cheeks burned as if he'd wandered into direct sunlight for too long, and his stomach twisted into an intricate maze of tiny knives.

Unfortunately, vampires still had to attend high school, so Max had found ways to cope. He spent most of his class time drawing little coffins in the margins of his notebook, studiously avoiding eye contact with everyone, human and monster alike. During lunch he snuck into the empty high school theater to drink his biosimilar blood in the wings where no one could see him. (Thank Cain he didn't have to drink blood from actual people like his ancestors had.) And, of course, he lurked. He was an expert at lurking. He'd find the nearest dark corner and stand there unmoving, gathering the shadows around him, as his unsuspecting classmates passed him by. It was safe and comfortable. It worked really well for him. And he was happy.

Sort of.

"Excuse me! Pardon me! Hellooooooo!"

Max froze. Was someone talking to him? The blood he'd been drinking pounded through his veins. His shadowy camouflage began to slip away. It was suddenly hard to breathe.

"I said *hellooo*! Hey, vampire boy! Mayday! Mayday!"

Max turned slowly, the muscles in his neck twitching. There was a girl next to him, glowing faintly in the dark. One person. Surely he could handle one person.

"Wh-who—?"

"Oh, thank purgatory, you can see me." She hovered slightly above the stage. "I've been trying everyone, even the other vampires, and either there's no connection or they're ignoring me. I can't really tell."

Max opened his mouth to speak, but before he could get out a garbled *Who are you?* the girl stuck out her hand.

"I'm Lila. You're Max, right?"

He was so shocked she knew his name that he actually reached out to shake her hand. When his hand passed right through her, she cackled. "I'm dead," she said, obviously finding this hilarious.

Max took a small step backward. Maybe if he made a run for it, he could still finish his biosimilar in the bathroom.

"Listen, we don't have a lot of time." Lila's voice was suddenly serious. "I need your help."

"Me?" He mouthed the word, but no sound came out. His stomach squirmed.

"This is going to sound really weird, but I've seen the future, and if we don't stop something very bad from happening, this whole town is going to be destroyed. *Tonight.*"

Max stared at his bottle of biosimilar. Maybe they'd given him a bad batch.

"Are you listening?"

He nodded.

"You know Greta Baker, head of the cheer team?"

He had a vague idea of who she was: beautiful and blond with a useful pair of shimmering wings.

"Well, tonight Dr. Edwin T. Abernathy is going to fire a laser from his private lab right into the Homecoming game mid-cheer and turn her into a ravening beast that swallows the entire town!"

Max's vocal cords finally cooperated. "Dr. Abernathy?" He had been one of the science teachers last year, until the exploding frog incident. And the carnivorous slime mold that took over the cafeteria. The last straw, apparently, had been the model volcano flooding the halls with genuine lava. The school had been closed for two weeks. Max dimly remembered something about Dr. Abernathy storming off campus, screeching about his unappreciated genius and vowing revenge. Still, destroying the whole town seemed a little extreme. Max squeezed his eyes shut. "This is a trick, isn't it?" he said, more to himself than to her.

"What? No!"

"Like that time the Doppler twins lured me into a tanning salon."

"That's terrible," said Lila. "Why would anyone do that?"

Max opened his eyes wide. "Or the time Matt Thorsen tricked me into going to a garlic festival."

"Um, what kind of people do you hang out with?" Lila asked.

"Well, I—I'm not falling for it this time." Max backed toward the stage door. If this was anything like the tanning salon fiasco, the whole school would be waiting outside to laugh at what a gullible loser he was.

Lila swooped after him. "It's not a trick, I swear. I see things before they happen. I think it's a 'being dead' thing. Maybe. I've only been dead for a few weeks."

Max's curiosity slowly overcame his terror. "What—what happened?"

Lila sank through the stage up to her waist, her glow turning slightly pink with embarrassment. "I was . . ." She mumbled something unintelligible.

"What?"

"I was reading a book."

Max stared at her, open-mouthed.

"It was humiliating, okay? We moved here this summer, and I was reading this amazing book on all the weird stuff that happens in Peculiar Falls. Did you know that more supernatural phenomena occur in this town than anywhere else in the world? My parents are paranormal investigators. Pretty ironic that they can't even sense their own dead daughter trying to make contact. Anyway, I stepped off the curb and bam! Hit by a bus. No more body for me."

"Wow," said Max.

"I was supposed to start classes here this fall. So much for that idea." She sighed. "Anyway, how did you become a vampire? Are you, like, a hundred years old? I know you guys aren't allowed to bite people anymore. They signed that treaty ages ago, right?"

Max shrank into himself, wishing for the millionth time that he had been bitten like a normal vampire. He turned away and muttered into his coat, "I was born this way." He was pretty sure his parents had violated several vampire laws in the process.

"Wait, that's a thing?"

He cringed. Here it came: the laughter, the mockery, the jokes about teething vampire babies. He'd heard it all before. "It's very rare," he said.

"I knew there was a reason you could see me. See? You *are* special."

"What?" No one had ever had that reaction before.

"It's perfect. You can stop the mad scientist, save the town!"

"Um . . ."

"I would try myself but I'm incorporeal, right? Limited. But you have a *body*. Plus, you can do cool vampire stuff." She waved her arms around like a demented bat. "You could be a hero!"

"Oh, no, no, no, no, no. I couldn't. I—" Just the thought of doing anything in front of others was making the room spin like a darkened carousel.

"Why not?"

"Because there'd be people and talking and . . ." And they'd all laugh at him or tell him how weird he was or threaten him with crosses. He was going to throw up.

"Look, I've tried everyone else. You're my only option here. The town's only option!"

"What about that human Janie Hernandez?" he said. "She's always saving cheerleaders and stuff."

"She's already fighting a secret cabal of demon librarians. And anyway, she can't actually see me, so . . ."

"Harsimar Brooks, then."

"Definitely not. Didn't you hear he was bitten by a werewolf last week? And tonight's a full moon."

"Of course it is." Max groaned. The bell rang and he almost dropped his biosimilar. "Um, I've got to go."

"So is that a yes?"

"I—I mean . . . this is all really weird. Maybe you were just having a bad dream?"

The glow around Lila turned a murderous red. "You know my parents are in this town, too, and they don't deserve to get destroyed any more than you do."

"Look, I'm sorry, okay? I just—I can't do this right now." Max scrambled to get his things together.

"Okay, Max," she said. "I didn't like those sunglasses anyway." Then she popped out of existence.

Max rushed out of the theater, wondering what his sunglasses had to do with anything and why Dr. Abernathy thought firing a laser into the Homecoming game was going to solve all his problems. Max hated Peculiar Falls as much as the next social outcast, but he didn't want it to be destroyed. He just wanted to go somewhere far away. Someplace they had proper mausoleums where he could lurk and they didn't put holy water in your biosimilar.

The quad buzzed with students—humans and fair folk, cryptids and other creatures, along with a handful of witches. There were even a few other vampires, way cooler than Max, clustered together under one of the pine trees. Everyone in a group of their own kind. But Max didn't belong with any of them. Vampires who were born instead of bitten belonged in myths and legends. Which meant that in a town full of strange creatures and weird phenomena, he was the oddest of them all.

Max grit his fangs and pushed through the crowd, trying to avoid notice, as the relentless sun beat down on everyone. His skin sizzled even under the layers of sunblock he'd slathered over himself, and he pulled his coat closer around him. There were so many people. Why did there have to be so many people?

One of them slammed into him, and he fell to the ground, black jeans tearing against the concrete. "Why don't you watch where you're going?" Matt Thorsen, huge and covered in fur, snarled at him, then shoved his way back into the crowd. Max blinked against the harsh light of the sun and felt around for his sunglasses. They were broken. Great. Now he'd have a pounding headache by the end of the day for sure. He snatched up the shattered pieces and fled into the cool recesses of the locker area, taking in deep shuddering breaths. Then he stared at the snapped frames in his hands.

"Told you!" Lila materialized so quickly that Max stifled a scream.

"Okay, okay." Max pressed back against the cold metal lockers. "So you can predict things. But that doesn't mean I'm capable of saving anyone. I've—I've got—I'm very busy."

"You're not going to be busy doing anything if Peculiar Falls gets destroyed."

"What do you want me to do?" He threw his arms up in despair. "I can barely make it through a normal school day. How am I supposed to stop a mad scientist? Eat him?"

"What? No! Heroes don't eat people." Lila looked genuinely horrified. "And I am *not* bailing you out of jail."

"I'm sorry." Max shook his head. "I just don't see how I can help. I can barely talk to people."

"You're talking to me right now."

"Well, you're dead. It's a little different." She also hadn't filled his locker with mirrors or done any of the other horrible things the rest of the students did to him on a regular basis. Not yet anyway.

"What are you so scared of?" asked Lila. "You're a vampire, and you're, like, a million feet tall. Everyone should be afraid of *you.*"

"You're kidding, right? Everyone here hates me." The other vampires didn't even consider him a *real* vampire.

"Look," Lila sighed. "All you have to do is find Greta. Stop her from going to the performance tonight."

The second bell rang. "I can't do this now. I'll be late for class!" He made a run for it.

"Who cares about class at a time like this?" she shouted after him.

When he finally got to room 207, the door was already closed, which meant class had started, which meant everyone was going to stare at him when he walked in. Stare and judge. He bit his lip so hard he tasted the bitter tang of his own blood. Then he took a deep breath and held it. He just had to do it quick, like ripping open a bottle of biosimilar.

He jerked the door open. Just as he'd predicted, every head in the room swiveled toward him. He stood there frozen for a second. It was the worst-case scenario. All the seats in the back were taken. Now he would have to go to the front of the class, and everyone would remember that he existed and what a freak he was. The vampire who wasn't even supposed to exist.

Max willed his body forward, not meeting anyone's gaze as they watched him, and wished desperately that there were a few stray shadows he could hide in. He sank into an empty seat and stared at his notebook, cheeks burning. He couldn't even hear the words Ms. Nguyen said as she droned on about their upcoming project.

He stuffed his hands in his pockets, fingered his broken glasses, and tried to suck in deep calming breaths. Lila had been right about the glasses. But did that mean she was right about the town being destroyed? Probably. Why did she have to make it *his* responsibility, though? Also, she had disrupted his routine. And it was clear she would keep disrupting things. How could you stop a disembodied spirit from following you around?

He chewed the end of his pen, then risked a glance around the room. Greta Baker was four seats away from him, passing notes to Victor, one of the "normal" vampires. Max frowned. Maybe it was a sign. Not that he believed in that sort of thing. He squeezed his broken glasses so hard his fingers went numb.

"Okay, let's split into groups." Ms. Nguyen turned to the whiteboard.

Wait, what? As if his day could get any worse. No one ever wanted to work with him, and Ms. Nguyen usually ended up having to assign him a partner. He stood uncertainly, eyes darting back and forth at the seats around him. Greta was *right there.* All he had to do was sit next to her. Take some initiative. But Victor was next to her, with his chiseled cheekbones and his flawlessly mussed hair. The perfect picture of everything Max was not. He dug his nails into his palms and inched toward Greta's desk.

They had already teamed up with one of the witches, Jamilah, and were chattering away like it was easy. He stood just outside their circle of desks, trying to figure out how to interrupt, for the first time in his life wanting someone to notice him. When they finally felt him looming over them, Greta looked up. "Um, did you need something?"

Max opened his mouth and cringed as his voice came out in a breathy whisper. "H-hi."

Greta laughed and mimicked his pathetic "hi" perfectly. Max burned hot, then cold. He was going to kill Lila the next time he saw her. Well, exorcise her, or whatever people did to get rid of ghosts. He collapsed into the empty desk behind Greta and tried to look very small, which was difficult for someone as tall as he was. The others shuddered and leaned away from him ever so slightly. Unlike Victor, Max hadn't died in a terribly romantic way or lived through a fascinating era of human history. Max was a quiet and unsettling abomination, even for a town like Peculiar Falls. On the other hand, he hadn't been repeating his junior year of high school over and over again for decades because he couldn't pass any of his classes.

"So what are we supposed to be doing again?" Greta went back to looking at her notes.

Jamilah sighed. "We need to pick a scene to perform."

"To be or not to be," said Victor. "That is the question."

Greta rolled her eyes. "Wrong play, Victor."

"Oh, right. Sorry."

Max shuddered. This was even worse than he'd expected. Group projects were one thing, but performing in front of the entire class? He'd rather swim through a pool of freshly pressed garlic juice. Maybe he *should* let Dr. Abernathy destroy the town . . .

The others tossed ideas back and forth for a while. Several times, Max thought of contributing his own ideas, but that would require talking. After Greta's humiliating imitation, he was never talking to anyone ever again. In fact, he was going to drop out of high school entirely and move to the Carpathian Mountains, where he could live in a forest with wolves because wolves did not mock people. Except you probably couldn't get biosimilar up in the mountains.

He tried to look as though he were taking attentive notes, but the pen lurched out of his hand and began to dance across the page in large bubbly letters: *What are you doing? SAY SOMETHING!* The pen glowed slightly.

"Lila?" he whispered, looking around desperately, but she wasn't there. Was she *possessing* the pen? Could ghosts even do that?

"Did you say something?" asked Victor. Max shook his head and tried to smile reassuringly. Victor gave him a look of pity, then turned back to the girls.

Great. Now they would all think he was talking to himself.

Tell Greta she's in danger, the pen wrote. *She has to skip the game tonight. Make something up.*

Max squeezed the pen. What would get a girl like Greta to skip the most important game of the school year?

"Um," he ventured, but the sound barely left his mouth. He tried again. "Excuse me," he whispered. Why wouldn't his vocal cords work when he wanted them to?

"EXCUSE ME."

Everyone in the room stopped and stared at him. He sat with his mouth open, stunned by his own sudden visibility, the pen crushed in his hand as black ink leaked onto the page.

"Okay, you definitely said something that time," said Victor.

"Greta, you can't go to the game tonight," Max blurted, surprised by the steadiness in his voice. "There's a mad scientist with a laser and he's going to turn you into a monster that destroys the whole town."

Greta blinked, then threw her head back and laughed, high and hysterical, the others joining her in a torrent of ridicule. Even Ms. Nguyen was shaking her head, trying hard not to smile. Max flushed a bright pink, dissolved into a cloud of mist, and wafted frantically toward the door. He seeped into the hall and drifted to the nearest bathroom. When he finally managed to pull himself back into a corporeal form, he took great gasping breaths and hid in the stall farthest from the door.

"You did it!" Lila poked her head halfway through the stall. Apparently not even his utter humiliation would stop her. "Why did you run away?"

"Are you joking?" he asked. "Didn't you see what happened? I told you I couldn't do this."

"You just have to explain—"

"You don't understand." Max buried his face in his hands. "It's easy for you to talk to people."

"You think I have it easy, Max? No one else can see or hear me. Not even my parents!"

"Why don't you just possess another pen? That seemed to work pretty well for you ten minutes ago."

Lila groaned. "As if I haven't tried that a hundred times! It only works when I'm around you. At least you aren't invisible to everyone."

"I want to be, okay? Then maybe everyone would leave me alone."

Lila turned a threatening crimson. "You want to be *dead* dead? You want to be helpless, just waiting around for your parents to join you—way before their time?"

"I'm sorry, Lila, but it's not my fault your parents moved to this horrible town. I'm not helping you save Peculiar Falls. Everyone here is awful. It's not worth saving."

"How can you say that?" Lila's chin wobbled.

"Just leave me alone." Max got to his feet, determined. "I don't want to have to banish you to another dimension or something." He didn't really know how to banish ghosts—although he was pretty sure some of the artifacts in his parents' museum could do the trick—but Lila didn't know that.

"You wouldn't." She backed away from him uncertainly.

"Try me." Max slammed out of the bathroom and fled. The thought of having to face his English class again after discorporating was too humiliating to bear. He was certain Victor had never discorporated like that in public.

Max lurched away from Peculiar High, glancing over his shoulder every once in a while to make sure Lila wasn't following him.

What he needed was someplace quiet, someplace he could be alone to think. He pulled out a pair of earbuds, cranked up the volume on his phone, and tried to take deep breaths to the sound of wailing and feverish strings. Then he turned toward the old cemetery on the hill, careful to avoid any of the busier streets. The trees had just started turning a spectacular scarlet, and the sun felt a little less oppressive under their branches. He could almost imagine he was off with his parents on their current expedition to the old country, photographing crumbling ramparts and mist-shrouded towers. There was nothing like that in Peculiar Falls. In that sense, it *was* better to let the town get destroyed. Then when his parents came back, they would have to take him with them. He'd get to see all the places he'd only known through photographs. But if the town did get destroyed, then everyone *in* the town would be destroyed, too. Including Lila's parents.

It wasn't fair. He was just trying to make it through high school. No one had ever said anything about saving entire towns from destruction. That was Janie and Harsimar's job. *They* were the chosen ones. Just because he could apparently communicate with ghosts, that didn't make it his responsibility.

"Maybe she's wrong," he whispered. "Maybe this isn't like the glasses at all." He wound his way up the hill, the sound of undulating violins thrumming in his ears with each step. The tombstones here were ancient, so worn by the elements that you could barely read the inscriptions on most of them. It was quiet and peaceful. He could almost believe he was the only person left in the whole world.

He picked out a weathered gray headstone covered in lichen and settled back against it, looking over the town. Would it really be so bad if Greta wiped Peculiar Falls off the face of the earth? For one thing, no one would laugh behind his back or tell him he wasn't a real vampire or stick crosses in his backpack anymore. He stared down at the ugly brick high school and shuddered. On the other hand, he didn't want to lose his parents' museum. Not with all those ancient, mysterious artifacts he had always wanted a crack at deciphering. He leaned his head against the stone, trying not to think about Lila's face when she'd mentioned her parents. Even paranormal investigators wouldn't be prepared for a monstrous cheerleader attack. And what if Greta came up here to the cemetery and started eating the trees and the stones and stuff? He *liked* those trees.

He could see it all now. Dr. Abernathy's laser shooting through the night sky, Greta growing larger and larger, glowing a sickly green. She'd be twenty feet, fifty, a hundred feet tall, and she'd be shoving everything into the gaping hole that was her mouth: football players, entire buildings, Lila's parents. Then she'd turn and stomp toward his sanctuary, ripping up trees and headstones and popping them into her mouth like candy.

He swallowed a low moan. He didn't want the cemetery to be destroyed. He didn't want *anything* to be destroyed, really. But going to the game to stop Greta, getting up in front of all those people . . . It would be like walking under the sun naked at the hottest time of the day on the hottest day of the year. He'd burst into flames. He'd turn to dust. He'd crumble. Lila had to understand that. Panic fizzed through his veins and his chest grew painfully tight, as if someone were sitting on top of him. He couldn't breathe. He couldn't breathe. He couldn't breathe.

Trying not to totally lose it, he grabbed his phone and swiped to his favorite meditation app, fingers fumbling to hit the right icons. A low growl filled his earbuds, then the sweet, calming sound of rain. He curled up in a tight ball and tried to breathe in and out as a soothing voice reminded him to relax the muscles of his face. He felt bone-weary suddenly, like he hadn't slept in his coffin for a week. The voice was telling him to relax his toes now. He settled deeper into the grass, eyes drifting shut.

Max jerked his eyes open.

The sky was dark, and the meditation app had stopped. How had it gotten so late? His phone said 7:30. The game had started at 6:30. For a minute he wondered if it had already happened and he'd missed everything. But no, if Dr. Abernathy had fired his laser, Max would have heard an earsplitting screech or felt a coffin-shaking earthquake. There was still time. He could make a run for it now, get to the edge of town before the chaos started. Or he could try to stop this. Lila's face seemed to swim before him, on the edge of tears. He gathered his last ounce of courage and ran down the hill toward the football field, then stopped. There was no way he was going to get there in time.

"Rats, rats, rats." He hopped from one foot to the other. Mist was too slow. Running was out of the question, even if he could manage to turn into a wolf, something he had never succeeded in doing before. Flying would have to do. He squeezed his eyes shut and willed himself into a bat. One arm shrank and beat wildly at the air, then the other. He was really out of practice. A humiliating shriek ripped from his throat. Thank Cain no one was around to see him do this. He flapped toward the football field, getting smaller and smaller until he was finally bat-size and echolocating his way across the night sky. He flapped past the stadium lights and the stomping fans below. He couldn't see them, but he could *feel* them. Was he too late?

He circled the stadium a few times, then juddered back into human form right next to the public bathrooms.

"Max?" Lila was floating behind the bleachers, looking gray and defeated, but she brightened when she saw him. "You came!" She launched herself at him. "Hurry! Halftime's just starting!"

"Lila, I'm really sorry about what I said earlier—"

"No time, Max! Go!"

He stumbled toward the field. There were so many people out there. More people than he had ever seen in his entire life.

"Oh, dear Cain." He couldn't even get Greta alone now. He'd have to walk across the field in front of all those people.

"You can do this!" called Lila. "I believe in you."

He squeezed his fists tight and took a step forward. He was going to discorporate again. But he couldn't. He *wouldn't*. Not now. Sweat trickled down his neck. How did Janie and Harsimar do this sort of thing all the time?

A sickly green light suddenly flooded the sky.

Max didn't think. He just ran, the lights and the cheers fading around him. The base cheerleaders tossed Greta into the air. As she swooped into a perfect figure eight, Max leapt and crashed into her with a hard jolt. Greta screamed. Then they were falling. A beam of acrid light slammed into the football turf inches from their heads, gouging a deep furrow into the ground. The crowd erupted into pan-icked shouts and screams.

Max glanced about him wildly. The furrow stretched across the field, glowing a putrid green. But it hadn't hit anyone. That was the important thing. Relief flooded him.

"I did it," said Max. He sucked in a glorious nonapocalyptic breath of fresh air. "I can't believe it."

Greta smacked Max hard. "Get off me, you freak!"

Max rolled onto his back. Holy sepulchre. *He* had stopped the destruction of Peculiar Falls. *He* had saved everybody. And there would still be time for him to lurk in the cemetery and puzzle over the secrets in his parents' museum. He laughed dementedly.

"Ugh, you are so weird." Greta stood and brushed herself off.

"Oh my god. Are you okay?" One of the human cheerleaders rushed to Greta's side. "That laser almost hit you. If he hadn't pushed you out of the way . . ." Tears filled her eyes.

Greta blinked, then turned reluctantly to Max. "Oh. Um, thanks . . . I guess."

"Max!" Suddenly Lila hovered over him. "You did it!"

"I did." Max smiled.

"What a relief! It's going to be at least a year before he can charge that thing up again," said Lila.

"Wait, what—"

But then the football coach swept Max onto his shoulders and paraded him around the field to the sound of raucous cheers. Everyone was staring at him and smiling. It was horrible. But also kind of wonderful.

"They love you, Max!" Lila floated beside him.

"I don't know how I feel about this." He was getting jittery and a little light-headed, as if he might float up into the clouds.

Lila laughed. "Did you see Greta's face when you went flying toward her? Priceless." She swooped closer. "So anyway, now that you're a hero, you should know there's a secret lab under the gym. Nurse Manderly is creating a virus that'll turn everyone into a mutant zombie horde."

"Zombies?" The euphoria left him suddenly, like he'd taken a stake to the heart.

"But now that you know, you could stop it!" She clapped her hands together, delighted.

"No, not again, Lila—no more apocalypses! I can't keep doing this."

"Dude, who are you talking to?" Victor looked up at him from the crowd.

"Er, my friend Lila," said Max. "She told me to stop the laser . . ."

Victor stared at the space to Max's left while Lila waved frantically on his right.

"She's a ghost," said Max.

"Huh." Victor nodded slowly.

Max frowned at Lila, hoping the other vampires wouldn't think he was even weirder now than they already did.

"Well, we're all going to Paradise to celebrate tonight," said Victor, keeping pace with the football coach, who still hadn't put Max back down. "Come with us and have a bloodshake. It's on me. Um, you could even bring your ghost friend."

No one had ever invited Max to the diner before. He shook his head, trying not to let the shock show on his face. "Thanks, but I've got something I need to do."

Lila floated above Max's favorite grave, a large marble slab with a weeping angel perched on top. "I guess all your precious cemeteries are going to be full of zombies soon."

"Lila," Max groaned. "Can't I enjoy our victory in peace?"

"Okay, but don't come crying to me when the zombie hordes knock over these tombstones. Some of them look pretty fragile."

Max settled against a stone carved in the shape of a tree trunk. "I was thinking maybe I could talk to your parents."

Lila's eyes widened. "You'd do that?"

"They should know that you're still here."

"Wow, thanks, Max! They'll be so relieved." She tried to sweep him into a hug and floated right through him instead. "This is great! First we'll make contact with my parents. Then we'll shut down the zombie apocalypse."

Max sighed and looked up at the stars. It was going to be a long school year if Lila insisted he stop every single catastrophe. But for the very first time, he thought maybe he could handle it.

A NOTE FROM JONATHAN LENORE KASTIN

* * * * * * * * * * * * * * * * * * *

Growing up, I didn't know that what I was experiencing was anxiety. I just knew that I would get stomachaches every day before school and that my mind would go blank when I was trying to talk to people I didn't know well. I've often joked that having social anxiety feels a lot like being a vampire. I have to be invited in or I'll just lurk outside of social circles for eternity. When I was asked to write something for this anthology, I knew I had to write about a vampire dealing with all the things that terrified me in high school: being late to class, people, and monster cheerleaders. Well, okay, maybe not the monster part.

AVALANCHE

NIKKI GRIMES

Content Note: This story references schizophrenia and severe anxiety.

HERE'S THE DEAL

I'm fine.
Grandma just called from Bellevue,
put a doctor on the line:
"Your mother is suffering
from schizophrenia."
Like I don't know that already.
"She'll have to stay in the hospital for a while."
Good! That's where she needs to be.
"Do you have any questions?"
Yeah! Is this thing hereditary?
Never mind. I don't want to know.

ANY QUESTIONS?

I'm fine.
Did I say that already?
I'm Shanti Glover.

Shanti means peace or tranquility.
My life is none of that,
not with a mother
who rides the pendulum swing
between paranoid and plastered
with too few moments
of sane and sober in the middle.
It's that part-time crazy
that gets you,
the never knowing
which Mom is going
to show up.
I'm a senior,
which means I'm one year closer
to getting the hell out of here—
if I graduate,
if I maintain my
high grade point average,
if I can snag a scholarship
to—wherever.
If. If. If. If.
Looking for my ticket
to a tomorrow
where sanity rules
and peace of mind
is more than
proverbial.

ROUTINE

My alarm
helps me beat the sun.
I rise first,

go to grab breakfast.
(This story is so cliché.)
I pour what's left of the cold cereal
into the one clean bowl I can find.
The empty milk carton
is the morning's
first disappointment.
Yesterday, Mom was supposed to
shop for groceries, but
she was too busy
running down the street naked,
then being carted off to Bellevue.
No biggie.
It's fine.
Who needs breakfast?
I can use the time
to finish my homework.
Five minutes in,
my stomach growls.
"Shut. Up!" I tell it,
and it doesn't growl again.

RESTING MEAN FACE

I book to the bus stop,
hop on the cross-town,
look cross-eyed at any boy
who even thinks about
messing with me.
I am not in the mood.

FOG

I float through the day like a ghost,
only break through the ectoplasm
when some unfortunate
substitute teacher
asks me how my mother is.
"What are you asking me that for?"
"Well, uh, the principal mentioned
that your mother was just taken to—"
"My mother is fine!
And why don't you mind
your own business?"
It wasn't really a question.
I suddenly feel
the drum of my pulse
calling the regular me
to attention.
What the hell?
You never talk to teachers like that.
A slight tremor
scissors through me.
Get a grip, Glover.

RUNNING

The change bell rings
and I bolt into the hall,
a bowling ball
striking the first pin.
Oops! It's Gloria, my BFF.

"Hey! Slow your roll!" she says.
"Sorry," I mumble.
Gloria studies me.
"The cloud you're carrying around
is darker than usual.
What's up?"
"I'm fine."
"Try again."
I exhale.
"Mom's back at Bellevue."
Nothing Gloria hasn't heard before.
She's been at my house more than once
when Mom was wandering the halls
talking to herself.
"Okay. You need me to come over
after school and hang?"
I shake my head.
"I've got that new part-time job
at Mickey D's.
But thanks."
"All right. I'll call you later.
You need anything,
I'm here for you.
Meantime,
try to go easy
on the world."

EASY AIN'T EASY

I spend the rest of the day
cocooned in silence.
Later, home alone,
I make it through

math homework
before it's time
to jet to McDonald's
for my four-hour shift.
Soon as I clock in
I grab a pen
to jot down a list of groceries
to pick up on my way home.
"Hey!" snaps the store manager.
"You better be taking notes
for the customer in front of you
waiting for service!"
"Sorry," I mutter.
I plaster on my best
Mickey D's smile and say,
"Hi! How can I help you today?"

DINNER FOR ONE

At the end of my shift,
I scarf down a Big Mac and fries,
call it dinner,
and head to Safeway.
Thank God my part-time salary
is enough to cover
cereal, milk, eggs, and bacon—
just till the hospital
cuts Mom loose. Again.
I buy lunch at school
and eat dinner for free
at Mickey D's during the week.
Grandma brings me
fried okra and oxtail stew

on Fridays,
enough to get me through
the weekends.
Otherwise, I'm on my own.
"I done already raised my babies,"
she sometimes reminds me.
"You big enough to care for yourself."
I shrug it off. Whatever.
I'm happy for Grandma's cooking, though.
That woman knows her way
around the kitchen!
Anyway, we let everybody think
Grandma's staying here full-time
so nobody drags me off
to foster care
"for my own good."
Damn. Why did I have to go there?
My daily headache returns
for a longer-than-usual visit.
God, are you sure you don't hate me?
Just asking.

IN HER ABSENCE

Our mailbox
bulges with bills.
I toss them on the table,
wondering how long
the lights will stay on,
wondering when
Mom paid the bill last.
Not my problem,

just my worry.
I count what dollars
I have left after Safeway.
Too few.
Mom'll be home soon,
I tell myself.
I need her home.
I don't want her home.
I wish it were simple.
The hospital
will kick her loose
before long,
once she's . . . better?
It will likely be
a few weeks. Or more.
But this is the lie
I can live with.

BLACKOUT

Curtains drawn,
I breathe in the darkness,
ready to shut out the world
even if it leaves me
alone with my pain.

NOW

Now is the one word
in my vocabulary.
Mom isn't in it.

WARNING SIGNS

The next morning,
my guidance counselor,
Mrs. Roberts,
calls me into her office,
which is never the best sign.
She gets right to it:
"Shanti, I've noticed
that your grades
have been slipping lately.
Down is not the direction
you want your grades to go in
when you're planning on college."
"I know."
"Is there something going on,
something you want to tell me?"
I fidget in my seat.
"No! No, I'm fine.
I need to concentrate more, is all."
Mrs. Roberts lets out a heavy sigh.
"Shanti, we both know
there's more to it.
When you're ready to talk
I'm here, okay?
For now, you can go."
I jump up from the seat
as if it's spring-loaded.
Glover, get your act together!

ONE JOB TOO MANY

Out of clean clothes, I
head for the laundromat since
clothes won't wash themselves.

LOST IN SPACE

Shit!
This essay is due in two days
and I can't even start it
until I make it through
Their Eyes Were Watching God.
Okay. Where was I?
The last paragraph was
something about
back from burying . . .
from burying . . . from burying . . .
Wake. Up!
"back from burying . . ."
There!
". . . back from burying the *dead*."
Finally!
Why can't I read for ten minutes
without checking out?
I'm fine. I just need sleep.
I'm so tired. So tired.
Isn't that what Mom always says
just before she breaks?

ESCAPE

Sleep is my best friend.
I'd marry her if I could.
How happy we'd be!

ALARM

I'm late! I'm late!
Overslept. Again.
School's already started.
I debate:
Is it really worth
dragging my bones out of bed?
Wouldn't it be better
to crawl back
under the covers instead?
Sleep's so sweet,
the way it keeps me from
thinking or feeling
anything at all.
I wonder, though:
How much sleep will it take
to make me
feel okay?

MY MESS

I wake up to a sink
stacked with dirty dishes,
an avalanche of me
not giving a damn for days.

"Okay," I say to no one,
and turn on the faucet.
Focus. Focus. Focus.
Dish by dish
I make something like
progress, or what I think
that looks like.
I move on to sweeping the floor,
then picking up dirty clothes
strewn around the house
like soiled confetti.
I'm on my way
to toss them in the hamper
when the phone rings.
"Hello?"
It's Gloria, my BFF.
"Hey! I've missed you at school
the past couple of days.
You okay?"
It's so good to hear Gloria's voice.
It's so good to not be alone
for a minute
because everything is
Just. Too. Much.
"I . . . I . . . I . . ."
I start to cry.
And. I. Can't. Stop.

OH. ZORA

I rally the next day,
lace up my sneakers
and race through the living room,

passing by my half-read copy of
Their Eyes Were Watching God,
abandoned on the coffee table.
"Sorry, Zora," I whisper,
wondering when
I'll get that essay written.
I head out the door,
mentally rehearsing
exactly how I'm going to grovel
at my teacher's feet.

TREADING WATER

"Good morning, class,"
says Ms. Harper,
my English teacher.
"Please pass your essays forward."
A quick check through the stack
is all it takes to tell her what's missing.
"Ms. Glover," she says,
her eyes like lasers,
"I need to see you after class."
I swallow hard enough
for the hall monitor to hear.
The guidance counselor's last words
still ringing in my ears:
Down is not the direction
you want your grades to go in.
Ms. Harper's eyes
are wet with worry.
She looks at me long and hard
before she speaks.
"This is the third paper in a row

you've been late on," she says.
"I don't see you leaving my class
with a satisfactory grade, do you?"
"But—"
"No buts, Shanti.
I know you've got stuff going on at home,
but if you're serious about college,
I suggest you plan on summer school.
It's your best shot at pulling up
your grade point average."
"But what about graduation?"
"What about it?"

DROWNING

What about it?
What about it?
I sleepwalk down the hall,
all my dreams of graduating
with my senior class
now slivers of shattered glass.
Oh God, oh God, oh God!
"Shanti? What's wrong?"
Gloria's voice pierces my fog.
Swimming in tears,
I land on the safe shore
of my friend's shoulder.
Then, for no reason,
I start to laugh,
and the tears hang around
for company.
Gloria guides me to
the nearest girls' room,

dabs cold water on my face
to erase the tears.
"Better?" she asks.
I nod.
"Okay. So, give."
I make it brief:
Slipping grades.
Summer school.
Bye-bye graduation.
"Ouch. That's a lot," says Gloria.
"You think?"
"But. It's not
the end of the world."
"Oh, thanks!" I say,
pushing Gloria away.
"I'm just saying
you could use the time
to get your head on straight."
My teeth clench.
"My head's just fine."
"I love you, Shanti,
but you need to quit lying,"
says Gloria.
"At least to yourself.
I think you need help."

A BREAK IN THE ICE

Help.
What does that
even look like?

Suddenly, there's an itch
in my brain,
some memory scratching
at the edges.
Oh! Yes. Maybe?

LIFELINE

A business card lay
heavy in my hand, a "gift"
from Mrs. Roberts:
Dr. Kimber Del Valle,
Clinical Psychologist.

Mental Health Center—
those last words slice me open,
leave me bleeding fear.
Am I like my mother now?
Am I crazy, or almost?

An earthquake of nerves,
I punch in the phone number,
shaking head to toe.
"Dr. Del Valle's office. Can
I help you?" *God, I hope so.*

There's one thing I know:
I'm not fine. Not even close.
"Fine" is the lie I just can't
choke on anymore.
"Better" is what I hope for.

DETAILS

But how will I pay?
"Don't worry about that now,"
says Dr. Del Valle.
"My clinic offers programs
that help. We'll figure it out."

PRESCRIPTION

Dr. Del Valle says
I'm beginning a journey
and this is Step One.

DOCTOR'S ORDERS

Face your feelings.
Face your fears.
Face your mom.

VISITING HOURS

I hurry through the hospital halls,
concentrate on the sound of my footfalls,
anything to keep from thinking about
where I am, or why.
I reach room 305.
Breathe. Breathe.

I knock on the door.
A voice weaker than I remember
says, "Come in." As if I really want to.
Breathe. Breathe.
"Hello, Mom. It's me. Shanti."

A NOTE FROM NIKKI GRIMES

* * * * * * * * * * * * *

I was never diagnosed with a clinical mental illness, but years of living with a mother who was, and developing her bad habit of holding things in, eventually led me to the verge of a nervous breakdown. I didn't start to pull back from the edge until I realized that I needed to talk to someone, that I needed to get my thoughts and feelings out.

It doesn't matter how strong you are. Everyone needs help sometimes. Everyone.

People always tell me how strong I am, but you want to know a secret? No one is strong on their own. Everyone needs support. Everyone needs encouragement. Everyone needs a shoulder to cry on. And sometimes, everyone needs a willing ear to listen.

Guess what? You deserve that support, that shoulder, that listening ear. If you really want to be strong, learn to ask for help when you need it. Trust me. A little help goes a long way.

BEGGARS WOULD RIDE

VAL HOWLETT

Content Note: This story references post-traumatic stress disorder and gender dysphoria.

When I first saw the wishing well, it gave me nothing. No tingling excitement, no creepy danger feeling, no sense of the extraordinary either way. Probably because I wasn't paying attention. I only had eyes for Larkin.

We were hanging at Larkin's mansion-home—Larkin and Emma and me. It was a Friday night and we'd just finished an issue of the *Oakfordian*, so we felt newly free. We'd gone to Stop & Shop and bought chips and seven-layer bean dip and a full strawberry pie, because that's the kind of friends we were, not so much the partying-with-booze type as the eating-over-the-top-treats-at-midnight type. We'd spread it all out on the coffee table and put on a movie, but the movie turned out to be slow and kind of annoying, so we turned it off and just talked while we feasted.

The talking turned into complaining, but not in a catty way. More like confiding in each other. Emma stressed about her application for editor in chief, even though I kept telling her she was obviously the top candidate. Larkin was really quiet, until she admitted how hard it was to see her ex, Michael Hart, at every single *Oakfordian* meeting, and how much it hurt when that living turd of a high school guy flirted with other girls on staff, like he was messing with her on purpose. It was heartbreaking to watch her try not to show how upset she was, her chin wobbling the tiniest bit when she said his name.

They kept looking at me expectantly, like they hoped I would unload, too, and part of me wanted to, because I felt the same way they did—like I was going through something. Gender was becoming a big thing in my head, and I had been thinking that I might not be a girl, exactly, that I might be more in between. But I hadn't said anything yet, was stuck guessing how they might respond, like a detective noting all remarks remotely related to guys and girls and trying to piece together how they would think of me, after.

They already knew I liked girls. That wasn't a secret. But gender stuff was different, more daunting to try and explain. And that whole night felt like Girl Time, with the treats and roasting boys we knew, like the magic and closeness of it depended on me being one of them.

So I tried to be. I told Emma of course she would get editor in chief and declared to Lark, "He didn't deserve you," which I one thousand percent meant. Larkin Priest was too good for most people.

Larkin set down her pie plate. "You guys?" she said. "I'm going to share something with you that I haven't told anyone, except Michael."

That shut my overthinking down.

She looked between us with a half-formed, nervous smile, like she was deciding whether to keep going. My heartbeats got really loud. *She's gay*, I hoped.

"What?" Emma said, and then Larkin stood decisively, grinned down at us, and said, "Follow me."

We did, of course, Emma with a slow "Oh-kayyy," but mostly we moved quietly, trading puzzled looks. Especially once Larkin led us downstairs to her back door.

I let out a giggle, too high-pitched. I had been so wrong.

The grounds behind Larkin's home were massive. You wouldn't know from the front, but her house was a high point on a hill that overlooked a forest and, below that, rooftops of a neighboring town. A kaleidoscope of lights went on as we stepped into the spring night chill and trailed her down stone stairs.

We cut past a fancy garden to the end of her yard and followed her into the border woods. The path was so narrow it forced us to walk single file, using our phone lights to see. Emma kept trying to make me laugh, and since I always laugh in uncomfortable situations, it wasn't hard. "We don't get reception in here. That's great, that's . . . great. Larkin, are you in a cult? Cough twice if you're in a cult." And my laughter got to the point where it kept refreshing itself.

Then Larkin's light stopped moving, and so did Emma's. I walked into Emma and she yelped. The lights illuminated vague shapes: a fence ahead of Larkin and a gated door with a lock on it. As Larkin did the combination, I fell into a hole of cry-laughing, and Emma said, "Kayla, you know if you keep laughing, you're going to die first," which did not help. The gate swung open.

We could barely see anything. It smelled faintly like there was a stream nearby, only I couldn't hear water. Larkin went somewhere and returned with two lanterns hanging over her arms, which made her glow like the Ghost of Christmas Past from a Scrooge movie. She moved toward the center of a clearing, illuminating a raised circle of old stone with a flat cover on top.

She said, "It's a wishing well."

I giggled. Emma said, "Sure it is," but Larkin smiled like she knew we would come around.

She went on to explain that it had been in her family since the 1600s; that she had learned about the well sometime in middle school and had her own wishing ceremony last year, when she was fifteen; that it only grants one wish to each person, and the wish only works if it's about you alone. Like it wouldn't work to wish for world peace or to end war or fix global warming. You couldn't even wish for a sick relative to get better. You had to wish for yourself.

"Okay," said Emma, playing along. "So do I just go up to it, and—"
She reached for the cover.

"No no no!" Larkin pushed her back.

I laughed again, but then Larkin said, "Listen," and her voice was
so urgent that it shut me up.

"You get one wish. You should not decide today. You have to really
think it through. Plus, I have a book that will help you."

"Great, now there's homework," Emma said, totally for my benefit,
but the mood had changed. It was too weird to see Lark this invested
in a prank. It didn't feel like her.

Whenever you watch a show about magic, the disbelief is the boring part. But that was where Emma and I were as we headed back
to the house—Emma cracking jokes about fairy tales, me watching
Lark, waiting for everything to make sense. Until we went in, and she
brought us the book.

It was ancient. Brown, bound in some sort of skin. Like a
centuries-old scrapbook. We cleared off the coffee table. Larkin set
the book down gingerly, and some pages slid out a little, like they
had been crammed in years after the book was made. It was all the
writing her family had done about the well, she said. All the things
they had learned about wishing over four centuries—which wishes
worked and which didn't and which had disastrous consequences.
She turned pages that were different sizes and hues of yellow-beige,
all soft with age, full of faded handwritten script. I made out phrases
like *one effective wish . . . competing desires could complicate . . . coins
best to drop include . . .* The book was hard to explain away. It made
the well feel real.

"Oh my god," breathed Emma, like it was a gift.

"It's a good secret, right?" said Larkin.

I didn't feel that way at all. I kept glancing from Larkin's told-you-
so smile to the thick book of instructions. It felt like I was in that
dream where you think it's a normal school day, but suddenly there's

a test and you haven't studied. I'd spent the past year getting myself above water, and when I looked at that book, I couldn't help seeing something that could drag me back under.

It was time for me to go. I don't sleep at other people's houses, and it was really late. I told Emma I needed her to take me home, and she gave me a long look that said she wanted nothing more than to stay.

"Sleep over!" Larkin said. "We have a guest room. We can make pancakes in the morning."

"I don't do guest rooms," I said.

"Not even for pancakes?"

"Not even for pancakes."

"Not even for the chance to read a book that will give you advice on your one wish?"

Emma moaned.

I didn't want to break up their fun. I thought about staying over and not sleeping. But I knew that when the others would sleep, panic would rise inside me like a tide, and if I got that upset, it could take days for it to fall back.

"We can come over next week and read it," I said. Then I added, because I knew it would make her smile, "You know me. I need my beauty rest."

Lark shook her head. "You're such a diva."

I wasn't. On, like, three levels. I stood rigid as she threw her arms around me for a goodbye hug, but then she gave me this extra squeeze that seemed to say she was glad to have me in on her secret.

In Emma's car, Emma was all *I can't believe it* and *we can become anyone we want.* When I didn't respond, she said, "You feel bad about leaving."

She was so sure she knew my mind. I hated that she was right.

"You should just tell her," said Emma. "Otherwise you'll keep feeling bad."

Like it was so easy.

Putting up with Emma's bluntness was part of the deal of being her friend. We'd been friends for eight years. I usually let it roll off me.

But there were moments when it was harder. Like the time last year when I finally told her what was going on with me, that I had been diagnosed with PTSD, and the psychiatrist also found that I had ADHD, a weird little side salad to the main diagnosis. Emma was great at first. She listened, she hugged me. She told me she was glad to know what was going on. But then she said, "You sure have a lot of initialisms."

"You mean, like, acronyms?" I had asked, and she corrected me like she was in newspaper editor mode, like I hadn't just shared this really hard thing. She said that acronyms were pronounced like a word. Whereas initialisms were just letters. They didn't add up to a single sound. ADHD, PTSD. Maybe she was thinking of LGBTQ, too.

When I got home, I performed my rituals—checked the locks, put the ornament with the bells in front of my bedroom door—all the time thinking about the parts of me I wanted to wish away. How was I going to choose?

But I woke up with an idea: to wish away my boobs.

Because I had read about top surgery. It would be really expensive. I would have to get a therapist's permission to get it, and my therapist was great, but I wasn't seeing her for gender stuff. I would probably have to get my mom's permission, too, which would mean explaining to her why I wanted it, which would be tough because I didn't know how to explain it to myself even. And it would probably hurt and recovery would be hard. But if I just wished my boobs away, then I could get around the whole thing.

I loved the idea so much it surprised me. I didn't usually think of myself as superficial, but what did it say about me that I had a chance to change anything and all I thought about were looks?

I considered wishing to be the most handsome genderqueer person ever and to stay that way for my whole life. Still shallow, but it felt smarter because it would do more. I'd probably still lose at least some of my boobs, plus my curves. I'd grow taller, more androgynous. So when I went back into the world, people wouldn't know what gender I was—they'd just see me.

I reached for my phone and saw that Emma and Larkin were already up, texting in our group chat.

Emma had asked Lark what she had wished for. Larkin had replied with a monkey-with-hands-over-mouth emoji.

> E: Are you serious?
>
> L: when you read the book, you'll get why. plenty of my ancestors were treated differently after they wished. like some of them got asked for favors all the time, and some of them got blamed for stuff
>
> E: Okay...but we won't do that!
>
> Me: Didn't you say you made your wish in front of your whole family?
>
> L: yeah but i whispered my wish into the well. nobody could hear me. I like to keep them guessing 😎
>
> E: 😩
>
> Me: 😩
>
> E: I think it's really unfair to tell your friends you wished for something and not disclose what it was.
>
> Me: I don't! People are allowed to have secrets
>
> L: yeah, I'm letting you wish on my family's secret well, aren't I? I told you the secret that matters
>
> E: We're going to figure it out eventually.
>
> E: 🔍
>
> Me: Lark, did any of your relatives wish for beauty?
>
> L: oh yeah. lots.
>
> E: Ugh, Kay, don't. What a waste of a wish.
>
> Me: Did it go okay for them?

L: depends. you know how standards of beauty are always changing?

Me: Sure

L: the well is this natural thing. it doesn't know what is considered "beautiful" in a given year. like there were times when curvy was the thing and other times when stick thin was in

L: so the well would make the wishers look like the prettiest versions of themselves, but it didn't change their bodies much.

E: Right. Because beauty is too ambiguous.

L: a lot of them still stressed about how they looked, even after wishing

Me: Got it

L: plus you're already pretty

I tried to be stern with myself. Larkin probably wasn't hitting on me. She was saying what girls say to girls to be nice. And I didn't even want to be pretty, exactly. Or that wasn't the adjective I was going for. And then Emma chimed in with **Yeah, you're the pretty one.** And then I was annoyed.

Really annoyed.

Unfairly annoyed, because Emma was just being Emma. But what a backhanded compliment. It was mean to both Larkin and me.

And maybe I was annoyed about the well, too. Because it was clear that wishing to be a handsome genderqueer person was too risky. I couldn't trust a four-hundred-year-old well to know what genderqueer meant.

I looked over all the emojis for a couple of minutes before hovering over the top hat. I wanted to send it so bad. But I was done talking. I hit the blushing face, then send, and dropped the phone.

The second time I saw the well, it freaked me out.

We weren't there for my wish. I hadn't gotten through the book yet, probably because of my ADHD. Emma and I had tried to take turns reading it, but from the first line I knew it was hopeless:

> *The well in the wood south of the Settlement we hath*
> *christened Oakford was discovered by my father Thomas*
> *Priest in the yeare 1654 . . .*

The groan came, unbidden, from inside my body.

"What?" Emma asked. She'd read thirty pages before scooting out of the way to give me a turn.

"Did . . ." I glanced between her puzzled look and Larkin's. Was it just me? "Did you have any trouble reading this?"

Emma shook her head. "It's really interesting," she said. "Like a history of our town and magic at the same time."

"It gets easier," Lark promised. "Once they start using a typewriter, it goes faster."

I flipped a chunk of pages at once, slowly, to find different, thinner paper containing print instead of handwriting:

> *Nellie's wish materialised the very moment her coin and water*
> *touched; having witnessed this, Clarence prepared his attire*
> *accordingly . . .*

I read the line over a couple of times, but my mind did the same thing it does with physics explanations or how-to instructions, where it lets the words pass through like skywriting but they are already moving away before I can make sense of them.

I pretended to read the book for a couple of hours each afternoon, turning pages occasionally for effect, but I wasn't fooling anyone. During one of my "turns," when Larkin and Emma were talking about senior staff applications for the *Oakfordian* (Emma, of course, doing most of the talking), I forgot to fake-read and asked Larkin about her managing editor application. They both gave me looks.

"Are you even reading at all?" Emma asked. "Because if you're not, I'll take another turn."

Larkin threw a piece of popcorn at Emma. "Let Kay read!" She turned to me. "You really should read it, Kay. There are so many wishes that sound good in theory but backfire on people."

"Like your wish? Did your wish backfire?" Emma tried to interrupt Larkin, but she didn't bite.

She told me, "It's useful. Even if the language is old-fashioned."

"I know," I said, and the hugeness of the book and enormity of the decision seemed to fill up the room, crashing around my head like waves, so I hardly knew what I was saying. "I really want to. I want to be initialism . . . I mean, informed." I giggled, which only made me more embarrassed.

"Oh, Kay," said Larkin, looking at me like I was a sweet, simple pet. "Never change."

My turns grew shorter. Emma stopped setting a timer for us to switch places. She'd soak in the book's wisdom while I drew doodles to make Larkin laugh and gossiped with Larkin and looked at Larkin. Her perfect olive skin, the way it crinkled around her eyes when she laughed. Her smile, impish and a little bit tantalizing, like she knew something we didn't. What had her wish done for her? Had it made her this magnetic, the kind of person I needed to know all of?

And then, shockingly soon, Emma shut the book with a clap that made Larkin go, "Careful!" and announced that she knew what her wish was going to be.

The well looked different in the daylight, when we could see the whole area. It was surrounded on all sides by two rows of low backless benches, which made it the tallest, most central thing—like a podium. Its stones should have grown dull with age, but they were weirdly shiny. Did Larkin's family polish them? Or was the shine because of its power?

Emma strode right up to it while Larkin and I hung back between benches. Emma seemed to know exactly what to do. She pushed hard at the cover, sliding it off slowly until it thudded onto the dirt. Then she looked in, leaning way down so we could barely see her neck.

Larkin grabbed my hand, squeezed it. I felt her grip all through my body.

When Larkin usually came here, she was surrounded by her family for a big ceremony. She seemed excited by our aloneness, the secrecy of it all, but those same things made me feel shaky, like it would be better to have more witnesses, maybe some expert to make sure Emma didn't mess up.

Emma pulled a coin from her pocket and muttered so low I couldn't hear her. Then we heard a plunk of coin hitting water, and Emma disappeared.

Larkin screamed.

But then we heard Emma's voice, laughing.

"You should've seen your faces," said Emma's voice, and she cackled again. It sounded like she was right in front of us, but before us was just a terrible emptiness of forest moss and the well.

It took me another moment to understand that she was invisible.

"You jerk!" said Larkin. "I thought I killed you." She was still gripping my hand.

"What?" Emma sounded giddy. "No! This isn't about *you*." Larkin's hair flipped up in the air, though there was no wind.

"Don't!" said Larkin, and we heard Emma laugh again, so close to me. I pulled out of Larkin's hold and took two steps back, fast, then scrambled over the bench behind us without conscious thought. Like my body did it without my mind.

"I'm invisible!" came Emma's voice. "I'm invisible, right? I'm looking down and I can't see myself."

"Stop it," I heard myself say. My voice sounded lower and slower than it usually did, like I was underwater. I kept backing up until I hit the wooden gate.

"Hey, Larkin! Do you have any supernatural skills? Wanna show off with me?" said Emma's voice.

Larkin looked down. Her shoe had come untied. "Emma, I know

you're having fun," she said, like she was talking to a small child, "but this is kind of creepy. Can you—can you turn back?"

No sound. Was she coming for me next? My heart throbbed in my ears.

"Are you still there?" Larkin cried.

Then she was—in the space between me and Lark, half Emma, half the shape of Lark behind her. Like a TV ghost, until she was all the way Emma, skinny and solid and grinning, her glasses askew. "Sorry," she said, adjusting them. "It took me a minute to figure out how to come back."

I watched Lark's face relax. Watched her laugh, and Emma laugh, too. Larkin ran around the front bench toward Emma, hugged her like she'd made a winning touchdown. "You did it!" she shrieked, and Emma said, "I can turn invisible!" and Larkin said, "*Yeah* you can," and they jumped and hugged together, looking at me like I should get in there.

I hated that even smiling felt like too much, that I couldn't marvel at Emma or her miracle, that all I could do was focus on my breath, try to slow it down.

We eventually returned to Larkin's house and gathered our things. I couldn't say much. Emma didn't even protest when I asked her to drive me home.

I had been in therapy for PTSD for a year, so I thought I knew all my triggers. Mostly they had to do with sleep, because the bad thing that happened to me involved being woken up from sleep. They included: Hearing noises when I was in bed. People visiting our condo at night.

I stayed up late if there were nighttime guests. I kept my windows locked. I did before-bed meditations to calm down, and set a bell ornament by the door to alert me if anyone did come in. Beyond bedtime, there were a couple of others: I couldn't be alone or even mostly alone with strangers. Which meant I wouldn't take an Uber or anything like that. When I got a ride, it had to be from someone I knew.

My therapist kept telling me it was okay. That my rituals weren't signs of how messed up I was; that I should instead think of them as steps I took to feel safe. And whenever I got overwhelmed worrying about the future and college and how was I ever going to cope with staying in a dorm or sleeping with someone I liked, she reminded me: one day at a time, I could make new plans as I needed them, I could just be here today, drawing and doing homework and hanging out with friends. I didn't have to figure out my entire future.

But when I discovered a new trigger, it was hard not to feel hopeless. Because how could I relax if I didn't know what would set me off?

Emma flicked on and off in the driver's seat, and I couldn't tell her to stop.

She knew what had happened to me. She probably would have stopped if I'd asked, even if she didn't understand the connection between her invisibility and what I had been through before.

But it would have been embarrassing to show her how upset I was. I rode it out, crying only after I made it inside. I had to assure my mom I was okay and do breathing exercises and watch *The Great British Baking Show* until my thoughts slowed enough for me to go to my room and set the bell ornament before the door.

The third time I saw the well, it called to me. Visiting it was my idea. Though at first, I thought it was only to cheer up Larkin.

We'd spent a lot of time just the two of us since Emma made her wish. Emma was off taking action. She'd explained her plan over group chat, that she was going to hunt down an amazing story for the paper in time to turn in her application for editor in chief, so she'd be sure to get the position. Hopefully the story would be so good it would win awards, which would help her get into Northwestern, which would help her become a big-time reporter someday.

I tried to be proud of my friend who had her life figured out. When she sent updates like **I think the field hockey coach is sleeping with a student. I'll be staking out the locker room after school** . . . or **Hid in the teachers' lounge today. You wouldn't believe what they say about us** . . . I would text exclamation points and try to think of good follow-up questions, ignoring the queasy feeling that came for me whenever I thought of Emma being so close to people who couldn't see her.

Larkin kept inviting me over to read the book, and I kept going, even though I couldn't read the book, because of Larkin. I'd lean over the delicate pages and try to scan them for instructions or warnings, but mostly I'd focus on how near Larkin's body was to mine, and did she mean to sit so close to me in such a huge room or was I reading into it too much? And when she'd talk to me, I'd turn from the book completely. It felt so different, being only with her. Less like a girl group I was trying to keep my place in and more like two people who had gotten close enough to know each other's fixations and mood swings and daily complaints and still wanted to float in the same water.

The day after she turned in her senior staff application, Larkin was so wound up that she didn't even pretend to let me read. She poked me in the side and rolled grapes across the table at me, and when I called her eight years old she delighted in it, firing off questions like an annoying younger sibling: "Do you have any ideas for your wish?" and "Are you afraid of wishing?"

"No!" I lied. "You're the one who keeps saying to 'read carefully' and 'use caution.'" I did a deep teacher voice and she smiled. But her smile melted quick.

"Do you know what Emma asked me yesterday?"

"What your wish was?" It was kind of a joke. Emma asked her that every day.

"That, and if I wanted her to spy on Michael."

I couldn't read her voice, couldn't tell if she was as creeped out as me. "Do you?"

"No!" Larkin pressed down on a grape until it squished. "I need to think about Michael less, not more. I think about him too much already."

It was jarring to consider Michael for more than a second, to remember there'd been a whole chapter of Larkin's life before Emma and me, when Michael was the person she told about the well.

Michael knew. He had probably made a wish.

"What did Michael wish for?"

Larkin leaned over the table, looking down at its surface so I couldn't see her eyes. Then she said, "I don't know, but I'm pretty sure it had to do with sex. The week after he made it was when he cheated on me."

She didn't sound like the usual Lark then. She spoke smaller.

I thought about the gift she had offered us, how none of us deserved it. She could have kept the well to herself.

I was keeping so much to myself.

"Do you ever just hang out with it?" I asked. "The well?"

She looked at me funny. "It's not alive. It has supernatural properties, but it's not, like, a creature. Kay, what do I have to do to get you to read the book?"

I ignored that last part. "I know, but it's this thing that's had a huge effect on your whole life, right behind your backyard. Don't you ever want to look into the water? Not to make a wish. Just to look."

"You can hardly see the water. The well is deep." But she smiled at me like she couldn't wait to try.

That's why I thought we went down there. Not to wish. To gaze into something powerful, because we could.

But as we ran through her yard under the sunset, I felt light, like I was giving in to a wave.

The well stood waiting like a little beacon, its stones reflecting the day's final sunbeams. I helped Larkin push the cover off until it hit the dirt. Larkin stood at the edge and leaned over. I joined her, our cold hands touching as they rested on the stone.

She was right. The well went deep. I couldn't see anything until she held her phone directly over it and the water reflected that little bit of light. If I hadn't seen that, or smelled the cavelike wet, I wouldn't have been sure there was water in it at all.

I don't know how long we stood together. Eventually Lark asked, "Should we sit?" and we moved back to the closest bench. I had barely sat down when she asked me, "Do you still want to know what I wished for?"

Before I could even say yes, she leaned toward my ear, smiling like a girl who had the juiciest gossip, and whispered, "I didn't wish for anything."

The feeling of her mouth almost touching my ear was so intense I couldn't take in her words. "What?"

"My dad made a wish when he was a teenager and he really regrets it," she rushed on. "All my life, he's been saying how teenagers are too young to know what they need. My mom made her wish as an adult, when he brought her into the family, and he's so jealous. It's, like, a thing in their marriage."

I didn't understand. "But you had a big wishing ceremony."

She smirked. "I just did that to get my relatives off my back. So I wouldn't have to listen to any more nagging about what everyone thought I should wish for. But when it was my time to look into the well, I didn't think anything. I just muttered nonsense, like, 'Banana banana, this is not a wish.' Just for the illusion." She was trying to make me laugh. I knew it, but I was too shocked to give her what she wanted.

"But actually," she kept going, "I'm going to take my time. I'm going to wait until I need something really badly, and that's when I'll wish."

She was so pleased with herself. I wanted to shake it out of her.

Because she had made it all the way to sixteen without needing anything badly.

"So if you don't think teenagers should make wishes, why are you letting us do it?" I was angry, I realized. I didn't want to be her experiment.

"Because I like you."

"Okay, but—" I was so agitated about the responsibility she'd given us, responsibility untested, that I was completely stunned when she leaned in and kissed me.

I didn't kiss her back. Not at first. I let my jaw kind of hang as she pulled back, smiling, a bit shy.

For a second, I wondered if I'd somehow made my wish by accident. Then I remembered that a wish couldn't affect another person. Larkin just liked me.

"Was that okay?" she asked. Like she was scared I didn't want her.

I kissed her like a flood, like an answer. I knelt on the bench, then straddled it, and my hands were on her broad shoulders, on her back, my leg over hers, our shoes touching. We were close, we were rocking together like one boat. The bench was awkward and shaky, but it didn't matter because I wasn't. I was my body, for once. Not a walking shell that moved my anxiety around. A real person, who acted. Like Larkin and Emma. Like Michael Hart.

After a while, Lark pulled back, smiling at me. She ruffled my hair, then turned to face the well. The sun was down, and it stood in shadow. It had gone back to being a secret.

I adjusted myself beside her, still in awe, sneaking glances at her—this surprising, bold person who'd confided in me and kissed me first. I wanted her to know me.

I wished for it.

Not out loud—I was way too cautious to make a formal wish on a rush of feeling. But inside, I wished. I wished for Lark to look at me and see all my inner currents, even the hard ones—instantly.

So we could skip over the explanation part, the part where I'd have to put words to states that were too big, where I'd stammer inadequately while watching her face, needing too much for her to take me in and think I was deep and brave and doing my best—not someone too messed up to love.

But I didn't wish it over the well.

Larkin turned to me, grinning. "*Now* will you sleep over?"

I could barely say it. "I can't."

"My parents aren't here," she went on. "But even if they were, they wouldn't suspect anything. Since you're a girl."

I almost flinched. I was so far from the person she thought I was. "Actually . . ."

I tried to convince myself to keep going. I looked down at my jeans so I wouldn't have to watch her expression change. "I don't know if I am a girl."

"What?"

I made myself face her. She was giggling a little, like she couldn't tell if I was joking. Or maybe she was doing what I always did, laughing because she didn't know what was going on.

"I think I might be more . . . in between."

"Oh-kay," she said. She squinted like she was trying to read me. It felt important to hold her gaze, make it clear I was serious.

Then she said, "This sounds like a thing we can talk about when you stay over."

I didn't know what to say. I'd expected something else. I didn't know what—just more of a reaction.

She wasn't being mean. She wasn't rejecting me. But she sounded like she was proud to have steered us back to a minute ago, when she'd been coaxing me to stay over like it was a fun game she knew she would win.

Like she wished I hadn't been honest.

"I can't" was all I could say. Again.

"What if I told you my parents took their cars? So I can't drive you home." She was going for a sexy tease. I started to panic.

"Lark, you don't understand," I told her. "I have to get a ride." I could hear my voice. It sounded terrible. I had wanted this for so long, and now I was ruining it. I was going to ruin every potential relationship before it could even start.

I got up, stumbled out of the gate, fumbled with my phone light, and ran up the path. I didn't know if she would chase me or take what I said as a burn and let me go. Either way, I needed her not to see me fall apart.

When I reached her yard, my phone started vibrating. I had gotten a wave of texts while it had no signal. I unlocked it and saw that most of the texts were from Emma, an hour ago.

E: Can you believe it?

E: Can you believe that backstabbing piece of shit?

"Oh my god," said Lark, looking at her phone. She was behind me, had followed me back. "They announced the senior staff."

The email had been sent to everyone on the *Oakfordian* staff, with the subject "The Big Decision." At the very top:

Larkin Priest: Editor in Chief

Not Emma.

I turned on Larkin. "I thought you applied for managing editor."

Larkin looked up from her phone slowly. I watched her face as she registered what I'd said, as if she had momentarily forgotten I was there.

"I was going to. But then I thought, why not aim for the highest thing? You know, just in case? I really didn't think I would get it." The edge of her lips hinted at a smile.

I stepped back. I didn't know whether to believe her. Because she had kept it from us, from me. Even if she had changed her application at the last minute, she'd had this whole afternoon alone with me to let me know.

I didn't wish for anything, she had whispered to me earlier. Had that been a lie, too?

I looked back at Emma's texts.

E: I guess we finally know Larkin's wish.

E: To get whatever she wants.

E: It has to be.

E: I was there for deliberations you know. I stood in the corner of the room and listened to the seniors talk about how great Larkin is. Know what they said about me? That I'm "not leadership material." That I'm too intense and weird to be in charge.

E: The whole things so fucked. Like its my college applications on the line and I spent three years working my butt off for the paper and it all turned into a popularity contest because of Larkin's stupid wish

[Missed call from Emma Murphy]

[Missed call from Emma Murphy]

E: Are you going to say anything???

E: You're with her right now aren't you

E: You're pathetic too you know that? Choosing that backstab-ber over your oldest friend because of a crush

E: You can't even read a book.

"Kay!" Larkin called to me from a window. She had retreated to the house. "The book is gone!"

By the time I reached Larkin, she was pacing around the trashed rec room, typing madly on her phone. Eyeliner streams marked her cheeks. She told me she was getting an Uber. She wanted the two of us to ride to Emma's house and demand the book.

"I'll claw her eyes out if I have to," she stormed. "I have to get it back. My family is going to kill me. I'm going to be disowned."

She assumed that I would help her.

She didn't realize I was not there.

My body was. The shell of me. But the combination of the invaded room and this frantic version of Larkin set off my mind. They were triggers I'd never planned for. People turning out different from how I thought. People twisting into their most unstable parts.

I was full-on overalert exit planning.

Emma had been in Larkin's house. Emma was mad at Larkin. And Emma was mad at me. I had to get to my house before she could.

I pulled out my phone. Emma's last message about how I couldn't read popped up again. My text blurred as I typed. I needed to lock the doors and windows and put the ornament out, and still I probably wouldn't be able to sleep.

"Uber's here," said Lark. "Let's go."

I followed her outside. I could not speak. I could only move my body, put one foot in front of the other, try to breathe more slowly than the thoughts in my head.

An unfamiliar car pulled into her circular driveway. Larkin ran up to it, her hair half out of her ponytail. She opened the door, then turned to me, her cheeks still streaked. She called my name, wobbly and unsure, the way she sounded when she talked about Michael Hart.

Another car drove in behind the Uber, a familiar sight.

Finally, I found words.

"I'm not going."

I did not stay to watch her take in my betrayal. I turned and fled to my mom's car.

I couldn't tell if Emma was in my room, or had been. Nothing seemed out of place. Maybe I'd made it home and locked the doors and windows before she reached me. Or maybe she knew me enough to understand that even though she was furious, invading my room was a boundary not to cross.

I hoped so. But I couldn't know. I climbed into bed with my clothes on, pulled the covers over my knees, and looked around, jumping every time there was a creak, saying "Emma?" pathetically to the probably empty air.

I wished I could be the person Larkin had wanted to kiss. Or the kind of person who saw things through, who could insist on talking over gender stuff with Lark, who could confront Emma about sneaking around instead of sinking under the creepy feeling. Who wasn't held captive by my own inescapable panic.

That was when I knew what my wish should be. Because it all came down to one initialism: PTSD.

If it wasn't too late. If I could find a way back onto Larkin's grounds and make it to the well.

Of course, I couldn't wish away the bad thing that had happened to me, because it involved another person. But I could wish for its continued effect on my life to disappear.

I could almost see it.

I would turn away from the well after wishing, after witnessing the dark shadow of my reflection rippled by a coin. I would see the day again the way Emma had once described getting glasses for the first time, realizing that leaves were crisp, that every single one had distinct edges. I'd see my friends anew—Larkin and Emma each with their faults and ultimately good intentions. Not versions of them blurred by my own pain.

And if I tried to think back to how I had felt before, or to the incident itself, that time in middle school when I'd been so unfathomably scared that my body didn't let me feel it until years later, when it drenched my whole world, I would feel sorry for the kid I had been. But in a distant way—the way you feel about someone in an article or a storybook. *Poor thing*, I'd think. *They got something they did not deserve.*

But the feeling would be small. Manageable. A tiny penny in a deep well.

A NOTE FROM VAL HOWLETT

✱ ✱ ✱ ✱ ✱ ✱ ✱ ✱ ✱ ✱ ✱ ✱ ✱

As someone who lives with multiple initialisms, I set out to write "Beggars Would Ride" about the fear of being too much, of having too many problems to ever be loved. I did not expect it to end where it does, with PTSD at the forefront and Kay feeling such despair. But once I wrote it, I knew it was right. Not because I don't feel optimistic. But I believe that when writing about mental health problems, acknowledging pain is as important as communicating that recovery is possible.

My experience with recovering from trauma has not been a simple path, a bruise that hurts less until you forget it's there. It feels more like waves. Doing the hard work of finding a therapist, facing the unbearable, and practicing coping techniques has helped me experience peaks—stretches of months, years even, when I feel relatively unburdened. These peaks are worth the work. But I've also had frustrating dips that can feel like I'm back where I started. If you've been there, I want you to know that you're not alone.

MY SISTER RAFAELA IS A GOOD PERSON
MERCEDES ÁNGEL ACOSTA

Content Note: This story references complex post-traumatic stress disorder, rejection sensitive dysphoria, and severe anxiety.

I can't stop thinking about what Titi Celia said.

I trust Dr. Emilio. It's not that I don't believe in him.

But anytime Auntie criticizes me, I just can't stop focusing on it—

Grrr!

You OK, chica?

I'm fine!

But even more, I worry about Rafaela not liking me.

My older sister is the coolest person I know. She's pretty. She's studying to be a vet tech, and she has great taste in music, lots of friends, and is super talented at a lot of things. Like healing people, making music, and public speaking.

And I'm just . . . me.

Stupid, anxious, sensitive me.

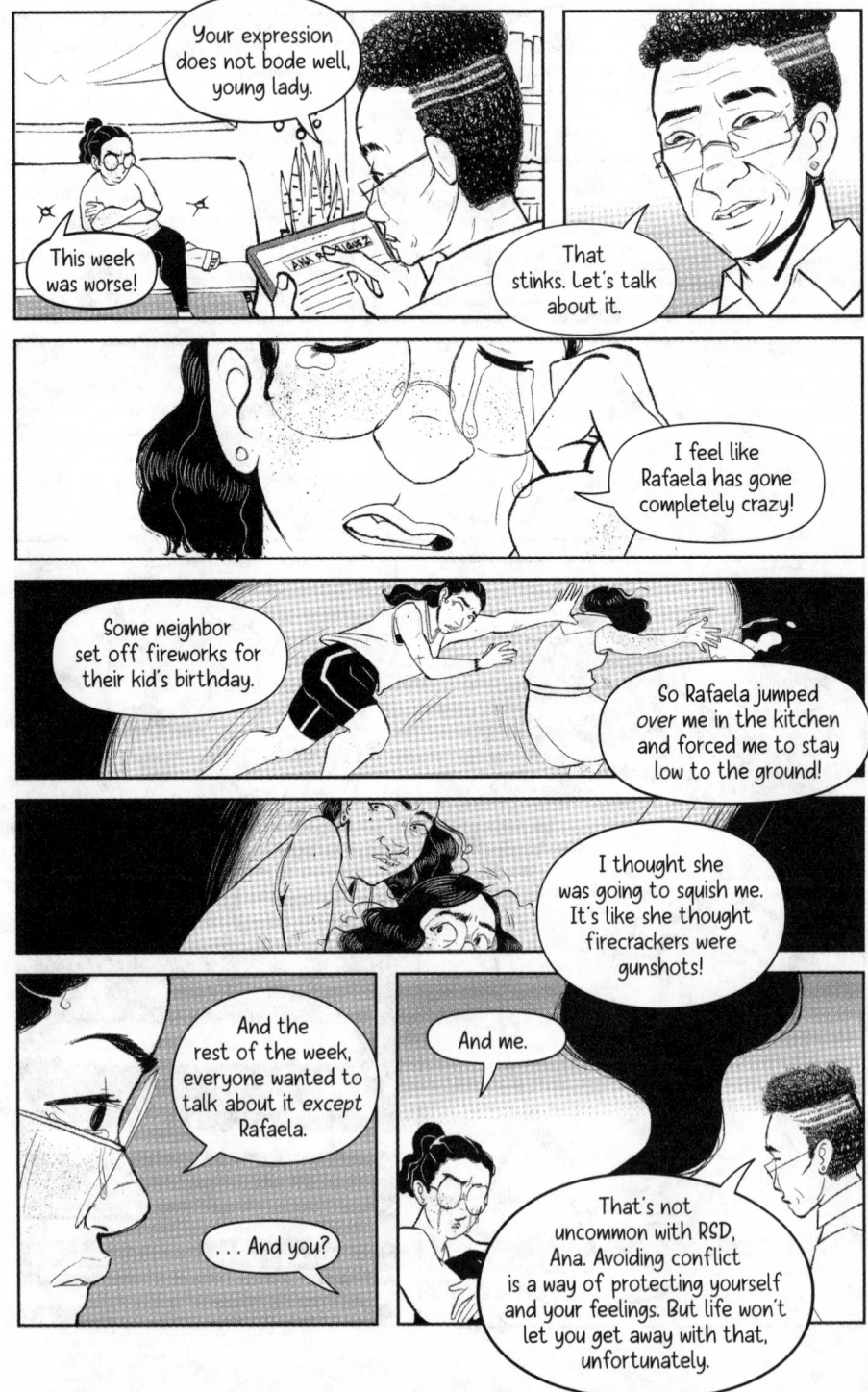

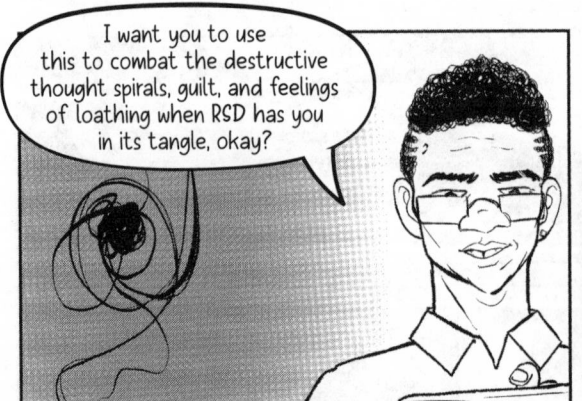

I want you to use this to combat the destructive thought spirals, guilt, and feelings of loathing when RSD has you in its tangle, okay?

You want your positive experiences and thoughts to balance the negative ones . . .

"Like swimming, it's going to take a lot of practice."

"It won't happen overnight. But you can try to cultivate these experiences, just like you'd go to swim practice."

Wanna get ice cream afterward?

Sure thing, Ana.

For you, mija. Té. Now go before you are late for Torah Club!

Thanks, Abuela.

Here, Ana. I know you like yours cold.

What is it?

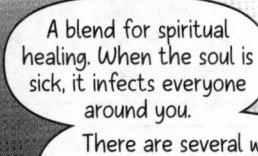

A blend for spiritual healing. When the soul is sick, it infects everyone around you.

There are several ways to heal, mija. And families like ours, they heal or break together.

Gracias, Mamá Hilda.

Cultivate *these* experiences.

And don't punish yourself when they don't last.

Do you know what a street medic is?

I do. People with medical training who aid injured folks at protests, riots, and disasters, right?

Rafaela's got paramedic training and she's great at healing people. She's been all over to provide support. Standing Rock, Louisville, Virginia . . . places where it got ugly.

She doesn't talk about it. But she remembers it. More than she wants to.

Ana, it is very likely that your sister is suffering from PTSD.

I know.

Therapy and treatment might help her manage better.

Yeah.

A NOTE FROM MERCEDES ÁNGEL ACOSTA
* * * * * * * * * * * * * * * * * * * *

It is actually amazing to me how much attention deficit hyper-activity disorder (ADHD) and complex post-traumatic stress disorder (C-PTSD) can mimic each other sometimes. As someone with both, I wanted to tell a story that showed how family members can impact one another when more than one person under the roof is struggling. More important, I wanted to show how families can also heal together. Like Rafaela, I am a street medic whose work at Black Lives Matter protests, water protection sites, and homeless camp evictions haunts me. And like Ana, my rejection sensitive dysphoria that stems from my ADHD can make me nervous, obsessive, and hyper-vigilant, questioning my every move and those of the people around me. Though coping with my conditions is a lifelong effort, I want to grow and flourish in my own space like Ana and Rafaela. My family doesn't always understand my mental health struggles. We've grown more distant since the summer of 2020, when my heart broke into pieces at the things that I saw and suffered in the streets. Giving Ana and Rafaela safe spaces to heal and ways to hold on to each other felt a little bit like healing myself, too.

VERBATIM

PATRICK DOWNES

*Content Note: This story references grief,
hallucinations, and disordered eating.*

. . . and I'm here because I fell apart.

When was that, Abraham?

Only my brother ever called me Abraham.

What would you prefer?

You can call me Abe.

All right, Abe. Do you remember when you fell apart?

I was falling apart for months. But I remember the day . . .

The day?

The day when things—I don't know—turned.

What was the day?

October the fourth. The feast day of Saint Francis.

You deserve the truth. I was admitted to the hospital after being hit by a car. I was hit by a car because I pushed my little brother out of the way. The only trouble is, my little brother wasn't there. I only thought he was.

That was a year ago, the night of October 10.

Even if I'd never been hit by a car, though, I would've ended up in the hospital. It's not just that I hallucinated my brother. The dreams and headaches; the anger; the sadness; the walking at all hours, talking to myself; the fits of laughing and crying. The fasting. Food was dust in my mouth. I didn't want to eat, and I thought fasting would clear my head.

It didn't.

I'd already given up playing rugby and basketball, given up wrestling. I'd stopped playing piano: when we play music, just like when we listen to music, we feel it; we might lose ourselves, forget where we are, break down.

In five months, I'd changed. I didn't know myself. I couldn't guess what I'd feel or think from one minute to the next. I fell silent. I said nothing to anyone, ever.

I was wild.

This scared me, made me sad, and soothed me all at the same time. Scared me because our minds can become a wilderness, uncharted and totally unknowable. Everywhere, creatures we never want to meet face-to-face; plants we never want to smell or taste or see, poisonous fruits and leaves; hills and valleys and dark lakes we don't want to cross; wide, black, endless forests we don't want to enter. Made me sad because I was tired and lonely and had nowhere to turn, no one to understand. Soothed me because it gave me an answer: I felt this way because I was losing my mind.

That explained it. Phew.

The morning of October 4, a week before I threw myself in front of a car, everything I'd been feeling came to a head. I woke to wind and rain. I woke in my bed, but I *felt* like I was lying in the ground under the cold storm. I was soaked and shivering, a six-foot-four-inch exposed nerve. I wanted to be done with my skin and muscle, my sadness and fear and all the other feelings, the endless emotions. This didn't mean I wanted to die. I didn't want to *be anything*, not even dead.

Six days later, I was brought to the hospital because I jumped in front of a car. I meant to and didn't mean to. I remember the weak sun pinkening the sky, almost no one in the street. The occasional shop owner, getting an early start; a delivery truck; a dog walker or two; almost no buses or cars: the city asleep, mostly. I had walked for three hours but, in all that time, made it only four miles from my parents' house, as the crow flies, walking in a spiral, out and out and out. My brother met up with me, out of nowhere, surprising me. We talked—I had some questions for him—and he lost track of the sidewalk. He wandered into the street. A car, one headlight out, not speeding or anything, just moving along, and my brother, invisible it seemed. I had to do something. I leapt at my brother. It didn't even occur to me to yell—

In the hospital, I asked to talk to the chaplain. I don't know why. Not really. I only know I wanted to talk.

The chaplain came. We talked. He suggested I write, that I write down what mattered to me. What mattered was what we talked about. This is what I remember of our first conversation.

The feast day of Saint Francis. That's a very interesting fact, Abe. How did you know October fourth is the feast day of Saint Francis?

On the Sunday closest to that date, every year, my dad would take my little brother and me to church—it was the only time all year we went to church, but it was a tradition. We went for the blessing of animals.

The blessing of animals?

People could bring their pets, small and large, to be blessed by the priest. You'd see little dogs, medium dogs, and big dogs; iguanas and ferrets and cats; snakes and rats and hedgehogs. Goldfish in a bowl. Birds in cages, parrots on shoulders. Someone once brought a miniature horse, and the horse pooped right in front of the big altar and cross and all that.

Well, if you're going to bring the animals in, I guess you have to expect poop. What was the strangest animal or the one you remember most?

The leashed camel. Its giant, soft, long-haired feet. It ploofed down the nave—isn't that what they call it, the big center aisle? It ploofed down the aisle, grinding its teeth. Its hump bare and hairy at the same time. Its head high—noble, you know? It seemed above it all, all the emotions, all the people. Seven feet tall, taller than anyone except maybe Tyson Graver's dad, who played ten seconds at center for an NBA farm team before his knee exploded. So, yeah, the camel.

A camel. That's pretty memorable, for sure.

I think someone must have arranged it in advance. I never saw it before or after. I mean, who keeps camels around here?

No one I know. [Pause.] Is there anything else you remember from this time, Abe, from the blessing of the animals?

[Closing my eyes.] I remember the damaged animals, the animals that were hurt.

The damaged animals?

Yeah. A wingless crow. A blind raccoon. A two-headed lamb, though one of the heads was hanging down at the end of its own neck, dead. My brother cried at the sight of them.

Did your brother find these animals frightening or saddening? Both?

Both, I guess. I never asked.

How about you? Did they sadden you?

Yes. [Pause.] So, so sad. [Pause.] Who wants to see an animal sick or suffering, or see . . .

Or see . . . ?

Or see a child suffering, a kid? Who wants to see a kid sick and dying? But the damaged and sick deserve to be blessed, too. They need the blessing, the help of God or the gods, way more than any of the other animals.

Abe, we moved from animals who suffer to children.

[Sighing, sinking into my pillows.] Can we move on?

Of course. [Pause.] May I ask, though? Your father would take you and your little brother to the blessing of the animals, right? So did you have animals for the blessing?

I thought you said we could move on.

You're right. You're right. I—

No. We weren't allowed to have animals, pets. My parents wouldn't let us.

Your parents wouldn't let you have pets?

My mother said she would be left cleaning up after them, that the pets would become her responsibility. My father said they wouldn't live long. They both said pets burn a hole in your wallet, that they're expensive, and then they die. But . . .

Yes?

Kids can die, too. I mean, why have kids, when they cost a lot and can die young?

I'm not sure we expect children to die. Do you?

My brother died. [Pause.] My brother. He died. Nine years old. My parents would probably take in all the dogs and cats and camels in the world if they could have my brother back.

I was almost five years old when my little brother was born. I was five when my parents and teachers started describing me as sensitive— too sensitive. That was also when I started getting my headaches. And when the nightmares woke me and woke me. I hated sleep; I feared sleep.

So maybe it's a surprise I made it all the way to fifteen before I cracked up. But it's when something happens, with an event, when we might lose ourselves, fall apart.

Hard times land on a spectrum between *bad* and *really, really bad.* But where do we put the unthinkable? There's not a lot that's truly unthinkable, truly unimaginable. The unthinkable when it's thought, the unimaginable when it's imagined, drives us into the ground, turns us mad, makes us beg for mercy. Sometimes it might kill us.

Maybe getting hit by a car to save your invisible brother is only really, really bad. But that happened because the unthinkable happened.

People like me—

People like you? I lost you for a minute there, Abe. You were thinking? Remembering?

People like me, who watch their little brother die of brain cancer, an inoperable tumor, and then watch their parents' relationship come unraveled and the tree their little brother liked to climb turn black.

[Pause.] What was your brother's name?

Connor. I don't even know what kind of tree it was. Something climbable, a dogwood maybe, a small, kind of fragile-looking flowering tree. It grew in our backyard. My brother was freakishly strong, which is weird to think about since he died before he was ten. I remember finding him up in the tree when he was four. I didn't know he was up there until I heard him laughing. And there he was, eight, ten feet off the ground, giggling. The tree held him in its arms, and I said, "Connor, get down here," though I wished the tree would just let go of him, let him fall right on down through its branches to the ground. He stopped laughing and came down. I said something nasty to him, I'm sure.

What do you mean?

I probably called him some kind of name or hit him in the back of the head or something equally mean.

Why?

I didn't like my brother for most of his life. I had no good reason for not liking him. Jealousy, I guess, my own messed-up heart. But I was trying to tell you that tree died when my brother died. Can a tree grieve? It's like the tree missed my brother almost as much as I did. So, yeah, I was thinking about people like me who feel like they're starving for understanding, for something, anything, that makes sense, for one thing that could help them feel an emotion other than fear, other than sadness, other than grief, and I was starving for answers; I was starving for my little brother who died . . .

[Silence.]

That is a terrible, deeply painful wound, Abraham.

It was worse for my brother. [Pause.] I'm not sure why I'm telling you any of this.

I don't think we can always know why we talk or don't talk to other people about what's inside us, what we're going through. Some people talk; some are silent.

When I stopped talking, people thought I was being rude, that it was a way of being violent, of punishing the world. As if silence is war. Maybe it can be war—the silent treatment and all that—but it wasn't for me. I just didn't know what to say. I didn't know how to speak about what was inside me. I thought it was best to stay quiet so I didn't confuse anyone or say the wrong thing.

Who'd ever imagine I'd jump in front of a car to save my brother, dead for five months already, as if I were doing something heroic? The accident cracked my head open, shattered my jaw and eye socket, broke my arm, one leg, and four ribs, burst my spleen. That the driver of the car had a blood alcohol level three times the legal limit and only one functional headlight didn't really matter. He might have gotten lucky and arrived home safe and sound without hurting anyone. His life changed when I dived in front of him.

I was a solid athlete once. And I was a solid B-plus student. I played the piano. That was probably what I was best at: piano. Piano and math. And French.

But those all went away.

No. I wasn't best at piano, math, and French. Wasn't best at fighting and running. I was really best at suffering.

I was best at *being* pain.

That's what having a movable, untethered mind is. That mind is pain.

And that mind became a no.

No to everything.

No food. No appetite. No hair.

No books. No reading. No math. No crosswords.

No Bach or Monk. No covers of Bon Iver or Alicia Keys.

No talking, either. For months and months, I didn't say anything, ever, to anyone.

No. No. No. No. No.

You're surprised you're talking to me at all, Abraham?

[Frowning.] Yes. [Shaking my head.] I don't even remember your name.

That's easily fixed. My name is Julius.

And you're a chaplain here.

That's right.

What religion?

I'm here to support anyone who wants to speak to me about what's on their minds or in their hearts. You can call me interfaith.

But don't you have your own religion?

I do, yes.

And . . . ?

We can discuss this if—

Do you believe in God?

[Smiling.] Yes.

Why?

You're asking important questions, but maybe we can talk more about this, about why I believe in God, another day. I want very much to get back to you, if that's all right.

[Shrugging.] I guess so.

Are you ready to return to why you're here, and why we're talking together?

[Nodding.]

Good. Thank you. I'm very glad you're talking to me, that you asked to talk to me, especially when you're surprised by it. Can you tell me more about why you're surprised?

I think about God. I don't know why my brother died, why he suffered. I'm like everybody else who doesn't understand why God lets the horrible happen. What's unthinkable to a human is thinkable to God, right? But it's hard to believe in a God who watches children die of cancer, their heads ruined and rotten on the inside.

Is this why you're surprised to be talking to me?

Maybe. Maybe it's connected. I haven't talked to anyone in months. Not a word. None, except to myself. So why now?

Do you have any kind of answer for that? Anything that makes sense?

Nothing that makes sense. I can't even say I'm especially angry at God. I never really believed in God much anyway. But my brother's death clinched it. I mean, for sure there's no God. Never was. It's pure fantasy. The facts speak for themselves. [Pause.] No offense.

None taken. You're saying what you think based on your experience, your extremely painful experience. Do you think, if there were a God, that God wouldn't let children die?

No. I'm selfish. I'm saying he, it, she, they, whatever wouldn't let *my* brother die. *My* brother wouldn't have died. [Closing my eyes, turning away, feeling kind of sick to my stomach.] Maybe there's nothing to talk about.

A verbatim is used to teach social workers and psychologists and counselors and therapists and chaplains how to talk to people who might be going through a hard time. These people who want to help other people study the verbatims, the word-for-word transcripts between a caregiver and a person who's hurting. Sometimes they read them out loud or even act them out, to hear what worked or didn't work. They practice talking to people who've gone through some-thing difficult. A trauma. A painful event. Maybe a loss, a death.

Their own rough minds.

But this verbatim is for you, my friend, the one who's suffering like I did, who's troubled, who's seen the unthinkable. I will let it play out. I'm not saying it's perfect, the first conversation, that it solved everything all at once. It didn't make me want to talk to the world again, or fix anything that turned me so sad and wild, or get me to sleep easier. My brother stayed dead. My thoughts and feelings were still a dammed river. I'm saying it mattered. It was a start.

Everything here is the first talk between that chaplain, Julius, and me. It wasn't all that long, but it mattered. It helped. I realized while we were talking, or Julius realized, that I had hope. I had hope. More of it than I knew.

Abraham, can you tell me what you feel when you say there might not be anything to talk about?

[Silence.]

I'm here when you're ready.

[Deciding.] There's a lot.

Start by naming one feeling. Naming what we feel helps clear our thoughts, helps sort what's happening in us.

Sad.

Sad . . .

[Nodding.]

Good, Abraham. Do you want to say more about that sadness?

[Suddenly laughing.] My brother was five years younger than me, a little less, and I wasn't happy when he came along. I'd gotten pretty used to being the only child, the prince, you know? He took every-thing from me. Or so I thought. What explains that? Why is my heart wired that way, where I could feel jealous of a baby—a baby!—and then hold on to that jealousy . . . for years? Let it poison us, make us sick? He took away my specialness, right? And he gave me headaches and bad sleep and night terrors. He didn't, of course, but it felt that way. He must have felt how much I hated him, so he never made a sound around me. If he was crying, he stopped when he saw me. If he was laughing, he stopped. He was a baby, and he knew. He *knew* I hated him. And he must have thought, *If I'm going to live until tomorrow, I'd better shut up.* So he might have been the best-behaved baby and kid because I hated him.

But if I understand what you said before, his death hit you hard and is still a deep wound.

It's why I'm here, right? Like this, banged up. [Pause.] I came to love him, my brother. But before I loved him, I hated him. I hated him even more for a little while because he would be so patient with me, so soft, like he already loved me, in spite of everything. "Do you want to play with me, Abraham?" "Can I get you something to drink, Abraham?" "Abraham, are you sad?" Like he felt sorry for me, sorry for me for hating him. Like he could *see* the trouble inside me, all the invisible stuff. As if he wished my heart were more peaceful, not for his sake, but for mine. That seriously killed me. [Pause.] But I remember, I remember something terrible I can't let go of.

[Waiting, then:] Are you able to say what that is, Abraham?

I wished him dead. I was still young, too, but I wished him dead. I wanted the strange creature that was my brother gone. He was four— a little four-year-old boy, skinny, all legs and curls and nose—probably exactly around the time he climbed the tree, when I found him and told him to come down. I wanted him gone from my life. [Pause.] So . . .

So . . . ?

So he died. I wanted him gone, and he went, sick and in pain. I'd thought the unthinkable.

You think you're the reason Connor died?

Now? No. I know I didn't give him the tumor or the cancer. I'm not making his dying about me. But then, when I was nine or ten, if I could've given him cancer, or a tumor, killed his brain and made him suffer, I would have. And that, that makes me the worst person I've ever known. That makes me ugly. That makes me cruel. That makes me—

Human.

Not everyone wants his brother to die.

Our hearts and minds can go through so much we can't necessarily explain, but—

I *thought* I gave him his cancer. He died, my brother died. And I loved him. Once, he found me crying about I don't know what. I wasn't really a kid who cried, or cried outwardly, but there I was, and he came right up to me and hugged me. I was the person who shut him up when he cried. I was the person who scared him into submission. I was the person who might have buried him alive if I thought I'd get away with it, and he came over and put his arms around me. Didn't say a word, either. Nothing. He just breathed in my ear. And I could hear his little breath going into my ear and into my brain and down into my own lungs, my own heart, my own *bones*, my *bones*. And that's what turned everything around. I felt him so deep, and I couldn't go on hating him. I don't think he was more than eight . . . [Angry.] And this must have been just before they found the tumor. I can't even remember why my parents were worried or what made them think something was wrong. I was wrapped up in myself, selfish. I didn't even know anything was wrong. But he'd breathed his life into me, like he knew. Like he *knew*! [Angrier.] God, why am I telling you all this?

You've carried a lot in you, Abraham.

[Angrier, or maybe sadder; just more upset.] You keep using my name, my full name, even though I told you only my brother called me Abraham. Not even my parents call me Abraham. And even though I don't know you . . . like, you're a *stranger* . . . ! [Deflating, as if

I popped on one of my own sharp thoughts coming through my skin like a horn.] It's like, when you use my name, you're closer to me than anyone. Anyone since my brother.

You're saying you feel I'm close to you.

You see me, and I don't want to be seen.

You don't want to be seen.

Not like this. Banged up and broken, body and brain. But I'm always seen. Even when I think I disappear, I can always be seen. Maybe I'm two people now, though, which is why I grew so big. I have my brother in me. I have my brother's breath, like I said, in my bones. Maybe if I starved myself, maybe if I went down to the bone, if you could only see my bones, you'd see him, my brother, and not me. He was the beautiful one.

That is a deeply sad thought, Abe.

Please call me Abraham.

All right. Can't you be beautiful, Abraham?

[Shaking my head.] I don't want to be seen like this.

It's hard to be witnessed in our pain. But sometimes, in spite of ourselves, even at our quietest, we're crying out to be seen.

[Silence.]

It takes a lot of strength, a lot of willpower to suffer without help. You're a strong boy.

[!] I've never thought that.

You must be very strong. A strong mind to go with strong feelings.

I've always felt people judging me—my teachers, parents, friends—for being weak, for being sensitive, for being alive to everything in my heart and mind and body, to the whole world, to everything said and not said, to every color.

That sounds tiring.

It is. There are days and weeks when I won't turn off. I can't sleep—maybe an hour or two for days—but I also can't *do* anything but feel and think.

That sounds like a painful thing, Abraham, a form of suffering. Do you think so?

[Shrugging, yawning.] I'm really tired.

Do you want to get some rest? I can come back when—

No. Don't leave yet.

Would you like to keep talking?

Yes. Please.

Sure. I have some more time.

I like talking to you. [Embarrassed.] I think you're really listening.

Does that bother you?

I just didn't know it could happen. I didn't know I wanted to talk, and I didn't know I could be heard, or listened to. I don't know what I think.

Do you have friends to talk to?

My friends aren't my friends anymore.

How about your mom and dad?

My family's a mess. I don't know if my parents will stay married. Once Connor died, my parents didn't know what to say to each other, or to me. And my mother gets really angry at me for my silence. Like, last week, she said, "So my second son died, and now my first son won't talk? Why won't you talk?"

Could you answer your mother?

No.

How does this make you feel, your mother's upset?

Not great. She's devastated, and I don't know what I am. Maybe I'm just crazy.

Crazy?

I thought I was saving my dead brother when I threw myself in front of that car.

You saw your brother, Abraham?

We were walking together. We were talking. It felt very real. [Pause.] But it wasn't the first time.

Had you seen your brother before then, before you were struck by the car?

[Nodding.] That's what I meant when I said everything turned on October fourth. The fourth, two weeks ago, was a Sunday, by coincidence. I woke up feeling like I was lying in a grave under the rain, and then I took myself to the blessing of the animals, to the church where Connor and my father and I would go, and I sat at the back, alone, in the corner. I don't know why I went. Maybe I thought—

I had been watching a man and his alpaca when my brother put his hand on my leg. He said, "Oh, Abraham, look at that little dog." I looked over, and a woman was walking next to her ancient dog. His hind legs were gone, and he sat on a little wagon. He used his front paws to pull himself along. Connor said, "Do you think he's in pain?"

Were you surprised to feel and see and hear your brother?

Surprised? Why? We'd sat in the church together so many times watching the blessing of the animals. We sat there again together, his hand on my leg. Then we left.

And did he come back again?

Not until the night I walked, when he found me. The night he walked into the street.

Was there any part of you that wanted to die, when you jumped out to save him?

[Closing my eyes.] I have thought now and then about killing myself. [Pause.] But not that night. That night, I wanted to save my brother. [Pause.] What sense does that make?

It seems as if you felt your brother was with you, that it felt real. The danger he was in, from an oncoming car—a danger not at all like cancer, when you could do nothing to help, when you felt helpless— [Pause.] You felt you could save him from that car. And you would sacrifice yourself for him.

[Tears spiking my eyes.] But that doesn't make sense, does it?

It makes sense, but the sense it makes is based on something else.

Do you think it's possible to invent a reality, Abraham? Can something—or someone—be both gone and present?

My brother is dead, but he never left. [Pause.] Am I crazy, Julius?

You'll be talking to other people as part of your care team, and those people will want to hear what you say, if you can talk to them.

But what do *you* think? Do you think I'm crazy?

I think you're in pain. I think you're suffering. And I think you should talk to the doctors if you can.

I'm not sure I can.

It might be good for you to say more. You might be helped to suffer less.

You mean no more headaches, no more nightmares? [Pause.] Will I stop seeing my brother?

I really can't say. But may I ask you a question? What do you think pain sounds like?

[Frowning.] You mean if you get hit with a hammer or cut your hand?

Well, that's physical pain, for sure. But I mean . . . [Pointing at his chest] . . . in your heart . . . [Pointing at his head] . . . in here, in your mind? What is the sound of suffering that's invisible?

I think it could sound like words, if we can talk about it, talk about what hurts us, or what upsets us. But it could be moans or sobs or screeching or wailing. Or like nothing.

Nothing meaning silence?

Yes, since it's inside us and invisible.

So . . . what does pain sound like inside of us, when no one else can hear?

Is there a right answer? I mean, do you want me to say something specific? Am I supposed to be saying something that makes sense? You said you believe in God. Do you think I should say our pain, the pain that's inside of us, should sound like, I don't know, a *prayer*? Like I should be praying quietly, to God?

I'm very sorry, Abraham. I didn't mean to upset or frustrate you. There's no right answer, no one answer. And I wouldn't tell you that our pain sounds like prayer. Maybe to some it does sound like that, whatever prayer means to a person. No, I was asking with genuine curiosity, because I like you, and so I'm curious. Do you think your decision to stop talking and the phenomenon of seeing your brother are connected to grief?

You don't have to say you're sorry.

I wanted to acknowledge that you felt upset, and that you seemed to think I wanted something specific from you, something specific I knew but you didn't. That can sometimes make us feel small, insulted, unheard. So I wanted to apologize to you for asking a question that seemed to hurt you.

You didn't really hurt me. I'm just—ha!—sensitive. I only like the big questions I ask myself. I'm not good with the big questions anyone else asks.

That's interesting, too, and something maybe we'll talk about.

I don't think I'm that interesting or strong.

Maybe you'll have to reconsider that.

I don't know what invisible pain sounds like. It sounds like saws. It sounds like the wind, a really strong wind that gets in your mouth and your ears, and you can barely breathe, barely think. Like you'll suffocate. Pain sounds like waves crashing over and over again on the beach. I haven't been able to go near water because I'm afraid of the sound. Like it will never, never stop. Like the water is always eating the ground, and crashing and crashing. It sounds really small sometimes, too, the pain, like trying to light a match or a lighter, or like the littlest fire, the smallest hissing flame, a candle. The crackling . . . [Noticing the chaplain has closed his eyes.] Julius?

[Opening his eyes, smiling a little.] I was just listening closely to you, Abraham. I didn't want to miss what you were saying, so I closed my eyes to hear better.

Oh, I do that, too, close my eyes to hear better. Did it sound okay, what I said?

Your answer is your answer, Abraham. I can't take that from you, doubt you, ask anything from you. If that's what the pain inside you sounds like, then I believe you.

I guess it does. And all those sounds added up to one thing.

What's that one thing?

Grief. Like you said. Grief and orders.

Orders?

Stop eating. Stop music; stop sports. Stop talking.

[Long pause, maybe a whole minute. Julius looking at me. Me looking at him and looking down, looking at him, looking down, playing with the ID bracelet on my wrist.]

I miss playing piano. I stopped when Connor died. He couldn't play, but he could sing. Maybe a year before the tumor was discovered, when he was just going on seven, when I really started liking him, I'd play the piano, and he'd sing. He would have grown up to be a really great singer, if he wanted, better than me, for sure. I played; he sang. [Sighing.] I miss it.

Do you have a piano *piano or an electric one?*

Both. [Embarrassed, looking down.] I used to win awards and stuff. Compose. The whole package.

It sounds like maybe you're ready to play again. Maybe you could ask your parents to have your piano tuned for when you get home. Maybe dust off the electric one. Have them ready for you.

Yeah. Maybe.

Maybe is where we start, Abraham.

What do you mean?

Maybe is may be.

There's something more, right? Something ahead, a future?

That's right.

[Yawning.] I'm tired, Julius.

You can sleep a little, and I'll go to my next appointment. Is there anything I can do for you before I go?

Will you come back?

For sure. You'll be here a little while, and I'll come back tomorrow.

[Yawning.] Sorry. Okay.

Our talk ended here. I wrote it down, verbatim. Or close to it. And I'm giving it to you because I see you. You're my friend, and you're suffering.

We have the minds and hearts we're given. We have them. We have them our whole lives. We have our memories and ideas and feelings, all our hurts and sorrows. All that messiness, all our humanness, needs space, and the space is in us.

Chaplain Julius stood up. For the first time, I realized he was really tall, stoop-through-the-door tall, camel tall. And old. Like, I don't know, fifty or sixty. Bald, mostly; a neat fringe of white-gray hair on the sides. Glasses.

I didn't want him to go, but my mind was quieter, and I was tired. I could feel the sleep coming.

Julius stopped at the door.

Maybe *is hope, Abraham. That's all* maybe *is. Now, get some rest.*

A NOTE FROM PATRICK DOWNES

✳ ✳ ✳ ✳ ✳ ✳ ✳ ✳ ✳ ✳ ✳ ✳ ✳ ✳ ✳

We sometimes suffer; we sometimes grieve. Often we do this on our own, in our own way. Sometimes that suffering and grieving bring us to despair, make us wild, and send us into an impenetrable darkness. The dark may bring us near enough to losing ourselves. It may bring us to a hospital bed. For many of us, the return to light comes with a small hope. In spite of all the ways grief finds us, we must remember that if we draw breath, then life has asked us to keep going. Should any of you, dear, dear readers, need a reason to hope, reach for it. Reach and reach and reach and reach and . . .

For the readers who know one who suffers, remember: when you approach, you carry within you the sanctuary another might need. Within you lives the place where listening happens, where hope occurs. You are the sanctuary. You are the garden. You are the stand of trees and the quiet sun. You are the wide, calm sea. And that other, that weakened other, longs for the place you carry inside. They reach and reach and reach for you.

BACK OF THE TRUCK

ISABEL QUINTERO

*Content Note: This story references obsessive
thoughts and severe anxiety.*

1.

My friend Adrian tells me I think too much. About everything.

"Marichu, why can't it just be a salad?" he asks when I start talking about the hands that pick our produce.

"Don't you ever think about who killed that chicken you're eating?" I ask. "Like, where do they live? Do they get fair wages?"

"Jesus. Dude, I just want to eat this chicken without feeling guilty about it," Adrian says.

And he's probably right, but I can't help it. My brain won't stop.

My dad says it's good to ask questions; that's how people learn. He's right, but also, having questions run through your head nonstop is exhausting. And not all questions are created equal. "Are *King Arthur* and *Tortilla Flat* connected somehow?" was a good question to ask in English with Ms. Sanchez, for example. It led to a deep discussion about why Steinbeck would use those chapter titles. *What if Jeff really doesn't like me and he's pretending to like me to get me to make out and then he breaks up with me in front of everyone and then I'll be so humiliated that I won't be able to face anyone?* This is an example of a not very productive question and one I kept asking myself until Jeff broke up with me in front of everyone and proved me right.

"What are you thinking about?" Adrian asks from his side of the truck bed. "Oh, about how handsome you look, Adrian," he says in a high-pitched voice when I don't answer right away.

"My voice isn't that high," I tell him. "I'm thinking about a lot of things," I finally reply.

"What things?" He adjusts the bunched-up blanket under him. His long legs, only a few inches from the tailgate, struggle to get comfortable.

"About questions. Like, how some questions are good and some not so good and how they can lead to things we want or don't want to know."

"Of course that's what you'd be thinking about."

"What are you thinking about?"

He turns toward me and smiles. "About how many hot girls there'll be. And how maybe, just maybe, one will want to make out with me."

"Oh." All the muscles in my body tighten up.

"I know you were nervous about coming out tonight, but you have nothing to worry about," he says.

"Really? What if no one asks me to dance and I'm the only one who isn't dancing and people think I'm a loser? Or worse, what if the only person asking me to dance is someone's old-ass tío who preys on young innocent girls?"

Adrian laughs. "First off, of course someone will ask you to dance. Look at you. Secondly, you will definitely be asked to dance by some old-ass tío because you know how dudes be."

Adrian laughs again and shakes his head. He's tall, with dark brown skin, dark brown eyes with the longest eyelashes, and a dimple—he's the definition of attractive, even with his pathetic excuse for a mustache. He's so confident. Knowing who he is has always come easy for Adrian, so he has no clue what it's like to think about and replay over and over again the mean thing you said to a classmate in first grade, even if it was ten years ago and that first grader is now a good friend, because maybe that former first grader will bring it up one day and reveal that they never really were your friend but were faking it to get back at you.

When I told Adrian that, he said, "That's a lot of work to get you back for saying that she colors ugly. I don't think Steph would do that."

Adrian is probably right. But I can't stop the thoughts from form-ing—or lingering.

"I want to sit up," Adrian says. I can tell he's antsy and has been doing his best to stay down.

We are in the back of the truck because there isn't room for all seven of us in the cab.

"Sorry, but two of you will have to go in the back," my cousin Myra said when we realized we wouldn't all fit in her car.

I had begged my mom to let me go dancing at Mi Ranchito, in San Coyote, with my cousins and some friends. I knew I was going to get in trouble when I got home because I'd asked in front of my tía, and Mom *hates* when I do that.

"You didn't even bring clothes," she'd said, hopeful.

"Don't worry, Tía, she can borrow some of my clothes," Myra chimed in.

My mom gave in. "Okay, but don't stay out so late, and be careful. You don't know what can happen. Remember what I always say: The devil—"

"—is a pig. Yes, Mom, I know," I told her.

Adrian was already there, and when he heard my mom's favorite saying, he couldn't keep his mouth shut. "The devil is a pig? Well, good thing I'm in the mood for carnitas!" He was incredibly pleased with his cleverness.

"Ay, Adrian," my mom said, shaking her head. "I'm serious, be careful. ¿Me oyes, María de Jesús?"

I scowled at Adrian. "You almost ruined my chances," I told him later.

Myra did my hair and makeup and I helped with hers.

"You're not gonna fit in the truck," my tía warned, and my mom looked relieved.

"Yes we will!" Myra argued. Betin, Myra's older brother, brought a bunch of blankets to the truck bed.

The only fair way to decide who went in back was rock-paper-scissors between Lisa, Santiago, Adrian, and me. Yuri was wearing a miniskirt and platforms, so we decided to be nice and let her go up front.

"Shit," I said when I lost to Lisa.

"I'll go with you," Adrian said.

Adrian and I hopped in.

The way to the club was smooth on the city streets but has now turned bumpy. Mi Ranchito is on a back road somewhere in San Coyote, somewhere near the river where things begin to get rural.

The truck turns into a dirt-and-gravel parking lot. Little clouds of dust go up around us as Myra finds a spot. Music thumps and people laugh as they make their way to the door.

"This has got to be the most Mexican thing we've done this week," Adrian says.

"The blankets or the club?" I ask.

"It's a close call, but I meant the blankets," he answers.

The doors of the truck open and close.

"Let's go, prima!" Myra calls. I can tell by her voice that she's super excited. She's had a crush on Santiago forever, and she's hoping something will happen tonight. I told her not to hold her breath.

"Dude, you are so messy," I say to her.

Lisa is Myra's cousin on her dad's side, and they were really close until Emi told on Myra for sneaking out to see this guy she was dating, under the guise of being concerned for her safety. More important, Emi had dated Santiago, and Myra knew how much he had broken her heart back then.

Betin opens the truck bed, and I am careful getting out because I'm wearing Myra's faux-leather blue ankle boots, and she'll be pissed if I get mud on them.

"Me? Messy? Never," Myra says, winking as she refreshes my eyeliner.

Mi Ranchito is a Mexican dance club known for its rowdy clientele. (This is one of the reasons my mom didn't want me to go.) Everyone in line looks damn good. If the young women aren't wearing six-inch heels and tight-fitting dresses that look impossible to move in, they are wearing just-as-tight jeans and boots or heels, with short shirts or plunging necklines. I am wearing fitted white jeans, a loose pink blouse with blue flowers, and the blue boots. I feel a bit out of place.

"Okay, so I didn't tell you before because I know how you get when you have to lie to your mom." Myra holds up two cards in my face.

"Fake IDs?" I ask, dreading the consequences because my mom is sure to find out. "I thought this place was sixteen and older?"

Myra gives me an exaggerated smile. "It's eighteen and older. But you're almost eighteen!"

"Myra," I say, looking at the birth date on the ID, "this says I'm twenty-three. I do not look twenty-three."

"Not with that attitude. Look, I also brought this." She pulls out a piece of blue-and-red cloth.

"No." I recognize her turquoise shirt with red roses, the tight stretchy one that has no shoulders, which means I'll have to either show my bra straps or take my bra off.

Betin is getting anxious. "Can you two hurry it up?"

"Did everyone know about the fake IDs?" I look at my best friend. "Et tu, Adrian?"

"I thought you knew, dude." I can see he is serious. "And I don't need a fake ID unless I'm going to be drinking." Adrian likes to remind me that he's already eighteen any chance he gets.

Yuri speaks up. "Come on, Chuyita, you'll look super hot in it."

Reluctantly I give in because I am already starting to stress about holding up the group.

"I'll change when we get in," I say, taking the shirt.

Lisa and Myra give each other a look. "Um, and you're just going to hold on to my blouse in there, or what?" Myra says. "Nope. We'll hold up blankets."

The night just keeps getting worse and it hasn't really begun yet. I start wishing that I'd stayed home.

The shirt fits well, I have to admit, and it's tight enough that I don't need a bra really. When Myra and Lisa let the blanket down, Santiago and Adrian both whistle.

"Damn, Chuyita, why don't you dress like that more often?" Santiago looks me up and down. Myra rolls her eyes and shakes her head.

Betin turns to his friend. "That's my little cousin. What the fuck?"

"My bad," Santiago says. "She just looks extra cute tonight."

"Let's go, we're getting old out here," Myra rushes us.

The bouncer doesn't even blink at my ID and stamps my hand so the bartender will know I can drink.

Inside, the club is small. The dance floor is right in front of the stage, and surrounding it are tables and chairs; against one wall is the bar and against the opposite wall are booths. Old event posters paper the place next to Modelo and Corona neon signs. Mi Ranchito looks like it hasn't been redecorated since it opened in the '90s. My parents probably sat in the same booth we slide into.

As I take in every neon sign and cowboy boot, I spot an incredibly attractive guy in a black tejana leaning against the bar, talking to an older man. He's wearing a light-colored Western-style shirt, cinturón piteado, jeans, and beige ostrich cowboy boots. *I wish he'd ask me to dance*, I think.

"Do you see him?" Lisa whispers.

I nod. Almost immediately the hot guy comes to our table and asks me to dance.

"Told you," Adrian whispers. I smile sheepishly.

The hot guy's name is Moises.

"But you can call me Moy," he says in a deep voice.

"I'm María de Jesús, but everyone calls me Marichu."

He smiles. "Well, Marichu, I hope you like zapateado." Moy pulls me toward the middle of the dance floor just as the live banda, La Consentida Nopalera de Culiacán de Don Francisco León, starts playing one of my favorite songs, "El Sinaloense."

"Ha," I say. "I hope *you* like zapateado."

Something happens to me when I hear the tubas, trombones, trumpets, and the banging of the drums. Even though I'm not from Mexico, even though it's my parents who know what it is to live on a rancho and not me, I still feel the lyrics deep within me. As if I know the place where my father grew up well, instead of only through photographs and vague memories of visiting my grandparents. Moy and I start dancing, our feet moving fast to match the banda. Each time the cymbals clang, I stomp hard and spin and feel so free. The song ends and I'm almost giddy. I wanted it to go on forever. Moy smiles again and his eyes crinkle at the corners. He has long lashes and dark brown eyes. His eyebrows are perfectly done and his dark brown skin is glowing. He pulls me into him for the next song, and he smells sweet and woodsy.

We dance two more songs, and I'm feeling great. Then I'm not. I slip on some spilled beer and almost eat shit, and that's when I really begin to notice all the people around us. The dance floor is packed.

Sombreros, boots, and heels. Mixed scents of perfume and sweat and beer. Bodies bumping into one another. That one slip was enough to bring me back to a place I didn't realize I'd left.

Moy stops smiling. "You okay, Marichu?"

"Yeah, I'm good," I lie.

The banda plays another zapateado. My feet are off-key and I can't seem to find my rhythm. The space around me tightens, and my breath is coming faster. I feel disoriented and hot and like I can't breathe.

"You don't look okay," Moy says.

I'm scaring the hot guy. He's probably thinking I'm crazy, but I can't really breathe and the room feels smaller and why won't these people make more room I probably look like a dumbass and my feet feel weird and I feel weird and my chest hurts and I'm about to start crying oh my god I can't cry he's gonna think I'm crazy why would I cry this is stupid and here are the tears . . .

"Whoa, let's sit you down," Moy says. He looks worried as he walks me over to my friends. Immediately, Adrian stands up straight and unfolds into the full six-foot-two-and-three-years-of-playing-football body he's grown into.

"What'd you do to her?"

"Dude, nothing. She just freaked out," Moy says, standing straight in an attempt to make himself match Adrian but falling short about five inches and fifty pounds.

Adrian turns to me. "Did he hurt you?"

I can barely talk. "No. I need air."

Myra must have seen what was happening from the bar, where she'd been putting her stamped hand to good use with Lisa. She was there and suddenly she is next to me.

"What'd you do to her?" Myra asks Moy.

"I didn't do anything, she just flipped." Moy starts edging away. I can see he's worried, but he also wants to leave.

"I need to go outside." I start for the door. I can see everything but nothing very clearly. I push people aside and only know I do this because I hear annoyed voices say, "What the fuck, watch it" and "Excuse *you.*"

Outside, I lean against the building and slide to the ground. My chest hurts. I want to stop crying and hyperventilating, but I can't.

Myra crouches next to me, and Adrian brings me water. People arriving at the club just walk by.

"It's not even eleven and that girl is already fucked up," someone says.

"Leave the drinking to the adults, little girls." A woman in a tight red dress smirks at us.

"Shut up," Myra says.

"What'd you say?" Red Dress steps back.

"I said shut up and go inside before this *little girl* kicks your grown-woman ass." Myra stands up.

Adrian tries to intervene. "This is not the time," he says.

"You're lucky I don't wanna fuck up my nails," Red Dress says.

"Why? Walmart's just down the block, bitch!" Myra couldn't keep her mouth shut if they paid her.

"Fuck you!"

"Fuck you!"

The bouncer walks over. "Ay, you coming in or what, nena?" he says to Red Dress. Then he looks at me, still crying. "You ain't ready for the big leagues yet, niñas."

"I'm not drunk!" I shout through tears.

"That is exactly what a drunk person would say," the bouncer says, smirking at me. "This is the end of the night for y'all. Don't come back in."

Myra is pissed. "What an asshole."

Adrian hands me the water bottle he's brought as he sits down on the dirt with me. "You okay?" he asks, in a voice so gentle it doesn't seem like it comes from his body.

Myra looks at me guiltily. "I'm obviously worried about you, too, prima. What happened?"

My breathing is finally calming down, but I'm still semi-crying and now feeling weightless. "I don't know. One minute I was dancing, and the next minute I slipped on some beer and started worrying that Moy was embarrassed he was dancing with the girl who flipped out and that he should have never asked me. Then I began to feel trapped. I had to get out of there."

Adrian looks worried. "Has this happened before?"

I shake my head. Then I remember. "Once, in Michoacán," I say.

We'd gone on vacation to Janitzio, an island in el Lago de Pátzcuaro. There are several hundred steps to the monument of Morelos and then more steps to the revolutionary's fist. There are murals all the way to the top, and I hadn't been paying attention to how high up I was. About midway I looked down and began to get dizzy. It was a similar feeling to tonight but not as intense. Only minimal crying as I went down the stairs on my butt. Once at the bottom, I tried to explain to my mom what had happened, and she just said, "That's why you need to pay attention to what you're doing." And that was that.

"But it wasn't like this," I say.

Adrian makes a face.

"What?"

"It sounds like an anxiety attack. Lalo gets them."

"She's not like your crazy brother," Myra says defensively. "She just had a moment. We all have moments."

Adrian looks stung. "He's not crazy, Myra. So watch it. I'm just saying he also gets anxiety attacks. And this all seems like an anxiety attack."

"I don't think that's what it is," I say. Lalo is nice, but he's on antidepressant meds and was even put on a seventy-two-hour hold in a mental health facility. I am not like Lalo. At all. "Look, I just want to lie down for a bit. I feel exhausted."

"Okay," Adrian says. "I'll walk you to the truck."

Myra pulls out her phone. "I have to text everyone inside and let them know what happened."

I feel terrible that we all will have to leave, but there is no way I am going back in there even if the bouncer would let us.

Adrian helps me into the truck, and I lie down on the blankets. "I can hear you thinking by the way you're breathing," he says. "You're gonna get worked up again. Collect your breath. Count to ten."

Adrian's advice seems to help. Then a new worry creeps in: Will whatever this is happen again? Is there a way to stop it? Usually I would go to my mom with questions like this, but I can't tell her. She'd be like, *See, that's why you shouldn't have gone out.*

I hear our group approach the truck.

"What happened?" I hear Yuri ask. Then I see her brown eyes, lined with the sharpest wings, looking down at me.

"My only night off, prima, and you had to lose your shit," Betin complains.

"Sorry," I say, sitting up.

Adrian sits up, too, and glares at Betin. "It's fine, Chuyita. We can go get some tacos or something."

We do just that, and even grab some beers, and end up at Martinez Park, where we chill for a few hours.

Later, when I'm lying on Myra's floor and she is snoring, I look up "anxiety attacks" online.

"Shit," I whisper when I start reading the results.

Eventually, I fall asleep. In the morning, everything seems back to normal. Last night was a dream.

2.

The ambulance ride was different than I had imagined.

"How are you feeling?" the paramedic asks me.

I hate that question. "Like shit."

She nods. "On a scale of one to ten, how bad is your chest pain now? You said an eleven before."

"A solid ten, I think," I answer, holding my chest.

Adrian watches from where he's sitting in the ambulance—I've never seen him look so worried. He has his hand on my shin but moves it away to answer a text.

"Your mom is going to meet us at the hospital," he says. I nod.

"You're too young to have a heart attack, but take this just in case," the paramedic says, handing me an orange pill and a cup of water. "It's aspirin," she explains.

"Oh," I said, and tip the cup back.

Adrian, Myra, and I had been eating frozen yogurt at the Tyler Mall when suddenly my chest began hurting. It was as if my heart was getting crushed. And then I was doubled over in pain and clutching my chest on the floor. I couldn't even make it to the car. Each breath and step was excruciating. Myra called the paramedics, and Adrian called my mom.

Mom was already at the hospital. She told Adrian and Myra to go home and that I'd call them when I got out. Adrian seemed reluctant, but Myra offered to take him and they left.

The nurses have me get undressed and into a gown—I regret not shaving my legs when I see my nurse. He places sticky pads with wires all over my chest and explains it's an EKG machine and will show if I've had a heart attack.

"On a scale of one to ten, what's your pain level?" he asks.

The pain is all but gone, and now I feel silly sitting in the hospital. I've wasted everyone's time.

"I'd say, like, a low two. Or even a one. It's not like it was at the mall."

He nods.

Yup, I'd just wasted everyone's time.

The doctor came in quicker than I had anticipated.

"Hello, María, I'm Dr. Lee, the attending physician. I hear you had an eventful day at the mall." She looks at her tablet.

"Yeah, my chest hurt."

"What did you eat today?"

I try to remember. "Oatmeal at breakfast. Then we had tacos at Miguel's for lunch. And then the frozen yogurt. Plain with fruit."

"Hmm. Okay. Have you had pain like this before?"

"No, she hasn't," my mom answers for me. "I would've brought her in if she did."

"Of course, ma'am," Dr. Lee says, smiling at my mom. "We just have to ask."

"She probably just ate something spicy and was being dramatic." My mom looks over at me.

"No, Mom, I literally thought I was going to die."

"Ay." My mom sounds annoyed.

Dr. Lee smiles that way people do when they're trying to be professional but are about to say something you, or in this case my mom, don't want to hear. "María, would it be okay if I spoke to you alone?"

"You can't do that!" My mom stands up. "She's a minor."

"In the state of California, I can speak to your daughter alone," Dr. Lee says. "And please, Mrs. Ramirez, I only ask because I would like to get to the bottom of what might have happened to your daughter."

"María de Jesús, you don't need to hide things from me." But then she asks, "Is this what you want?"

"Yes."

My mom looks hurt but walks out.

Dr. Lee pulls up a chair. "So tell me about your week or month, if you can."

"Well, I've had finals all this week, and last week I went out with my cousin and I had a freak-out, for no reason, on the dance floor, which was super embarrassing. Earlier in the month my boyfriend broke up with me in front of everyone. Should I go on?"

"That sounds like a lot for such a short time," Dr. Lee says.

I shrug, embarrassed that I sound like a whiner. "It's life."

She nods sympathetically. "It sure is." Then I tell her about what happened in Mexico last summer and about another incident a few months back that I'd forgotten about.

"I see," she says. "Do you mind if we call your mom back in?"

"Do I have cancer or something?" I get worried.

"Oh, no," Dr. Lee assures me. "No. I just think it might be best to speak to both of you at the same time."

"Okay." I'm relieved it isn't cancer but worried about what it is.

My mom comes back in.

"Is she pregnant?" she asks.

"Mom, are you serious?" My face turns red.

"Um, no. And the good news is María has not had a heart attack, either," Dr. Lee informs us.

"Then what's wrong with her?"

"I think—and after talking to María, I am almost sure—she had a panic attack."

"A what?" my mom asks.

"A panic attack. Sometimes they can mimic heart attacks. For someone with generalized anxiety, especially with undiagnosed generalized anxiety, this can be extra frightening. And I think, after speaking with María, this is the case with her."

I feel like crying. Adrian was right.

"Ay, anxiety? No, no. She's fine," my mom responds. "She probably ate something that gave her heartburn. She's not crazy." She is beginning to get angry. The kind of angry she gets when things are out of her control and she doesn't know what else to do but get angry at whatever is frustrating or confusing her. Right now a doctor is telling her that her daughter has a mental health issue, and Mom isn't having it.

But neither is Dr. Lee. "It was not something that she ate, ma'am. Anxiety is a mental health issue, yes, but it doesn't mean she's 'crazy'—which is not really a thing, by the way. Anxiety is manageable. For example, I have anxiety, and I take medication for it, as well as see a therapist. There are lots of things that can help you."

"She's not going on medication." My mom raises her voice.

"She doesn't have to be on medication. As I said, there are lots of ways to manage it. Medication is just one way."

"So what do I do?" I ask.

"We're going home," my mom says.

"Ma'am, I strongly suggest that when you go home, María rests and then tomorrow you either make an appointment with her doctor and get a referral or find a therapist on your own. That would be a good start. Otherwise, these attacks could happen again."

My mom looks at me. "Attacks? This is the first time this has happened. She would've told me."

I shake my head.

"What? María de Jesús, why didn't you tell me?" She's been betrayed. How could I have told a stranger something I had not told her?

"I did," I remind her. "In Mexico. But you said it was nothing. So I didn't tell you when it happened again because you were going to say I was being dramatic."

"I wouldn't say that," she protests. I raise my eyebrows but don't say anything.

When the doctor leaves, my mom turns to me. "I can't believe you would trust someone you just met more than me."

"It wasn't like that," I say, feeling guilty. I put my clothes back on.

"You kicked me out to tell her in secret. Now you have her thinking you're crazy. A therapist? Please. You just need to keep busy. You can rest today, but tomorrow I'll think of a few things to keep you busy with. Starting with clearing out the garage. A busy mind is a strong mind."

I know my mom will be hard to convince, but I don't want another panic attack.

"But the doctor said I needed to make an appointment with Dr. Aguilar," I insist.

"Fine. You'll see that he agrees with me. He's known you since you were born. He would've told us if something was wrong."

3.

"What? She's crazy?"

Dr. Aguilar did not agree with my mom.

"Señora, she's not crazy. It's anxiety. It doesn't mean her life is over or even that she is destined to be on medication."

"But you've never brought it up before. Wouldn't you have known?" My mom keeps looking from the doctor to me.

"Not necessarily," Dr. Aguilar says. "Marichu never told me any of the things she'd been feeling, so there was no way to diagnose her, and there is no blood work that would've shown it."

"I'm sorry" is all I can think to say.

Dr. Aguilar shakes his head. "There is nothing to apologize for, mija. I'm going to write the name and number of a therapist I'd like you to see. She specializes in working with teens."

"I don't like that idea," my mom says. "I don't want her seeing a stranger. It's nobody's business but hers."

I sigh.

"Señora, please. You take blood pressure medication, right?"

"That's different. If I don't take it, I can have a heart attack."

"This is medical, too. And it's not different. You came to me twenty years ago and confided in me, a stranger at the time, about how you were feeling. About how your body was feeling. You were feeling dizzy, you had headaches. You remember? Do you remember you told me how you felt after drinking too much? Or eating too much salty foods?"

"You used to drink too much, Mom?" I ask the woman who told me she's never gotten drunk.

"María de Jesús, we are here to talk about you." She's flustered as she takes the paper Dr. Aguilar is holding.

"Call her," he tells my mom. "If you don't like her and want to talk to someone else, let me know and I'll give you some other names."

"Thank you," I say.

In the car, my mom puts the paper in her purse.

"So tell me about how you used to drink too much, Mom," I tease.

"Ay, niña," my mom says, looking embarrassed. "It was a long time ago. I don't remember."

"So weird, though, right?" I don't let it go. "So weird that it happened so many times that you finally got worried and had to go to the doctor."

"Ya está bien." My mom's voice is firm. "When we get home, we'll call the susodicha. Just don't blame me if it doesn't work."

"Thanks, Mom," I say. "I know this is hard for you."

"Hmm. A ver."

4.

My mom and Myra take me to my first therapy appointment. I wish I had come by myself.

"Myra, how do you feel about this whole anxiety thing?" my mom asks in the waiting room.

Myra looks at me and shrugs. "Like, why are you here? Because you had a little moment dancing with a hot guy? All of a sudden you need a therapist for that?" She shakes her head. "So dramatic."

My mom turns to me angrily. "María de Jesús, is all this nonsense over some boy?"

My therapist calls me in and saves Myra.

"I can't believe you," I growl as I walk past. Myra looks remorseful—she knows she messed up.

The therapist is a cute young Black woman in stylish red pants and a black polka-dot blouse. Her curly dark brown hair shakes as she leads me to her office. I am still angry when we get to the door.

"Is this the part when I tell you about my crappy childhood?" I ask, trying to feel comfortable on the gray couch she invited me to sit down on.

She smiles. This is not the first time she's heard that line, I realize. I look away and try to collect myself.

Regina's office is not like what I imagined. There is no fainting couch. Or big fancy desk. It is dimly lit, and there is a small fountain next to a terrarium on a side table by the couch. On the floor near the door and next to Regina, who sits in a matching gray chair, is a white-noise machine, giving us privacy.

"If you want to tell me about your crappy childhood, we can talk about that," Regina says.

This makes me uncomfortable. I was making a joke, but now I realize it was a bad one because some people really do have crappy childhoods.

"No, I didn't have a crappy childhood. My parents are pretty chill—for the most part. Both of them can be extra extra when they feel like it, but I imagine that's all parents."

"You imagine correctly," she says.

I nod. An awkward moment of silence passes.

"Soooo . . . what do I say now?"

"Well, we can talk about your being diagnosed with generalized anxiety," Regina suggests.

"So delve right in, huh?"

"No reason to feel nervous. I am not here to judge you or stress you out."

I nod again. "Hmm. Okay. So getting diagnosed was weird. I mean, everyone is always telling me I'm dramatic. Like, right now my cousin is outside telling my mom that my panic attack was about a boy. I can't believe she said that. It wasn't over a boy. I'm just worried all the time and it gets the best of me sometimes."

"I see. What kinds of things do you worry about?"

"Ha! How long do you have?"

Regina just smiles and my discomfort grows. It's embarrassing to admit to all the things I worry about during the day. This is one of the reasons I don't talk to Myra about how I feel. She always lets me know how unimportant all of it is.

"Just don't think about it," she'll say. "It's a waste of time."

And maybe it *is* a waste of time . . .

Regina can sense my reluctance and asks me if I'm okay.

"Yeah," I answer. It's easier to complain about Myra than to actually talk about what's going on. "It's just that my worries seem insignificant, and I'm embarrassed to even say them out loud."

"Well, let's talk about it anyway. I'm sure they are important since you actually ended up in the hospital."

I nod. "Let's see. I worry about my grades, about my friends not really being my friends, about my family dying. I constantly imagine strange scenarios in my head—what if someone shoots up our school? What would I do? What if there's an earthquake and we don't have an emergency kit ready at home? What if I get into a car accident?" Saying it out loud makes it worse. She for sure is going to think I am wasting her time. I wait for Regina to say the same thing that Myra or Mom always says: *You're being dramatic.*

But instead she says, "That is a lot."

I'm relieved that she isn't making fun of me. "Recently, though, it's more than usual. The thoughts just keep coming."

"I see." Her expression seems to change slightly.

Shit, I think. *Here it comes.*

"So I'm crazy, right?" I say, half joking.

"No," Regina says, shaking her head. "Not at all. Crazy isn't real, but anxiety is. Let's talk some more. Can you tell me what these thoughts look like?"

"Well, like, weeks ago when I went to get my nails done with Myra, I was worried I'd pick the wrong color and began getting worked up about the consequences of my choice—what I'd be able to wear or if I would regret it later. I sat there holding five bottles of nail polish until the nail tech finished prepping my nails, and I just ended up choosing all five because I was so overwhelmed." I start crying and can't stop. "Sorry."

"Don't apologize." Regina hands me a tissue.

I blow my nose and feel like such a child.

"I want us to try some things," she says. "I'm going to teach you some grounding techniques that might help when you are in that kind of situation."

The hour goes by fast as she teaches me steps to help slow things down before they escalate, and for the first time since I was in the hospital, I begin to feel like there is some hope.

5.

I keep going to my sessions with Regina and am learning a great deal about myself. I tell Adrian, and of course he is understanding because of his brother. But Myra still thinks it is a waste of time.

"Maybe *I'm* the one who needs a therapist—not you. This is a real problem," she says, pointing to the hickeys on her neck. She explained that they were a gift from Santiago, who didn't want a "real" relationship, though she did. "Getting nervous in front of a guy is not a real problem. Potentially missing out on the love of your life because he can't see it *is*."

I am getting tired of her shit.

In my last session with Regina, we talked about boundaries, and now I am going to have to put what I've learned into practice.

"Look, Myra—"

"Here she goes. I'm going to get a lecture." She rolls her eyes.

That is it.

"I don't have to explain myself to you for the umpteenth time, Myra. You don't listen to me or even try to understand me or what I'm going through. So yeah, maybe you do need therapy so you can learn to be a better listener."

"Dude, I totally listen. You're my cousin and I don't want you to be sad, but therapy is something white people do. What am I supposed to say?"

"Therapy is not just for white people."

"Marichu, you used to say the same thing. You go a few times and suddenly you're all 'balanced' and shit and think you're better than everyone else. That's some total white people shit right there."

I hate admitting I am wrong, but I know I need to do just that. "I was wrong. We deserve to know this stuff about ourselves, too. Not just white people."

"Wow, listen to you. Already light-years ahead of me in self-knowledge."

"You sound so ridiculous, Myra. Ridiculous and mean."

"See, you're already doing it."

I take a deep breath, my body shaking as I tell her, "I can see that we're not going to get anywhere in this conversation, and I think it's best if we cool off before this escalates."

Myra isn't used to me pushing back like this, and she looks mad and hurt. *Good*, I think.

"¿En serio? Okay, Miss Perfect, I'll go home and meditate before I call you."

Myra gets up from where we are sitting in my room. She slams the door as she walks out. Then I hear her truck leave our driveway, a corrido blasting so loud I feel the bass pounding in me long after she's gone.

6.

Myra brings the blankets out of the linen closet and to the truck. We're heading back to Mi Ranchito for the first time as a group since I had my panic attack almost five months before. On one of her trips there with Lisa and Yuri, my cousin sweet-talked the bouncer into letting us back in.

I volunteer to go in the truck bed, and of course Adrian joins me. He turns to me. "I can hear you thinking."

"Always."

"About what this time?"

"About the fight I had with Myra, and how I'm so happy she eventually came around."

It had been a month after our fight when Myra and I saw each other again. We had carne asada at our grandparents' house, so we were forced to be in the same space.

"¿Y ahora, ustedes?" our grandmother asked, annoyed when she saw that we weren't causing the same amount of chaos we usually did at these family get-togethers.

"Marichu wishes she was white," Myra said.

"What?" my grandpa said, walking by.

"I started going to therapy, and for some reason, that bothers Myra," I said, on the verge of tears.

"What?" Grandma said. "Everyone goes to therapy. Or everyone should, ha! Even I've been. Sometimes the old noggin needs a . . ." She finished her sentence with the Mexican hand gesture for adjusting.

I was shocked.

"Really?" Myra asked in disbelief.

"Really, Myrita. It was when I lost my first baby. I needed the extra support," Grandma said.

"But I thought Grandpa and your sister Ruth got you through that hard time," Myra said. "Weren't they enough?"

Grandma sighed. "I needed professional help to deal with great sadness and ultimately depression. Your grandpa was having trouble with it as well, and we ended up both going. It saved our marriage, and probably my life."

Myra and I just stared at our grandmother. She wasn't who she was five minutes ago.

"So yeah," Grandma said, and bit into the taco she'd been rolling. "Therapy ain't just for white people."

Adrian shakes his head and says, "I still can't believe your grandma was in therapy. She seems so old-school. What else are you thinking about?" He knows there's more.

"I'm thinking about the last time I was in this truck and how I'm not anxious like that right now."

"Good. Because I really don't want to be known as La Loca's best friend."

I playfully shove him. "Shut up." I wonder if Adrian means it but then I push it out of my head, like Regina has taught me. I don't have control over him, only over me, and I need to remember that.

The truck stops. The familiar sounds of people making their way to the club surround us once more. The women in their tight dresses, tight jeans, tight miniskirts. The men in their sombreros, hoping to get lucky, downing small (or large) bottles of liquor and beer to avoid the high prices of alcohol inside, smoking their last cigarettes before going in.

"Oh, and about how many guys I'm going to make out with," I add. "That was the other thing I was thinking about."

Adrian bursts out laughing.

It's going to be a good night.

A NOTE FROM ISABEL QUINTERO

✳ ✳ ✳ ✳ ✳ ✳ ✳ ✳ ✳ ✳ ✳ ✳ ✳ ✳ ✳

"Back of the Truck" is semiautobiographical. I was diagnosed with anxiety when I was about twenty-five, but I'd been dealing with it and panic attacks longer. I had my first panic attack at fifteen, on the dance floor of a small Mexican club

while dancing with a guy I was really attracted to. I remember feeling embarrassed because I hadn't even heard the word anxiety yet. Growing up Latine/Latinx meant that, for many of us, mental health and therapy were never addressed, and mental health issues were something that only affected white people—we worked (literally) through whatever unnamed disorder we carried (anxiety, depression, OCD, PTSD, etc.). I still have panic attacks, but they've lessened since I started regularly going to therapy, where I've learned how to manage my anxiety. It's not easy, but I've grown so much that I keep going. I hope newer generations understand that we are worthy of mental health treatment, of healing and thriving. While many of our parents didn't have access to the same tools we do, their struggles do not have to be our own. We owe it to ourselves and those who come after to break cycles that do not serve us.

DON'T GO BREAKING MY HEART

ANNA DRURY

Content Note: This story references premenstrual dysphoric disorder, anxiety, and depression.

The letter in Emma's hands was heavy with the weight of confession. Of hope.

It's funny how people talked about hope as a thing of lightness, with feathers.

"You're sure about this?" Becky asked.

"No." Emma closed her eyes and took a deep breath, reminding herself of how far she'd come this year. "But I'm doing it anyway."

She slid the letter into the locker and pressed her hand to the cool metal. There was no turning back now.

All she could do was wait.

Gabe wove his way through the halls, head down, dodging excited conversations about hair, dresses, tuxes, limos, and everything else prom-related.

Eli and Shayna had tried to convince him to go, but there was only one girl Gabe had ever considered going with, and that was out of the question. Even after a year, thoughts of her twisted him up inside.

He yanked his locker open, and an envelope fell out. Adjusting his bag on his shoulder, he bent and picked it up from the floor. When he flipped it over, he saw his name neatly typed on the outside. He knew only one person who liked to use a typewriter.

He scanned the hall, searching for Emma's dark curly hair or a glimpse of her red cat-eye glasses, but of course she wasn't there.

He considered the letter in his hands for a moment, and then opened it.

Dear Gabe,

Do you remember our first dance? It was the last slow song at your Bar Mitzvah. You'd been dancing with all the girls there, so it's not like I was special, but when you asked me and I took your hand, every butterfly flew awake inside me. I put my arms around your neck, like I'd seen the other girls do, and your hands rested lightly on my waist. When you started moving side to side, I swayed with you.

It was my first slow dance. I hoped to G-d you couldn't tell how nervous I was.

It's strange to think of now, but that's the only time we ever danced together.

You couldn't come to my Bat Mitzvah because you were sick. So many times, I'd pictured you being there, asking me to dance again and telling me how pretty I looked in my dress. I imagined all sorts of things about how you might see me. How I wanted you to see me.

Thinking about you was one of the very few bright spots for me that year. I thought of you like my own personal North Star and imagined you sparkled across what felt like a never-ending night just for me.

That secret pull I felt toward you, filled with ease and hope, was such a stark contrast to what I felt in the rest of my life. No one really knew the full extent of what seventh grade was like for me. Not my family. Not even Becky.

But looking back, that is when everything started.

This is the first of multiple letters, part of my teshuvah.

You don't owe me anything, Gabe. I know that teshuvah begins and ends with me, but I also can't help but hope that you'll forgive me. If there is even a chance of that, though, you deserve an explanation.

So, if you are willing to give me this chance to explain and you want to keep reading, go to the place where you asked me to prom.

Love,

Emma

His eyes lingered over the last two words.

Love, Emma.

He ran his hand through his hair.

Forgive her? There was no more "Gabe and Emma." She'd made that clear last year. It wasn't fair of her to ask anything of him, to send him on some scavenger hunt. Whatever Emma's problems were, they weren't his. Not anymore.

Then again, he knew that repenting and asking forgiveness from those you've hurt was part of teshuvah, and he couldn't deny that he *had* been hoping for something—apology, explanation—for a long time. He groaned. He hated that he always wanted to know what Emma had to say, even when he knew he shouldn't.

He started to head out toward the front parking lot, where he'd asked her to prom. It wasn't like he had much of a choice; that was where he parked. He'd decide on the way if he felt like looking for another letter.

As he worked his way through the halls, he thought about how he'd made sure to dance with all the other girls at his Bar Mitzvah so it wouldn't be obvious that Emma was the one he'd really wanted to ask. He'd asked her last because he'd always had a thing about saving the best for last. He remembered hoping that she didn't notice how sweaty his hand was when he led her to the dance floor, and how he kept his arms down in case he smelled bad, even though his sisters had made sure he didn't forget his deodorant that day.

It wasn't his fault they hadn't danced since. He absolutely would have danced with her at her Bat Mitzvah if he hadn't been puking his guts out, doubly tortured by the thought of her dancing with the other boys in their Hebrew school class. And he'd planned on having every dance with her at prom last year, but that didn't happen because *she dumped him* the same day that he promposed.

When he stepped out of the school into the glare of the afternoon sun, his memories shifted to that morning last year.

He'd picked Emma up for school as usual, and when they arrived, he opened the door for her and handed her a note that said: *Donut go breaking my heart . . .*

"Don't Go Breaking My Heart" came blasting across the lot from Eli's car, and when she looked up, Gabe and his friends were holding three dozen donuts in boxes, spelling out *PROM?*

Emma had laughed. It was one of her laughs that burst out of her, even though he could tell she'd have held it in if she could've, which was perfect. The goal was always to make her so happy that she couldn't hide it, even if she wanted to.

She'd nodded yes while grinning at him in that way that told him he was a corny idiot and she loved it.

He'd swept her up in a big hug, and she'd buried her face in his neck. Everyone cheered. It was one of those moments that was so perfect it felt like it belonged in the movies.

"Hey!" Eli called, jogging up to him, breaking the spell of Gabe's memories.

A white flash of an envelope in Eli's hand caught Gabe's eye.

Gabe's shoulders dropped. Finding the letter wouldn't be much of a choice at all, apparently.

"You're in on this?"

"Just the messenger." Eli grinned and slapped the letter against Gabe's chest. "But you know me. I'm a sucker for the Gabe and Emma story."

"Yeah, well, don't get too excited," Gabe said. "Pretty sure that whatever this is won't change the ending of that story."

Eli shrugged. "Whatever you say. I'll catch you later, man. I gotta go find Shayna."

Eli always had to go find Shayna. They were basically high school couple royalty. Gabe had thought that he and Emma were really good together, too, in a way that could've maybe gone beyond high school. But that possibility had been ripped away from him.

He looked down at the envelope in his hand.

Did he really want to do this? Was he a sucker for letting her break his heart, then coming back the first time she beckoned, even after all this time?

Maybe. But he would for sure wonder about the letters if he didn't see what this was about. Reading them would be good, he told himself. For closure.

He ripped the second letter open in hopes that it would all be over and done with quickly.

Dear Gabe,

I'll always be grateful that Becky dragged me to the Thanksgiving Day game junior year, interrupting my plans of napping both before and after the meal.

When we arrived, you got me a hot chocolate and told me you were glad I came. I remember grumbling something at you like, "That makes one of us." You looked down, and I felt like such a putz—you were being nice, and it's not your fault I hate mornings. And football. I bumped you with my shoulder and said, "But this hot chocolate definitely helps."

When you smile—I mean, really smile—the dimple that

appears in your left cheek is like this reward to whoever you're
smiling at. It's my all-time favorite dimple. And when I saw it that
morning, all I wanted was to make you smile at me that way again.

I expected you to spend most of the game with Eli and
Shayna and your other friends, but you stayed with me and
narrated the whole game like it was a wildlife safari. My stomach
hurt from laughing so hard. At one point, you got a blanket from
your car so we didn't have to sit directly on the cold bleachers,
which also meant you sat right next to me. Warmth radiated off
you. I remember leaning into it, into you, just a little, and then
you leaned back just enough to close the space between us so
that our shoulders touched.

I hadn't been this close to you in years, and every part of me
was a live wire, ready and hopeful, just like when I was twelve
years old swaying with you on the dance floor.

We started hanging out more after that, and by Shayna's
birthday party on New Year's Eve, you still hadn't made a real
move. When we counted down to midnight, I thought you were
finally going to kiss me, but you came in for a hug instead.

I was tired of waiting—sometimes a girl just needs to get
things done herself. So when you started to release me from the
hug, I grabbed your shirt, and I kissed you.

Gabe loved that Emma had kissed him first. He'd known she liked
him, but he hadn't known if she wanted to be kissed in front of so
many people—he wasn't actually sure how he felt about such a public
display himself—so he'd decided against it.

But when she kissed him, he didn't care if everyone in the whole
world saw, because he was finally, *finally*, kissing Emma Fischer.

We had a lot of seemingly perfect moments in the months
we dated. But for every one of them, there were countless others
where I was desperately trying to control my feelings and hide

*how extreme my moods could get. Still, you caught glimpses. It
was inevitable, I suppose—just like it was inevitable that I would
mess everything up. Our last perfect moment was when you
promposed.*

*I was in full-on PMS mode that day when you picked me up
for school, even though I was nowhere near my period: filled to
the brim with this fury that had no known cause. But then you
gave me that goofy, sweet note, and the song and the donuts . . .
It was all so cheesy and sweet and wonderful.*

*How was it possible that I could be so genuinely happy with
you at the same time a river of poisonous rage coursed through
me? It made me feel like I was losing my mind.*

*For most of that day, I existed in that space of both promposal
high and unwarranted, seething fury.*

Until gym class.

*Even though I know you saw everything that happened, I
want to explain it from my perspective.*

*We were set up for badminton doubles. You were across
the field with Danny Johansson. I remember you waving at me
while I was getting set up with Becky to play against Amber and
Shannon. You smiled at me, and I tried to smile back. I don't know
if you noticed I failed, because the whistle blew and everyone
started playing.*

*Unsurprisingly, I sucked at the game. But instead of laughing
it off that day, I felt every miss make the backs of my eyes throb.*

*The boys next to us, including Chris Connors, kept talking
about "cocks," because obviously knowing that the full name for
the birdie is "shuttlecock" was too much for them. And then they
started saying stuff to us.*

"Oooh, she just gave it to that cock!"

"Get after that cock!"

*Shannon and Amber rolled their eyes and told them to shut
up, but they were smiling when they said it. Flirting.*

I missed again, and Chris said, "Emma has no idea what to do with a cock! Must suck to be Gabe!"

"More like doesn't suck!" Troy Atkinson added in what I'm sure he thought was a stroke of teen-boy genius.

Their shitty jokes hit closer to home than I wanted to admit. I wasn't ready to do any of that stuff. You always said it was fine, but maybe it wasn't? And then I thought about how we were going to prom—what if you wanted something to happen after?

Gabe bounced his fist against his car. He wanted to rip Chris and Troy apart. He'd never, ever pressured Emma about anything when it came to sex stuff. He was perfectly fine with going at whatever pace she wanted and figuring it out together. It wasn't anyone else's business.

The next time the birdie came to me, I channeled all my pissed-off frustration into my swing, and I hit it. I mean, barely, but then I swung again and hit it again, and it went over the net. And they didn't hit it back! That was a crowning athletic achievement for me.

I was grinning, triumphant, but Becky looked at me with this pitying expression on her face. I heard giggling. Amber was covering her mouth with her hand, and Shannon was smirking.

"What?" I asked Becky, a little breathless from my supposed victory. "Didn't I score?"

Becky shook her head. "It was a foul."

"That's not how you score!" Troy called, and Chris added, "Maybe Gabe needs to give his girl some feedback on how cocks work!"

The river of rage finally broke through the dam I'd built up and came rushing forth. I screamed and hurled my racket at the guys. It missed, which just made me angrier.

I lunged at Chris, but Becky grabbed me, and he shot out

of my reach. I jerked away from her, screaming again, wild, uncontainable. I wanted to destroy everything and disappear at the same time. It was like being trapped in a cage, but that cage was also me.

And then, different arms were around me in a bear hug, pulling me back.

You. My vision had narrowed, and I could barely breathe. And there you were, holding me and saying my name over and over to calm me down. I leaned my head back against you, and your hold relaxed, just a little.

That was when I saw that Shannon had her phone out.

"Psycho," she said.

I yanked myself out of your arms. I marched right up to Shannon, snatched the phone out of her hand, hurled it to the ground, and smashed it with my foot.

Everyone was watching. I could hear my heart pumping my blood, pounding and pounding through my veins. My fire had gone out, and I felt like I was underwater instead, and if I stayed in that spot any longer, I would drown.

So I ran. I didn't care that it was the middle of the day, or that all my stuff was still at school, or that I am less athletic than my bubbe. I couldn't be there anymore. I was going home.

You didn't follow me. You'd finally seen how messed up I was. It had always just been a matter of time.

The next letter will hopefully give you context about how things got to the point last year that a stupid game in gym class could make me completely freak out. It's waiting for you where we had our first high school class together, with the person who's had a front-row seat to our story since Hebrew school.

Love,

Emma

Gabe rubbed the back of his neck. When they were dating, he'd seen Emma be moody and unpredictable sometimes. And yeah, she cried a lot. He'd chalked that up to her being more sensitive than he'd realized, but it never affected how he'd felt about her. She'd usually laugh through her tears, and he'd kiss her, and everything would seem okay.

He'd never seen her—or anyone—go off like she did that day, though. He'd frozen in the moment. His ears always got hot when he felt guilty, and they blazed at the memory. He'd wondered countless times if things might've been different if he'd gotten his shit together to go after her. He *should* have gone after her, even if it wouldn't have changed anything that happened later.

He headed back inside to Ms. Greene's room, their ninth-grade English teacher who had also been their Hebrew school teacher. When he showed up in her doorway, she greeted him with a smile and held out an envelope for him.

"Thanks," he said.

"Have a good weekend," she called after him. He waved half-heartedly on his way out.

He went down the hall before stopping to read the letter.

Dear Gabe,

This letter gets intense, and some of it's very female-specific, in a biological sense. But I know your sisters and mom are awesome, and I trust you to be able to handle it. That I'm even warning you reeks of the patriarchy, though, doesn't it?

Before I get going, I want you to know—I'm okay now. But I wasn't, not for a really long time, including when we were together. Which was not your fault. I don't want to activate your hero complex. I know you always want to do the right thing and take care of people. But you need to know that there is truly nothing you could have done that would have changed my situation. Okay?

Wow, okay, Gabe thought. Eli always gave him crap about being a hero, too. He just wanted to be a good guy, unlike his dad. Was that such a bad thing?

I started my period the summer before seventh grade, and with it came migraines and cramps that made me puke.

Delightful, right?

Between that and my Bat Mitzvah, there was a lot of talk about how I was "becoming a woman" that year. At twelve.

Twelve-year-old girls are not women any more than twelve-year-old boys are men. I mean, we were still at the kids' Pesach table for the community seder that year. Talk about mixed messages.

Anyway, there was more than the standard joys of puberty going on with me, though we didn't exactly know it at the time. Along with physical symptoms, I was depressed and angry and anxious in ways I'd never been before, and my mood swings could make a ballerina dizzy.

Have you ever felt like your body and mind were betraying you?

Twelve was the year we danced. It was also the year that I stood in my bathroom, looking at a Venus razor and a bottle of Advil, wondering if they were capable of the kind of destruction I was contemplating. It was the year I started fantasizing about throwing myself out of the speeding car when my parents were driving on the highway.

I just wondered what would happen.

I was twelve years old, apparently "becoming a woman," and the two things I remember thinking about the most were you and dying. My North Star crush to distract me during my steepest downward spirals.

Crushes are one of the most appropriately named things in the world, don't you think? They can really be devastating and wonderful all at once. I'm convinced that "It was the best of times, it was the worst of times" is actually referring to how it feels to have a crush. But also, Dickens sucked, so maybe not. My point is that having a crush on you meant some part of me hoped for something, and hope can be a real anchor to life.

Still, I wonder how no one saw how bad it was, even though I can't really blame them; I didn't want anyone to see. Besides, the moods—the anxiety and depression, especially—weren't there all the time. For about a week or ten days every month, I felt fine. "Normal." And in those precious days, I'd convince myself I was fine, that everything was okay.

But it wasn't, not really. Time went on, and intrusive thoughts about death, and the feeling that life was basically pointless, kept creeping in.

In ninth grade, I quit going to synagogue after the High Holidays. All the stuff about repenting and being made in G-d's image infuriated me. If I was made in G-d's image, what did that say about G-d? Why should I repent when G-d apparently made me the way I was?

By tenth grade, "PMS" basically ruled my life. Relatives regularly told me I was blowing things out of proportion. Even Becky would get annoyed with me for canceling plans last-minute when I couldn't handle things that had previously sounded fun.

I asked my doctor about birth control, because Becky said it helped her with PMS and cramps. Apparently, the kind of migraines I get put me at risk for stroke if I go on the pill, so that was a no. I turned to "natural" remedies, like supplements and acupuncture. They helped a little, I guess, but not enough.

All of this meant that there were times I'd be running around, manic and laughing one minute, and the next moment I'd be curled up on the floor in the fetal position crying, or absolutely Hulk-raging-out (emotionally speaking) for no

*reason. It was almost impossible to know how I would be in any
given situation.*

That's who you were dating junior year.

*Becky told me later, after you and I were over, that you'd
met her at my locker at the end of the day when everything
went to shit, and asked to be the one to bring me my things, but
she refused. She wanted to protect me, I think, but sometimes
I wonder if things would have been different in the moment, if
you'd been the one who showed up first.*

*For what it's worth, I don't think it would have changed the
eventual outcome. Some things just needed to happen, including
us breaking up.*

*The next letter is with Becky, where you at least tried,
unaware of what was coming.*

Love,

Emma

Gabe's stomach was clenched in knots.

He thought about the girl he'd danced with at his Bar Mitzvah. He
remembered holding her hand and then tried to imagine her being
gone. Twelve years old and wanting to die?

Growing up with three older sisters meant periods and stuff were
talked about all the time—he was basically immune to the subject.
He knew when his sisters started baking and crying at ASPCA commercials that he was best off keeping to himself for a couple of days.
He would never forget when one of them told him his "male energy
was grating." So he just made himself scarce and helped himself to the
baked goods on his way through the kitchen.

And yeah, Emma had mentioned PMS when they were together,
but he'd never taken anything she'd said or done during those
moments to heart. He knew it would pass, and to him, it always
seemed to.

He had no idea all of it could make girls suicidal. That it had made *her* suicidal.

That was terrifying.

He pinched the bridge of his nose and closed his eyes. Had he not noticed how bad things were last year because he'd just been happy to be the one who held her when she cried, to kiss her tears away? Had he really been that oblivious?

He started walking through the halls again, and a couple of turns later, he was approaching Emma's locker, where Becky was waiting for him. His mind shot back to meeting her in this same spot last year.

Even though he'd screwed up, by the end of the day, he'd known that he needed to check on Emma. But Becky had said no, so he texted Emma instead, figuring she'd see it when Becky returned her phone. But she never replied, which was why he went over that night, and well . . .

"Took you long enough," Becky said, waving a white envelope in his face.

"Yeah, yeah, okay," he said, taking it. "How many more of these are there?"

"I guess you'll just have to keep reading to find out," she said. Her arms were wide open in a shrug as she backed up before she turned and jogged away.

Gabe tore into the letter before she was fully out of sight.

Dear Gabe,

Becky found me after school, sobbing in my room. When she handed over my phone, the screen was a mess of notifications. Turns out my smashing Shannon's phone didn't stop her from logging in to her account on another device and sending the video out to everyone. The cloud can be a real double-edged sword.

There were texts from tons of people, including you. I didn't read any of them at the time, though. I was too ashamed of myself, too scared of what they would say.

Becky sat with me and let me cry.

When my parents got home early from work (the school had called them, obviously—turns out just running away from class is concerning to adults), they tried to talk to me about what happened, but I didn't know how to explain. They informed me that I would be talking to the school psychologist the next day.

After Becky left, I sat alone on the roof outside my bedroom, and I wondered what would happen if I got closer to the edge. What if I just let myself fall?

I distinctly remember thinking that I didn't want to die. I just didn't know how I could keep living.

Then I heard my name.

You, standing in the yard below, calling up to me. There could be no more running or ignoring.

I saw myself in the hall mirror on my way downstairs: messy bun, red eyes, splotchy face. And still only a fraction of how bad my insides felt.

You moved to hug me when I got outside, but I flinched. I saw the hurt and confusion on your face. I didn't know how to tell you that if anyone touched me, especially you, I would shatter into a million pieces.

I hugged myself instead, to keep everything from spilling out.

"Are you okay?" you asked, no sign of that dimple I love so much.

"Do I look okay?" I was incredulous that you would ask that question, but I understand now that that was also the only question you could ask.

You didn't answer, which was kind of you. Instead, you asked, "What's going on? How can I help?"

G-d, I didn't know how to answer you. So I didn't.

You shifted tactics. "Are you coming to school tomorrow?"

"Not for class." I looked down at my sneakers. They were dirty.
A mess. Just like me.

"Talk to me, Em. Please." Your voice was gentle.

I looked up at you. I will never get used to the deep blue of
your eyes.

"And say what?"

"Whatever you want." You reached for my hand, and I let you
take it.

Hope. I saw it there, in your eyes, but I couldn't find it in
myself.

My insides cracked.

"I'm humiliated," I said. "And the video . . ."

"Everyone will forget about it soon," you said. "You know how
people are. Something else will get their attention, and it won't
even be a big deal anymore."

"But I won't forget," I whispered, taking my hand back. "It's
a big deal to me." I know you only meant to make me feel better.
But my happiness was completely out of your control.

"Why are you with me?" I asked.

You blinked at me, like I'd woken you from a dream. "What?"

"What do you see, when you look at me?"

I don't know what I wanted you to say.

You were quiet, and then you said, "I just see you."

And G-d, I didn't want to cry. I don't even know how my body
could keep producing tears, but there they were, streaming down
my face. I didn't have the energy to wipe them away.

"No, you don't. You see your idea of me. And that's the
thing . . . I think that maybe I'm just an idea that exists in other
people's minds. I don't feel real. But if I'm not real, I don't know
why everything hurts. So. Damn. Much."

"Emma." The sound of my name in your mouth had felt like

an anchor back to myself that afternoon, but right then, I didn't know who "Emma" was anymore.

"I'm too broken for this," I said. "Please don't pretend I'm not."

"What are you saying?" When I didn't answer right away, understanding seemed to begin to dawn on you. "What about prom?"

I knew I had to say it, finish it, even though it nauseated me.

"I'm saying that I can't do this. No prom. We're done. There is no 'Gabe and Emma,' not anymore."

I'll never forget your face. The shock. The hurt that I caused.

You tried to say something, but I didn't let you. I kissed you instead, one last time, and then I went inside.

Gabe could still taste her tears on his lips when he thought about that night, which made his throat ache.

He'd stayed there in her yard after she went back inside. He'd expected her to come back out, to say she hadn't meant it. He hated himself for asking *What about prom?* As though prom was of any consequence at all.

The last few weeks of school were full of doctors' appointments. I finished the year from home, which also meant I didn't see you. And I didn't have the capacity to deal with your texts or calls, so I ignored them. Blocked you. I told myself it was better that way. A cleaner break.

And during that time, something big happened.

I got diagnosed with PMDD, which stands for premenstrual dysphoric disorder. For the longest time, I'd felt crazy. But I wasn't. I'm not. What I experience has a name, and it's different from the PMS most menstruators get. It's a mood disorder, and the mood swings and the anxiety and the depression are all symptoms of this other thing.

I started medication and had regular checkups to monitor my reactions and progress. And it worked. There were some side effects, sure, but it was like my body and mind could get to know each other for the first time. Like all the parts of me could even be friends.

Over the summer, I asked Becky if this was how she always felt, how other people feel.

"What do you mean?" she asked.

I'll never forget what I said then. "Like, you know that life isn't perfect, but you'll be able to handle things that change or happen or whatever?"

She gave me this puzzled look. "Well, yeah."

But Gabe—I'd never felt that way before.

This was how people lived. It was astonishing. It still is.

When I came back to school for senior year, it turned out you were right. No one said anything about the video. Things were pretty normal, except for you and me. I made sure to stay away from anything you might go to with our friends; I didn't want to ruin stuff for you. Becky told me that you were staying away from group gatherings, too, and I knew that was my fault.

You deserved so much more from this past year—senior year—than what you got.

I'm good about taking my medicine. I cut out caffeine (and made it to my first class on time all year, if you can believe it), and I even started meditating. It's all helping. I'm not saying life is perfect. I get mild mood swings for a day or two before my period sometimes, and cramps still exist, but none of it is like what it used to be. I am me again. Or maybe for the first time. I'm my own North Star, which is how it's supposed to be.

I also decided to go back to synagogue, starting with the High Holiday services in the fall. It felt good to be back, to sing the prayers and feel the Hebrew words in my mouth again.

I'd managed to avoid you all summer, and even for those first weeks back at school. Until Yom Kippur, when my dad and I were making an early exit, and I was outside waiting for him to pull the car around. It was the first truly chilly day in September, but I hadn't dressed for it.

You came outside for some air and, of course, noticed me shivering. You said, "Here, it's cold," and gave me your suit jacket. It smelled like you.

We just stood there in silence. I wondered if maybe it wasn't that you hadn't seen me when we were together, but that you'd been able to see the good in me, even when I couldn't.

I wanted to say so much then. That I was sorry—it was the Day of Atonement, after all. I wanted to tell you that I was different and more myself than I'd ever been.

I wanted you to see me again, healthy and whole.

But I didn't say any of that, and all too soon, my dad drove up. I managed to at least thank you when I handed back your jacket. I missed its warmth, and your scent, as soon as I took it off.

I didn't have the words then, Gabe, but I do now. That's what these letters are.

My teshuvah.

My truth.

All these letters have been about the past, but I'm finally living now. And I'm thinking about the future.

I started all of this hoping you could forgive me. And if you can grant me that, I'll be grateful—it's probably more than I deserve. But I'd be lying if I said that's all I was hoping for, and these letters are all about being honest.

Here is the thing I've learned about teshuvah. It's not just repentance. It's also about returning.

I'm sorry. And I'm returning. To myself, and, if you'll forgive me, maybe to something more.

There is another, final letter in the place where I ran from you
last year.
I'm not running now.
Love,
Emma

Hope pounded through Gabe with every heartbeat, finally driving away his hesitation and his hurt.

When Emma hadn't responded to any of his texts or calls, he'd realized that she wasn't going to take back the breakup, so he'd tried to let her go as best he could. A self-preservation thing. And as for not hanging out with their friend group, well, it wasn't as fun without her, and their friends' attempts at cheering him up grated on his nerves. Eli had been just about the only person he could handle for a long time.

When he'd seen Emma outside the synagogue that day, muscle memory had taken over. He was so relieved that she didn't protest or pull away when he reached over and placed his jacket on her shoulders. It had physically hurt to step away from her, the space between them wide and silent, unbridgeable once again. When she handed his jacket back, the collar smelled like her shampoo, and he breathed her in for the rest of the day, a secret way to keep her close.

These letters were Emma's teshuvah.

Repentance and returning.

Maybe teshuvah could be the bridge between them. And the thing about bridges, he realized, was that they went both ways.

He sprinted through the halls, headed toward the fields behind the school.

He hoped he was right about who was holding the last letter for him.

Emma was sick with nerves, waiting in the field.

It was a beautiful spring afternoon. There were practices happening and students hanging out, waiting for friends or siblings or rides home.

She could almost taste the bittersweetness of the end of the year—the end of high school—in the air. She shifted the envelope and wax-paper bag she was holding so she could wipe her sweaty palms on her legs.

Becky ran up to her, with Eli and Shayna in tow. "He should be here soon!"

Emma bit her lip. "What if he doesn't show?"

"He will," Eli said. He was fiddling with a small wireless speaker and his phone.

"Seriously," Shayna added. "This is Gabe we're talking about."

Emma started to say something, but Becky stopped her.

"No *buts*. No matter what happens, Em, you're a badass. And if this is an alternate universe where you are somehow right, I have a freezer full of ice cream and a book full of curses we can cast on him. Okay?"

Emma smiled at her friend's ferocity. "Okay."

"Good," Becky said, a smile spreading wide over her face. "Because here he comes."

Emma turned and saw a familiar tall figure walking toward her.

Gabe vaguely registered Becky, Eli, and Shayna in the background, but he was focused on Emma. He knew he was finally seeing her fully, not as an idea in his mind like she'd written but as the real, beautifully complicated, and brave person she was.

He slowed his pace down even as his heart sped up when he got closer to her and saw that she was holding an envelope.

"You came." Her breath caught on the words.

"Of course I did." He couldn't believe he'd considered not reading her letters.

She smiled shyly and handed him the envelope. Their fingers brushed against one another, and a blush crept up her neck.

"Before I read this," he said, "I need you to know something."

Emma's eyes widened and her smile faded. "Okay?" It came out like a question, her voice uncertain.

"I'm sorry," Gabe said.

Emma's mouth dropped open. "For what?"

Gabe took a deep breath and caught a whiff of her shampoo on the wind. His entire body buzzed at having her so close. "Lots of things, but especially for asking about prom, like an idiot, when you were so clearly—"

Emma reached out and put her hand on his to stop him.

"Just read the damn letter," she whispered. She was smiling again. It took all Gabe had to tear his eyes away from hers.

Dear Gabe,

   I'm sorry for all the hurt I've caused you.

   I'm sorry for not trusting you with all of me.

   I'm sorry for pushing you away.

   Please forgive me.

   And if you can do that, I'm also hoping for a return to us—to "Gabe and Emma." It could be a do(nut)-over of sorts.

   Maybe we can start with prom?

   Love,

   Emma

When Gabe's dimple appeared, Emma thought she might actually sprout wings.

"Don't Go Breaking My Heart" came blasting through Eli's speaker, and Gabe laughed. Emma held out the wax-paper bag for him, and he smiled even wider when he withdrew a heart-shaped donut.

"Because you've always had my heart," she said.

He cocked an eyebrow at her. "I thought I was the cheesy one?"

"I may not be as good at puns as you, but I still know how to cheese it up," Emma said. Then more words came tumbling out of her. "I hope you weren't weirded out by everything I wrote. I know it's a lot. I needed to tell you, and there was no way to do that without telling you all of it. And—"

Gabe was shaking his head, and she wanted to ask him why, but before she had a chance, he pulled her to him and kissed her.

She rested a hand on his chest. His heart was beating fast, an echo of her own. She smiled and kissed him back, oblivious to the cheers of their friends around them.

When they drew apart, he leaned his forehead against hers.

"So . . . is that a yes to prom?" Emma smiled up at him.

"Yes." Gabe leaned closer and whispered in her ear. "We'll finally get our second dance. And all the ones that come after."

He kissed her again, and it tasted like forgiveness and hope and coming home.

A NOTE FROM ANNA DRURY

✳ ✳ ✳ ✳ ✳ ✳ ✳ ✳ ✳ ✳ ✳ ✳ ✳

PMDD is categorized as a depressive disorder in the DSM–5 (the fifth edition of the Diagnostic and Statistical Manual of Mental Disorders*). I was diagnosed with PMDD in my early thirties, but I showed the signs and symptoms of it on and off from the time I started menstruating at eleven years old. Many of the moments Emma describes are taken directly from my own experiences. It is rare, but not impossible, to be diagnosed with PMDD as a teenager; the symptoms can present as other issues, both physical and mental, and getting the* *diagnosis can depend greatly on the doctor you are seeing. This story is part wish fulfillment for me, imagining what my life might have been like had I been diagnosed earlier, and part call to action for young menstruators to pay attention to their cycles and to advocate for themselves.*

WE ARE STARDUST

ALECHIA DOW

Content Note: This story references depression and obsessive thoughts.

A star shines brightest when surrounded by the dark. The farther you are from other entities, the more vibrant you appear. And I, far from all because I am not only new but different, am brilliant.

But I've always wondered if a star only shines bright as a way to say, *Hey, I'm lonely. Anyone want to be friends?*

The truth is, being a star above worlds—too young to be seen by entities scattered across the universe and yet old enough to feel, think, and have a mind—is unbearable.

My mind has become my enemy, jealous of the life elsewhere, wishing for my own adventure, wishing for friendship and love, loathing the being I am. Loathing my own stardust. One moment I'm enraptured by the universe I'm part of. The next, I'm an abyss of dark thoughts. The other stars do not think these things. They are content in ways I can't understand.

The loop replays in my mind over and over: I am destined to be alone. I am to be trapped in space, shining for everyone but myself. Shining, despite my overwhelming . . . feelings. Feelings I don't always have the words to describe because I'm a star. Not part of a constellation or anything exciting like that. I'm too new to be part of a system. Too new to know my place.

I have nothing.

I am no one.

I am worthless.

And yet here I am, sparkling soundlessly in the tapestry of space. Where it ends, I don't know. I'm not old enough to know the secrets of the universe, and there's no one here to tell me, no mother to share her knowledge and care for me.

I know some things about stardust, life and death within the galaxies, words that I can never use, but nothing about how I came to be. Or what will happen to me. Or when.

Which is why, when a cloud of red spirals flecked with purple energy engulfs me, I don't know what to do. I can't move. I can't call for help. Nothing like this has ever happened before. This energy wants to change me.

But I am unchangeable. I am an immovable star.

Until I'm not.

Until I'm transforming into something new.

Something other.

And I'm falling through space and time and I think I hear myself. I think I have a voice. Because that voice comes from somewhere within me, and it screams. And it laughs. And it wonders what's happening.

If I have a voice, I must have a mouth.

If I have a mouth, I must have a body.

If I have a body, I must . . .

It's hot! And cold. Yet there's a warmth within me. There's sound, too, and limbs. I have a body, and my body will break if I don't stop falling. I feel . . . in my gut . . . some new sensation. My eyes blink. I have eyes! I see. I always could see, but now I see brilliance. Blue and green brilliance that's coming closer and closer.

And then there's that feeling in the pit of my body—*my body!*—again. Telling me fear. And that pounding sound grows quicker, louder, and there's not enough air or there's too much air.

The ground comes closer. I don't have names for stars and planets. They can't tell me who they are. But this one has life on it. Life I've seen. They have bodies and joy and they aren't alone. They have words, words I know!

Now that I am something, I have everything to lose if I can't stop falling.

My limbs move slowly through the strange substance surrounding me to cover my eyes. To prepare me. For the impact. To prepare me for destruction.

If this is the end, what an end it'll be. To have been more than I ever was. In this moment in time, I am a falling star. Briefly, I will be the entity creatures wish upon. Perhaps some of those wishes will come true.

It's beautiful, this end.

My body burns and strips away, and air streams over my limbs and my face. The wind caresses my skin, and I've never felt so alive. Never felt so beloved. And as more of me breaks off, I feel closer to what I was always meant to be. Where I was always meant to be.

My end happens.

Boom!

Or does it?

I crash into the green grass sticking up from the brown dirt. There are roots deep into the earth of this world, but I sink deeper. And what's surprising is that I'm still alive.

My upper limbs—arms, they're called—thrust outward through rock and nature, speckled with dust from the cosmos. Light from the sun shines down on me through the cracks of the rock I once thought was my body. But it wasn't. It was my protection.

And in that sunlight, I look at my real body.

Brown skin that's coated in pearly stardust. Thick, sturdy limbs. Appendages—the word escapes me, but I know they are normal—hang from my chest. My hands—hands!—with spindly brown fingers lift to my eyes. They are beautiful. And they can wiggle.

I laugh. It's a sweet sound that comes from somewhere in my chest and bursts from my mouth, and it represents the amusement I feel. Because I am star and not. I can laugh. I have fingers. With a wayward glance, I notice my feet.

Toes. Symmetrical. With nails.

Above them, there are knees.

And before I can wonder more about all these new developments, and what this means for me, and the cool air that nips at my limbs, the loop begins again.

You don't belong here. You don't deserve this. You are not a star anymore; you are something new and terrible. You are alone. Over and over these thoughts rush through my mind. Clawing at me.

Why, if I am something wholly new now, does my brain remain the same? Why couldn't it change like the rest of me? Why?

Something splashes down my face, something warm. I bring my fingers up to feel the silky fluid—water, yes, that's what it's called. I look up to discover the source of the water. But there is nothing above me except stone, dirt, and roots, and beyond, only sky. Blue, dotted with white clouds.

The water slides down my cheeks. It comes from my eyes.

This is emotion. This is feeling. This is sadness, I know. I'm sad. I've been sad before. I'm scared. I'm a star, but now I'm something else, too. I'm smaller. Less brilliant.

And I'm alone. Again.

The other stars are gone. Points I could see and recognize. Points I wish to know, wish to speak to. They are somewhere behind this blue sky of this new world I am not a part of.

I'm cold. I'm lonely. I'm—

"Hello?" A voice calls to me, and though I've never spoken before, I understand. My mind may be my enemy, but it also knows things. It knows these words, this language.

Before I can think of how my mouth will shape these sounds into words to respond, an older creature comes into view above me.

Human, my brain tells me.

A human, not creature, although I wonder if all humans are creatures, and if stars are, too.

What am I?

"Are you okay down there?" the human asks, and I stare up at it. Long gray spirals flow down its shoulders, and its skin is brown, similar to my own. Its face carries lines etched by time, and its eyes hide behind spectacles. It wears long white clothes on its body, and I wish I had some, too. I'm so cold. "Are you hurt?"

"I," my mouth says. *I* is me. My first word. "I am a star."

There's a moment of silence. Did I scare it? Did I trigger the loop in its head that tells it sad things like mine does?

But if the human's mind is its enemy like mine is, it has no impact. The human just stands there, looking down at me.

"I know, honey. I saw." The human steps closer to the edge of the cliff created by my fall.

A warning springs from my lips. "Be careful! You don't want to fall."

The human laughs. Something about the sound warms my insides, though my outsides are still very cold.

"I already have, child," it says with amusement. "I'm a star like you."

A million questions replace the loop in my mind, and I feel my eyes enlarge in relief and wonder . . . and uncertainty. But before I can ask, the star raises its hands and, with them, the air. I'm plucked from the earth and floating above the rocky protection that broke from my impact.

My limbs shift in the nothingness before I'm set down on the earth beside this star-human.

It looks me up and down. "You're just . . . You must be only sixteen or so. I've never seen a star so young here before. There, there," it says. "You must be freezing." It takes a heavy cloth from the ground and wraps it around my shoulders. Warmth envelops me. "My name is Dione. On this planet called Earth, I present as a woman—and an old one at that. Will you come with me?"

I regard it—her—slowly. She's a star, but she's old. Does she know the secrets of the universe? Does she know why I fell? Does she know what I've become?

Can she be trusted?

Why does she want to help me?

I may be new and young, but I do know there is evil in the universe, no matter how kind it presents itself. Black holes were once stars, too. Instead of shining bright, they consume life if it gets too close.

Dione says she was once a star. What is she now? How is she human? Will she consume my energy like a black hole?

"No," I answer carefully. "I don't know you. I don't know this world." I snuggle the cloth closer.

Her head tilts to the side and the corners of her lips rise. "I'm not a threat to you, dear. I'm just an old star offering to help a new one."

I glance around at the nothingness of this world. The sun is low in the sky; the grass is slick beneath my feet. I don't know where I am. What I am. What I'll do.

Dione knows.

I choose my words carefully. "I'll come with you if you'll agree to answer my questions."

Dione laughs softly. "Of course. In the meantime, do you have a name?"

I shake my head in a way I hope means no. "I'm too new."

"Yes, you are new, and how lovely that is." She smiles at me as she slides her arm through mine and leads me away from the crater I created. "We should call you Nova."

I think on it as my legs take one step at a time, my whole body in motion. My bare feet sink into the moist grass. Nova. A name. I've never had a name. Never had a body. I was just a mass of energy before, but now I'm this. Nova.

I'm Nova and I know Dione. There are two of us now. I am not alone. Even if I can't yet understand why Dione wants to help me.

My cheeks pull my lips, and now I, too, am smiling. "I like that."

She walks slowly as if her limbs are stiff. In the distance, a structure made from nature—wood—comes into view. It's red, with brown doors, and there are glass rectangles in the walls. It's unusual. It's small, unlike space. This is where she must keep her weary human body.

"A long time ago," she says suddenly, "I didn't have a name, either. But I chose Dione for myself. And when I became Dione, I decided to be something else. So I wished to come here, fell to Earth, learned to be a human, and . . . then eventually I grew old."

As we reach this structure, this home, I ask one of the many questions circulating through my mind. "You wished to come here and you just did?"

She nods once and silence spans between us.

I try another question. "Are you lonely?"

She turns to me, and I see warm eyes behind her spectacles. What makes them warm, I don't really know, but they reassure me. "No, I'm not lonely. Not anymore."

Hope rises in my throat, and I have to swallow it quickly. Soon my mind will tell me how pointless all of this is, but right now, I want to appreciate the beauty of newness. "Are there other stars here?"

"We're the only stars, but there are many humans. You'll meet them in time . . . when you're ready." She opens the wooden door and gently eases me inside. Immediately heat and smells and sensations surround me. The pads of my feet and tips of my toes tread on hard, smooth stone. Sharp sounds pierce my ears, and small creatures look up at me from their little nests on the floor. There are colors and strange items sitting on a wooden board. A table. I know words, though I don't know why.

"This is my home, and now it'll be yours, too." She beams at me again, and I wonder, briefly, how she can still beam like a star now that she is human. There's that warmth in her eyes, the richness in her dark brown skin, as if there's stardust at the center of her being. I wonder if she can burn her house down with the energy inside her. I wonder if I could or if this new form keeps it all carefully contained.

She pulls a chair out from the table, cutting through my thoughts. "Sit, eat. I'll go get some clothes for you. I know you have questions, but we have time."

Before I can object that I want answers now, that I'm not sure I trust her yet, she slides a porcelain slab full of . . . things . . . in front of me. I don't have the words for these yet, but they smell . . . good. Enticing. My stomach rumbles like a thunderous storm within. I laugh and place a hand to my bare stomach. This is hunger.

Stars eat dust. Not because we're hungry but because it swirls around us and we breathe it in and out. It's how we live and grow. I may not know how the universe came to be, but I know it's because of stardust. I know we need it. Without it, we're nothing.

But these things on a plate must be what humans eat to survive. Suddenly, though, I question whether Dione is using my human needs to trap me here.

My brain does this to me all the time, so why should now be different? Yet my stomach rumbles again. I must eat this food to make my new body work.

Dione has led me to this table. Prepared these items, knowing I would need them. I should be scared, should push the plate away, but even the thought of not consuming this makes my limbs sag. Hunger makes my vision darken, my stomach needy.

I will have to risk this. Even if the loop's telling me that no one is this kind or giving, not without wanting something in return. That I don't deserve this. That I'm nothing, no one, insignificant. What could Dione possibly want with me? I'm useless, not worth ensnaring in her diabolical plan . . .

With a slight hesitancy, I pick up a utensil with my fingertips and stare at it. I know I'm supposed to somehow use this strange slotted shovel to feed myself. Though my fingers shake, I slap the utensil onto the plate and drag it back up toward my mouth. But all the food falls off. I try again. And again. It all falls off the plate, onto the floor, everywhere but my mouth.

I let out a groan of frustration as my brain tells me how foolish I was to think I could do this, and I drop the tool. *Worthless. Useless. Hungry.*

"You can use your hands. It's okay," Dione says, a short distance away. "Go on."

I nod to myself and look down at my brown hands. Yes, they can hold things, too.

The food is warm in my hands. It's sticky and dirty, but I can't care. I take tentative bites using my teeth. I taste. I close my eyes. Flavors other than stardust burst onto my tongue. I don't have all the words to describe them. Maybe there *aren't* enough words to describe them.

Each bite is different from the last. Some leave tinges of salt on the roof of my mouth; some leave a tangy coating on the back of my tongue. And then there is the sweetness. And color. It brings me . . . joy. It makes my stomach feel happy.

I keep eating. Keep closing my eyes because that makes it easier to taste. Because somehow, my mind can only focus on a few new things at once. The creatures watch me closely from across the room, with their floppy light brown ears, fur-covered bodies, and piercing black eyes that track me from their cushioned nests. One walks over and its snout sniffs at me. Though they are different, they do not seem to want to harm me.

I shift on the chair, which bites into the backs of my legs, the wood cool beneath my bottom.

"Are you okay, Nova?" Dione's voice stirs me from my thoughts. "You're very quiet. New stars usually talk so much when they arrive."

At that, I open my eyes and sit taller in the chair. "I thought . . . You said we're the only stars here."

Are there more stars? Has she met them? Where are they now? Has she consumed them like a black hole?

This *is* a trap. It must be. My brain is right—no one is this nice or giving. She's making me feel safe, satiated, comfortable so she can use me. Stars may see one another across the expanse of space, but we don't know one another. Not in the way Dione and I can now. She knows I'm new and that I don't know the universe the way she does.

She can use this closeness to her advantage . . . She could—

"We *are* the only stars here. There are others in the worlds beyond. When you're a bit older, you'll understand how to communicate with them. We're a community. Anyway . . ." She pushes cloths—clothes—toward me and points to a door down a tunnel. A hallway. "There's a bathroom on your left. Get dressed, and I'll tell you everything you need to know when you're back."

I regard her slowly. *Will* she tell me everything I need to know, or will she withhold information like the universe always has from those too young and deemed unworthy?

Only time will tell, and I'm cold. I want to cover my body and feel warmth.

And so I walk down the hallway with the clothes in my arms, the cloth around my shoulders, and I push open a door into a small area. My brain knows what I'm supposed to do in this space, but I don't feel any urges. How wondrous that'll be when I do.

There's a garment meant to cage my chest appendages—breasts—and I spend a very long time trying to understand how I can buckle the pieces in the back. I close my eyes to let my brain give me the solution. It knows things. Surely it knows this.

But it doesn't. Instead, I try again and again. The frustration I feel at my hands, my body, my brain causes water to trickle from my eyes again. Tears.

Why can't I do things easily? Why must all things be difficult? Why can't I have fallen from the sky and been a better version of myself and not the same version in a different form? Why must my brain still loop and loathe me? Why don't my own limbs know how to take care of themselves, feed and clothe and sustain us?

I don't belong here.

I don't belong anywhere.

Though Dione is outside, I don't know her. I'm alone on a new world, out of my depth. Even if Dione is beneficent, she will quickly learn I am useless. She will send me back up into the sky or out into this strange world, where I'll surely perish.

My mind says I have squandered this chance. I'm worthless.

"Nova, are you all right, dear?" Dione's voice thrums through the walls. "Do you need help?"

"No," I lie through the tears. She can't know how helpless I am. She can't know. My chest heaves and my gaze blurs at the edges. I sit on the cool tiled floor, undressed. Unsure. My mind tosses insults at me. Tells me I don't matter. I never did. I was once a star, and now I'm nothing. I don't shine anymore.

There's silence on the other side of the door. She must think I'm strange and realize I'm here by accident. She must regret that she wasted her precious time and food on me.

"Do you need me to explain how to put the clothes on? They're tricky for beings who never had arms and legs before . . ." Her voice is kind and maybe she understands. Maybe she experienced the same thing when she crashed here and became something new. Or maybe she's lying so I'll depend on her. She will take my stardust until I am nothing.

"Please," I blurt, even though my brain repeats that I'm a burden.

Through the door, she guides me as I dress. It takes time, and it's difficult, but her words help me succeed. It's not beyond my capabilities. I can learn. I can listen. When I emerge from the room, she stands there with a smile.

For a reason I'm not quite sure of, I suddenly want to tell her the truth. Maybe because she is the only being I've ever had the chance to talk to. Maybe because she stayed with me and helped when she didn't have to.

"I'm not . . . My brain . . . it speaks things I don't want to hear. And though it . . . though I know words and gestures and food, I don't know why my brain says I'm foolish. That I don't belong anywhere. That I'm worthless. The other stars didn't have this." I take a large gulp of air and let my hands drift down the cloth along my sides.

My eyes don't meet hers, and I feel shame. She could use this against me. Somehow, though, in the back of my mind where the mean voice isn't, there's hope. There's belief. There's an idea that Dione won't betray me.

She steps closer to me and touches a finger to my chin and lifts until I look at her. Until I see the stardust in her eyes. She doesn't need stardust; it's within her. She isn't a black hole. She isn't what I feared. She's a star and a human.

"We may be stars in different forms, made by the same universe, but we aren't all made the same. Some of us struggle with old knees, like me." She laughs. "Some of us can't sing a song; some of us can't see or hear or walk. There's beauty in difference. There's beauty in how our stardust combines."

I nod, though I'm not really certain what this means. Not yet.

"Do you remember the stars?" She takes my arm and leads me down the hallway, through the room where I ate, past the creatures in their nests, and through the front door where I came in not long ago. "Look up."

And I do. The sun has set, and now there's a darkness in the sky from its absence. I wiggle my toes in the grass and breathe in the fresh air. The stars sparkle. Though not bright, they are there. They haven't fallen like me. They are immovable energy, trapped in time and space.

"Every star is different, but each one has found its way to survive and stay in our universe. You belong here. And oh, how you shine. See?" She points down to my brown skin, which shimmers.

I gasp and run my fingers over my skin. The shimmer stays. I'm still me but something else, too. Maybe this version of me *is* better, unlike what my brain said.

"You will always be a star. You will always be wanted. You are beautiful." Dione's words cut through my ever-running thoughts. "You are you. And there is nothing your brain can say that will change these simple truths."

The tears prickle my eyes again, but I hold them back. "Why am I here, Dione?"

"Because I wished for you," she says simply, without regret or shame. With joy. With honesty and something else I don't quite know the word for yet. I stare at this star-woman as the moon brightens and rises above. The wind plucks at my tears and dries them to my cheeks. "Stars show entities the way through the universe. Yet sometimes we also need to know the way. Sometimes we . . ." She pauses as her face tilts upward to the sky. "Sometimes the loneliness is too much to bear."

Her hand slips into my own and squeezes.

"The universe chose you to shine in its space and show the way to all those lost and looking. When I called out, lost and looking, feeling alone, you must've heard me. You decided to come here. I wished for you," she repeats, "and you came true."

For a few moments, we stand there, hand in hand, staring up at the sky we know better than our own bodies. Than our minds. And I realize then that I was wishing and wanting to be somewhere else, to do and be something different. Wishing to not be alone anymore.

"I think . . . I wished for you, too," I admit. "I was alone with only my mind, which isn't always the kindest."

She smiles at me, though her brows furrow. "This won't be perfect. I've been here a long time, and I don't remember what it feels like to be so young. But I will show you this world, and teach you how to care for it, and for yourself. Though I may not be here long enough to watch you grow up and grow old, I will make sure you're not alone. Ever again."

Warmth spreads through my chest, and that feeling I couldn't quite place before blossoms. It's happiness. It's hope. It's relief. My fears were misplaced. My brain tried to steal my joy, but it couldn't. This time, I wouldn't let it.

"How do we care for this world?" I ask as that hopeful combination swirls within me along with my stardust.

"By shining bright for the humans." Our hands still clasped, she pulls me . . . up. Off the ground. Into the air. "We must show them grace and kindness. We must help them save themselves or else this planet will crumble. And though some of them won't like us for how we look and our power, we must show them the way."

Still gravity threatens to pull me down. "I can't . . . I don't . . ."

"You do," she interjects. "You can. Use your stardust and fly. I may have asked the universe for you, but you fell here by choice. You belong here."

I close my eyes.

My brain tells me that I can't. That none of what she says is true. There is no beauty within me, only energy. Worthlessness.

But my brain is wrong.

I was hungry . . . but I taught myself to eat.

I couldn't dress myself . . . but here I am, dressed.

Life is a struggle . . . but I am strong enough for the fight.

My brain is my enemy . . . but it's mine, my own, a part of me. And I can show it the way.

I know that I'm strong. I know the universe created me to do great and beautiful things. I know that I'm scared and tired, hopeful but unsure. I also know, somewhere deep within me, that I'm not worthless. I chose to be here. I chose to fight.

I know many things, and there's still so much more to learn.

When I open my eyes, my skin aglow from the starlight streaming forth, my feet hover above the ground. The voice that leaves my mouth is more confident than the one I used before. It is happy. It is brave. It is . . . full of wonder. It is Nova.

I am Nova.

"Where do we go, Dione?"

"Wherever the stardust takes us."

I am ready.

A NOTE FROM ALECHIA DOW

✱ ✱ ✱ ✱ ✱ ✱ ✱ ✱ ✱ ✱ ✱ ✱ ✱

I'd just entered first grade when I was diagnosed with anxiety, I was a teen when I was diagnosed with depression, and I was in my thirties when I was diagnosed with bipolar disorder. Mental health struggles have been a huge part of my life, and I've always wanted to write about it in a kind, thoughtful, and considerate way. I hope I succeeded with "We Are Stardust." And I hope readers are reminded that they are stars, even when there are voices—theirs and others—telling them they can't shine.

RIVER BOY

JAMES BIRD

Content Note: This story references racial slurs.

They say up to 60 percent of the human body is water. The brain and the heart are composed of 73 percent water. The lungs are 83 percent water. The skin 64 percent water, muscles and kidneys 79 percent water. Even our bones are 31 percent water. So it should be perfectly normal for someone like me to exist. But it is not perfectly normal. No one is like me.

My name is Hank and I cry. All. The. Time.

Hiding in a stall in the boys' bathroom is how I spend most of my time at school. It's like my own private cry closet. I just wish it smelled better in here.

I have detention after school today, but that's not why I'm crying. Detention was part of the plan.

Getting detention is pretty easy. All you have to do is say the wrong thing to a teacher.

Why did I do it? One reason: Eve.

Everyone calls her Evil Eve. She is a Mexican girl with a strong chola accent. She wears black lines for eyebrows and black lipstick, and her long black hair is always styled tight against her skull like it was glued there. Like me, she has quite a reputation here at school. Unlike me, her reputation inspires fear. Maybe a little awe.

She's kinda like lightning that way, I think.

See, most people are afraid of lightning, too. But I'm not. I love watching it streak down from the sky. It's scary, sure, but also beautiful. Powerful. Sometimes Eve seems like she could burn people to ash with just a look.

That's the kind of different I'd like to be. Awe-inspiring.

I don't have any classes with her, but we have talked before. It was two months ago during fourth period. I started crying and rushed out of class, straight to the bathroom. I don't know if it was because my eyes were blurry or if I was just so upset that I got confused, but I darted into the girls' bathroom. I realized as soon as I dived into the nearest stall and sank to the floor. (The girls' bathroom definitely smells better than the boys'. Plus, there are those little trash cans attached to the walls of the stalls.)

Before I could fix my mistake, the door opened and someone walked in. I couldn't stifle my sobs, so I just hoped whoever heard me would feel uncomfortable and leave—that's what most people do.

But this person didn't. Instead, this person said seven words that my soggy brain will never forget: "Let it out to get it out."

It was Eve, and I guess I was so startled to hear her voice that I actually stopped crying.

I wiped my tears from my face, stood up, and opened the door. Eve was propped up on the sink, near the open window, smoking a cigarette. When I stepped out of the stall, she raised her eyebrows, but that was the closest she got to showing any surprise that I was a guy in the girls' bathroom.

I approached the sink. "You should quit," I said.

I don't know why that was the first thing I ever said to Eve. Who the heck am I to tell someone, especially someone like her, someone powerful, what to do?

She took another long drag. "Tell you what—I'll quit smoking when you quit crying."

As she blew out the smoke, she stared into my eyes in the mirror's reflection. I felt a jolt of electricity at the intensity of her gaze. She was so direct, so matter-of-fact, that it didn't feel like she was making fun of me, so I didn't even mind that she knew about my reputation. Everyone does, after all. But more than that, her words were a spark, a little bit of lightning power she spent on me, and I felt better as a result. I realized right then that if I had Eve as a friend, unlikely as it was, maybe her power would rub off on me a bit. Maybe she could help me be lightning strong, too.

"Deal," I said, because even though I had no idea how to make the whole friend thing happen, this bargain at least tied us together, even just for a moment. I washed and dried my hands, pushed opened the door, and left.

That was two months ago. I haven't quit crying, and she hasn't quit smoking.

If you're wondering why I'm always crying, well, that makes two of us. The truth is, I don't know why it happens. All I know is that it happens nearly every day. About nearly everything. Even for things no one should be crying about, like cheesy commercials, dead bugs on the sidewalk, hearing a sad story or a sad song. I sometimes cry from just a sad thought. *2Pac is dead.* Boom! I'm crying. *The Crocodile Hunter is dead.* Boom! I'm crying. *Kids go to bed hungry, some cats and dogs don't get adopted, Native Americans were slaughtered for their land,* all boom, all crying. I hate it. The doctors can't explain it, either. They always say the same thing: it's mental, not physical. But it sure feels physical to me. I'm like one of those lawns overflowing with water because the sprinkler's broken and it just runs constantly all day. Soon I'll flood the streets, too.

Half of tenth grade has now passed already, and Eve has landed in detention at least six times that I know of. Mostly for fighting. She fights a lot. Yeah, I know fighting is bad, especially at school, but there's something to admire in someone who always sticks up for herself. I mean, you touch a lightning bolt, you're gonna get burned.

See, our school is predominantly white, and unfortunately, there's no shortage of racists. So her being a brown-skinned girl, especially an *immigrant* brown-skinned girl, makes her an easy target for some people. Most of the things said about her are said behind her back. But today at lunch, a white girl tested her luck and called Eve a wetback right to her face. Eve pushed her onto a table, soaking the back of her shirt by dragging her through spilled sodas, milks, waters, and orange juices. "Who's the wetback now?" Eve asked her. And even though no one laughed aloud, I found it both funny and beautiful, another gorgeous bolt of brilliance.

Despite wanting to become friends with Eve, I haven't had the courage to approach her since that day in the bathroom. But that's going to change because I've come up with a plan. The only thing is, it requires both of us to have detention. Eve got hers at lunch. I got mine right after.

The bell rings and the halls burst with students. I go to my locker, where I've kept my detention outfit for days, ever since I came up with this idea. I borrowed my older brother's clothes without him knowing: a pair of jeans that are two sizes too big and an extra-large shirt that I'll basically be swimming in.

After changing, I try to ignore the nervous energy swirling inside me like a flushed toilet as I walk toward detention. I reach the room, take a deep breath, and open the door.

As I walk in, I remind myself that I did my homework on how to make Eve like me. All I need to do is stick to the plan.

Eve's not in here yet. That's okay. She's always late. I approach Mr. Koenig. He's a scowly-faced math teacher, assigned to watch the bad apple kids this week. I wonder if the teachers hate detention as much as the students do.

I hand him my detention slip. He looks up at me. "What are you in here for?"

"I flipped off Mrs. Hayward after lunch."

He grunts. "That'll do it. Take a seat."

I sit in the very back. This way, when Eve arrives, she won't have the chance of sitting behind me, which will make it less awkward when I switch my seat to be near her and strike up a conversation.

I watch the minutes crawl by. Nine of them. I get hungry, so I pull out one of the many Fruit Roll-Ups I brought. Halfway through my third one, it happens. The door opens and Eve enters the classroom.

She hands Mr. Koenig her detention slip but ignores him when he asks why she's in here. She scans the empty seats, popping a pink bubble of her chewing gum, and as her eyes hit mine, I look down. I doubt she recognizes me.

She sits in the middle of the room and props both feet up, resting them comfortably on the desk in front of her like she's in a hammock on a tropical beach.

"Feet off the desk," Mr. Koenig says.

"What do you care? Like honestly?" she pushes back.

He sighs and returns to his crossword puzzle.

I stare at the back of Eve's head for ten long minutes before gathering up enough courage-clouds to move the storm forward. *Legs, move! Stand up. Walk. Sit.*

I take the seat behind her and inhale. Hairspray fills my nostrils. She smells like a CVS. Like cigarettes. She smells imperfectly perfect.

I've imagined this moment many times, but now that I'm in it, I have no idea what to say. I made notes for what to say and do, but *crap*, I left my notebook on the desk in the back. I got too nervous when she walked in. I need to get it together. I need to make this work.

Before I can go back for my notes, she turns around. Her eyes lock into mine and she sniffs the air. "Are you eating a Fruit Roll-Up?" she asks.

I smile. She was smelling me, too.

"Hola," I reply. "I was, yeah."

"¿Tienes más?" she asks.

This is awesome. We are speaking Spanish together. Part of the plan is working!

"Yeah. I mean, sí. A red, I mean, rojo one. ¿Lo quieres?"

"Hell yeah, I want it," she says, and sticks her chewing gum under her desk.

I get up and return to my backpack. As I grab it, I also snatch my notebook and bring it with me and sit down behind her.

I hand her the red Fruit Roll-Up. She smiles. "Cherry. I haven't had one of these in, like, two thousand years," she says, and unrolls it.

I watch her ball it up into a tumbleweed of red gooey yum and stuff it into her mouth, closing her eyes while chewing.

She mumbles something to me in Spanish, but I don't understand her for two reasons: One, I have been studying Spanish for only two months. And two, she's talking while chewing.

"In English, por favor. I just started learning español."

She smiles. "I said this is so fuckin' good," she clarifies.

Eve makes bad words sound like good words.

"Muchas gracias," I say.

She laughs. "I say 'gracias.' You say 'de nada.'"

"But I'm thanking you for taking it," I say.

"Okay. Then de nada," she says, and turns back around.

I want to hop on my desk and do a victory dance. We conversed. We spoke Spanish. I fed her a Fruit Roll-Up. And now that my notebook is with me, I open it and scan the topics to discuss. My hand is shaky as I search the page. I'm nervous but I keep talking anyway.

"So . . . you volunteer at Oak View, huh?" I ask.

"Yeah, how'd you know that?" she says, but doesn't yet turn around.

"I do, too. On lunes y miércoles." I practiced saying Wednesday in Spanish because I kept tripping up on it in the middle. I want her to see that I can speak Spanglish like she always does under her breath when our classmates annoy her. I want her to see that I can fit into her world that straddles languages. Just like in my own home, where English and my broken-tongued Anishinaabemowin collide. That's the language us Ojibwe speak, or at least try to.

"I'm Tuesdays and Thursdays," she says.

For reasons unknown to me, my mind remembers another Tuesday. The Tuesday morning of September 11, 2001. Then it hits. The sadness. 2,996 people dead, 35,000 people injured. So many families broken. I swallow hard. *Please, brain, not now.*

My brain is a traitor and doesn't listen. Tears. I wipe them away quickly. *Shit!* I begin sniffling and breathing funny from trying to hold a cry back. *Please don't hear me. Please don't turn around.*

"You okay?" she asks, and to my horror she does in fact turn around.

I bury my face in my hands. "Fine. I just . . ."

Mr. Koenig asks what's going on, but I ignore him. I hear Eve say something to him, but my sobs crack me open and drown out her voice. Whatever she said must have satisfied him, because when I look up again, he's back to his crossword puzzle.

This is so embarrassing. I can't believe I'm crying in front of Eve. Again.

"You look like you're in pain. Are you, like, bursting your appendix or some shit?" she asks.

I shake my head, but I'd be lying if I said crying was painless. What people don't realize is the toll it takes on your body if you do it enough. Constant crying gives me really bad headaches. It exhausts me. I pretty much always have a sore throat. But I'm here to be tough, to show Eve I can hang with her, so I am not going to tell her how much hiccups can hurt.

"Hold up! I know you. You're Chico Rio!" she says.

"Chico what?" I ask as I wipe more tears from my face. All the Spanish words have leaked out of me. Another failure. Another burst of tears.

"Chico Rio. River Boy! It all makes perfect sense now. You're the guy that cries in the bathroom at Oak View."

Oh, crap. Any chance of me ever seeming tough was just thrown out the window.

"That place has thin walls. Those kids have a little chart for every time you cry. I thought they were making that shit up."

Embarrassment paints my cheeks pink. I sink deeper into my chair.

But she doesn't tease me. Instead, she says, "It's all good. Everybody cries."

I am grateful that even though I'm a puddle of tears, she doesn't lightning-strike me. She says it's okay. I can't imagine her crying, though. "Even you?"

"Me? Nah, I was saying that to be nice. But most people cry, I'm sure. I'm just built different."

"You don't cry?" How amazing must that feel? "Like, ever?"

She bites her bottom lip, which sends my heart into a backflip. And okay, fine, maybe in my wildest dreams she becomes more than just my friend. But I can't think about that now.

She looks up to the ceiling, as if the answer were stapled to it. "Does almost crying count? I almost cried, like, three weeks ago."

"You're so lucky. I have to drink, like, a gallon of water a day just to keep up with my eyes."

She laughs. "Whatever you gotta do to get you through the day, homie."

She called me her homie. Crying in front of her was not good, but homie means amigo and amigo means friend. So that means my plan *might* still be working. I need to keep talking. "So what made you almost cry three weeks ago?"

Ugh. Why did I ask that? For someone who wants to not cry so much, you'd think I'd avoid the subject.

"My abuela. She's sick in the hospital. Down in Oaxaca. She's tough, but she's old. And I'm afraid . . ." She shrugs. "So I almost cried."

"Can you go see her?"

"Nope. I miss any more school, they said, I would have to repeat tenth grade. I hate it here."

"I hated it when I first moved here, too. Everyone was so mean because of my, you know, cry-sis. That's what I call it."

"Clever," she says. "But I bet I get called worse than you do."

Ooh, a challenge. "Wanna bet?" I say.

She smiles. "You're on."

"I'll go first. I'll start with the most obvious: crybaby."

"Please, that's weak. I get called beaner. Beat that."

"Waterworks! No, Faucet Face," I fire back.

She scoffs. "Wetback. Which would also work for you, if you change it to wetface."

I laugh. "Sometimes I'm called the Sprinkler, Sir Cries-a-Lot, Snoop Sobby Sob, and Chippe-wah-wah, because I'm Chippewa."

"I like Snoop Sobby Sob. But I've still got you beat. I've been called spic, greaser, wab, Taco Belle, Burrito Brat, Pepperbelly, Berry Picker, Border Hopper, Homie Depot, Mudbaby, and my personal favorite, 'Aren't you my gardener's daughter?'"

"Wow. People are dicks."

"Like I said, I win."

"Not so fast. You seem to forget that I also live in Huntington Beach."

"What's your point?"

"We just covered half my issues. But I got a whole lotta targets on my back. I belong to the only Native American family around here. I've been called savage, Casino Boy, Chief Tear-Maker, Dirt Worshipper, Featherhead, Buffalo Boy, and redskin. But my personal favorite is when people sing, '*Injun, Injun number nine, father drowning in moonshine. If he ever reaches graduation, toss him back on the reservation*.' Sorry, Eve, I win."

She takes a deep breath. "Shit . . . We can call it a tie?"

"Deal." We're both quiet for a moment before I add, "What's the one you hate the most?"

"It's ridiculous."

"They're all ridiculous. I'll tell you mine if you tell me yours."

"Okay. I hate . . . brownie. Not only because it's super lame, but because I fuckin' love brownies. Now every time I see one, I hear some racist white kid whispering it into my ear. It kind of makes me not want to eat them anymore."

"That sucks. Brownies are so good."

"And yours?" she asks.

"I hate being called Fish Outta Water," I say.

"That's so random. Why would someone call you that?"

"I was so terrified of coming to high school and crying all the time that during the summer after eighth grade, I begged my mom to send me to see more doctors. Just in case there was, like, some medical breakthrough that could fix my brain," I say.

"And there wasn't?" she asks.

"No. But the doctors still loaded me up with pills. The first set of them made all my thoughts cloudy. And even though they stopped me from crying my first week at school, they also stopped me from thinking. I couldn't hold on to a thought to save my life."

"You went from soggy brain to foggy brain," she quips.

"Exactly. And to counteract those, the doctors put me on a new set of pills. Ones that were supposed to help me focus and hold on to my thoughts again."

Eve reaches into her backpack and pulls out a prescription pill bottle and rattles it in front of my face. "I got diagnosed with ADHD. Hello, Adderall. I told the doctors I just don't like school, but they insist I take these."

"Do you take them?"

"No. I sell them to all the rich kids after school. They pop 'em like Skittles." She raises her eyebrows. "Do you take yours?"

"I did for a while. But I was always nauseous and in a bad mood. I couldn't sleep. I hated everything. I went from soggy brain to foggy brain to groggy brain."

"Damn. No one gets between me and my dreams. I'd die before giving up sleep," Eve says. "For real."

"My mom was pissed and wanted me to stop taking everything, but the doctors convinced us to give it one more try."

"More pills? Dude! You're like a walking, talking Rite Aid pharmacy."

"Yup. To counteract all this new shit I was going through, they put me on pills to help me relax and up my mood. These had the worst side effects of all. They made me scared. I started having anxiety. I was worrying about worrying even though I wasn't worried about anything. I heard screaming in my head. I developed seizures. Kids began calling me Fish Outta Water. Like how you see a fish flailing about for air. And they laughed. It also just makes me feel like I don't belong. Like maybe I never will. It just got so bad with the medication. I even started shitting my pants. Then I got called Shit Stain." I suck in a breath. I cannot believe I just told her that.

Eve is cracking up. "How is Shit Stain not the worst insult?"

"It is. I was just too embarrassed to tell you that one. I wasn't going to. It just slipped out."

"It just slipped out. Ha! Like the shit slippin' out your butt," she says, and laughs again.

I laugh, too. It is funny. And I realize this is actually the first time I ever found humor in my situation. And it wasn't even me that found it. Eve did.

"Keep it down!" Mr. Koenig shouts from his desk.

"You're the one shouting," Eve fires back at him.

He doesn't respond. He just sighs and averts his eyes to his watch.

"I saw someone have a seizure once," Eve says, turning back to me. "This dude was just standing in line at Subway, then boom, he started spitting and his body collapsed like it forgot how to work. Then it was like he was having his own personal earthquake. It was freaky."

"Yeah, I had days where I would wake up in the hospital, connected to all these tubes in my arms, not knowing how I got there. I was always afraid that, one of these times, I would not be able to breathe and I'd die. I was constantly terrified."

"Well, if I ever hear someone call you Fish Outta Water, I'll sock them in the mouth for you," Eve says.

I smile. "That's the nicest thing anyone has ever said to me," I reply. "But I haven't had a seizure in months. The epilepsy pills burned as they traveled through my body. It felt like there was fire in my veins. So I told my mom I quit."

"Tears over fears," Eve says. "Good call."

"Yeah, the moment I started thinking that I was gonna die, I knew something was wrong. I haven't taken any pills in a few months."

"Crying is definitely better than dying," she says. "And here I thought my life was fucked up," she adds.

"Language!" Mr. Koenig shouts.

Eve looks over at him again, giving him the stink eye. They have a stare-off. And she wins.

Eve smiles and turns back to me. "Giving up is for bitches," she whispers. "People like you and me, we fight until the end." She holds her fist out to me.

I stare at it. This is going to be the first time Eve and I have ever touched.

I extend my fist to hers, knuckles to knuckles. The greatest fist bump ever.

A minute later Mr. Koenig clasps his hands together and stands. "At last, it's three o'clock," he tells us. "We are free."

Eve launches out of her seat and collects her bag. "I volunteer today. I'm already late, but I'll see ya around, Bawler," she says, and shoots me a wink.

"Bawler?"

"Yeah, you know. In the streets, a baller means you got your shit handled. It means you're flashy and confident. Like you're ballin' through life. But bawlin' also means you're crying, right? One fits you now, one will fit you later. You're the Bawler," she says.

"I like that," I say excitedly, and sling my bag over my back.

My notebook falls out and slides toward Eve's feet.

She picks it up, but before she hands it back to me, she reads the three words written on the cover. The three words I wrote and lived by for the last two months. The three words that will make Eve either punch me in the face or never want to see me again. Or both. *The Eve Plan.*

I grab at the notebook, but her years of fistfights have gained her lightning-quick reflexes, and she pulls it out of my reach. "What is this?"

"It's . . . I . . . It's just a thing," I stammer. "Please don't open it."

She gives me a look, then she walks out of the room with my notebook. I follow her through the halls and out of the building.

Halfway into the parking lot, I finally break the silence. "Can I have it back?"

"No. You're walking me to Oak View. I'm teaching kids soccer today. You can be the assistant coach," she says without stopping.

"But I don't volunteer today," I say.

"You do now. I need someone to watch the kids as I read this. If I don't like what's in here, I'll tell every single one of those kids to kick you in the nuts. And trust me, they know how to kick."

Kick. The word jumps out and contorts into how I hear it most often used. Kick out. *Kick the Mexicans out! Take back our country!* It's the same during every election, these words shouted over and over again. Immigrants damning immigrants. It's so stupid and heartless. So sickening. And sad.

I swallow, but the tears return. This is the worst possible time ever to cry. *Please, brain. Not again.*

"Cry it out," she says, and I feel her hand rest on my shoulder.

I look up at her through my wet eyelashes. "No one knows how nice you are."

"It will be our little secret. You spill it, I spill you," she says, and hugs me.

Right then and there, in the middle of the parking lot, I break down and let it all rush out of me. And even though she's late, she doesn't walk away—she just lets me cry into her shoulder. Her shirt's soggy and snotty and she doesn't say a thing.

After about five minutes of torrential downpour from my eyes, I finally feel spent.

"You ready?" she says.

I nod. She continues walking, and I continue following.

What Eve doesn't know is that I'd be walking this way anyway. I live near Oak View. My neighborhood is called the Slater Slums, and it's the only nonwhite area of Huntington Beach. If she doesn't like what's in my notebook, I could probably outrun her and forty kids and make it home. I run almost as fast as my tears do.

We pass through Murdy Park, which is dubbed Murder Park by everyone who lives around here because there have been a few bodies found in the park over the years.

This is usually where I go when I have to ditch school because I can't stop crying. It's where all the ditchers go. I've even seen Eve here a few times with all her friends. They hang out on the picnic benches and blast West Coast rap music. I've never approached her, though. All her friends look much older, and I don't know how they'd react if some stranger walked up and started crying all over them. So I've kept my distance.

"I know the doctors don't know, but why do *you* think you cry so much?" she asks as we cut through the park on our way to Oak View.

"Honestly, it's all too much. Even when it's not," I say.

"What's all too much?" she asks as she removes her flannel shirt and ties it around her waist, revealing a black 2Pac T-shirt.

"Everything," I say, and point to her shirt as an example. "Even seeing this makes me sad. It's not just Tupac being dead, which is sad enough, but his family must be so heartbroken, which doubles the sadness. And what if he had cats or a dog but he never came home to feed them? Those pets maybe starved to death. Then I think about all the animals that actually *do* starve to death. I think of all the wolves being hunted down and shot, just for being wolves. Some of them are pregnant when they're killed. Did you know that? Did you know that all those cows we drive by, you know, those smelly cattle lots where you see hundreds of cows waiting to be slaughtered, are all female? It's literally death row for them. They just stand around and await a gruesome execution. And we drive by and say, 'Hey, look at those cute cows.' Then all the kids who die, too. Then I think about my cousin who died. He was only ten. Then my brain breaks all over again."

"Holy shit," Eve says. "Your brain is an asshole for doing all that to you. But I don't know, maybe think about happy shit. That's what I do when I get sad."

"Think happy thoughts? Believe me, I've tried. I lose that fight every time."

"That's because you don't know how to fight. I do. You gotta fight the sad with the happy. Pit them against each other. Let them battle it out. Let them both fight for your attention. You won't always win, but you always get to choose which one to root for. Look at me: I hate it here. Huntington Beach is racist as fuck. But . . . look at all the grass around us. It's so green. And it smells like it was just cut. I love that smell. The world is full of good shit, too. You've just gotta notice it," she says.

I take a deep breath and inhale the fresh aroma of recently cut grass. She's right. It does smell nice.

"See?" she says, seeing my smile. "What else makes you happy? Video games? Sports? Sexy blond surfer chicks with big boobs?" she asks.

"You," I blurt.

She laughs it off. "Me? You don't know me."

"I know you enough. I hated life. Middle school was a nightmare for me. Ninth grade was, too. It all sucked until you came to school."

Eve stops. Her drawn-on eyebrows rise.

"Yeah. You're, like, the strongest, most beautiful person I've ever met," I say, and hope she is not creeped out. I want to tell her that she is like lightning. I want to tell her that I wish I were as strong as her.

She laughs. "You're lying."

"I cry, but I don't lie," I say, and point to the notebook in her hand. "That proves it."

She lifts the notebook to her face and looks around in all directions.

"What are you doing?" I ask.

"You tell anyone about this, and I'll cut you," she says, and pulls out a pair of the dorkiest black-framed reading glasses I've ever seen.

She puts them on. "I have to wear my dad's until we can afford a nicer pair. If you laugh—"

"Then you'll cut me. I know. But I think you look pretty hot in them," I say.

"Shut up. My eyes are shit, but I know what I look like in these," she says.

This is the first time I have ever seen Eve vulnerable. A part of me wants to reach out and hug her, but the rest of me reminds me that she's just made it abundantly clear that cutting me is an option if I press my luck. So I settle for saying, "Read that, and you'll see how you appear to me, even in dorky glasses."

She looks down and opens the notebook.

THE EVE PLAN:

1. LEARN SPANISH TO SHOW YOU CARE ABOUT HER HERITAGE

2. VOLUNTEER AT OAK VIEW

3. *DRESS LIKE HER: BAGGY PANTS, EXTRA-LARGE SHIRT*
4. *SMILE LESS, SCOWL MORE*
5. *TALK ABOUT WEST COAST HIP-HOP*
6. *GET DETENTION WITH HER*
7. *TALK TO HER!*
8. *ABSOLUTELY NO CRYING IN FRONT OF HER*

After she reads my plan, she takes off her glasses and stands perfectly still. An entire minute crawls by where she doesn't move. Is she pissed? Is she planning on how to kick my ass? Should I run?

Finally she says, "So you normally don't dress like that?"

I look down at my outfit. Jeans that are two sizes too big. So is the shirt. I'm swimming in them. "I wanted you to think I was tough, like you. So maybe you'd want to be friends, and then maybe I could actually learn to be tough instead of crying all the time."

"Why's there a lightning strike near my name?"

I swallow hard, nervous.

"Tell me," she commands.

"Because that's how I see you," I admit. "Powerful. Brilliant." I pause. "Beautiful. Like you could strike the world down and be so bright that we would still want to open the curtains to watch you do it. I want to be like that. Like you." Her eyes narrow like she's thinking, but she stays quiet. "Are you mad?" I ask.

"No." She shakes her head. "I mean, you're weird as fuck, but I'm not mad."

My insides light up. My blood flows fast through my body. My heart races. I feel warm everywhere, even in my toes. And I'm probably wearing the goofiest smile ever. *Weird* I can live with. Being weird still means I can be a good person. A lot of good people are weird.

"Why do you look so happy right now?" she asks.

"Because everyone has a weird friend. So maybe . . . maybe I can be yours?"

She lets out a small laugh. "So the Spanish? Volunteering? Detention? You really did that all for me?"

"Sí," I say.

She lets out a long sigh. "This"—she holds up the list—"*is* so weird. But your number four is wrong. You shouldn't smile less," she says.

"Why not? You hardly ever smile."

"I'm always mad. It's hard to smile when you're mad. But I'll work on it. Remember, dead people don't get to smile. We're alive. We should smile for them."

She hands me back my notebook and points to a concrete wall. "Meet me at that wall tomorrow after school."

"Aren't I going to Oak View with you?" I ask.

"No. Your nuts are safe. Go home. There's something I need to do," she says, and walks off.

The next day, I search for Eve all throughout the campus but don't find her. I guess she ditched today. And after school, I find myself walking toward Murdy Park with an extra pep in my step. I am finally excited about something. Even if it's something so strange as "meet me at that wall."

I enter the park and head toward where I saw Eve last. I wonder if she wants me to punch the wall. You know, as a metaphor or something to break down the barriers in my life that cause me to cry. I hope not. I don't want two broken hands.

When I reach the wall, I stop dead in my tracks. Wow.

An image of a boy sitting against the wall, covering his head with his hands, two blue streams flowing from his eyes. The streams connect and blend into a spray of paint—a spray shaped like a lightning flash, coming from a can held by a girl.

She drew both of us, connected, giving to and drawing from the other.

"Water is the perfect conductor of electricity," a voice says from behind me. "You don't always need to act like lightning to be strong."

I turn and there is Eve, but I can't speak.

She walks over to stand beside me, shoulder to shoulder. "I cried last night," she says.

I finally regain my voice. "You did?"

"My abuela passed away three weeks ago." She stares hard at the painting. "I was afraid to say it out loud. I was *afraid* to cry. I figured if I started, I'd never be able to stop. So yesterday, after our talk, I went home. I told my mama how much I miss Abuela, about my fear. I told her that's why I haven't wanted to talk about Abuela, why I walked away whenever she would try. Then *she* started crying and said it is good for the soul. It washes it. And I thought how my abuela would have held my mama then. I thought about how she might have told me stories and braided my hair like when I was little to make me feel better. And I just felt it. The tears. That wave of feeling that I couldn't hide from anymore.

"And then . . . I cried."

Her voice shook when she spoke. I feel my own tears welling up. This is her moment, but my eyes don't care.

"I'm sorry you lost your grandma," I say.

Eve puts her hand to her heart. "Mami says you can't really lose someone if you always know where they are."

I look back at the painting, and I realize that Eve has done more for me than any doctor. I don't need to be fixed, because nothing about me is broken. I'm not a fish outta water that doesn't belong. Different, maybe, but not troubled or problematic or any of the other dozen things I've been called over the years.

"You see me," she whispers. "And I see you."

And instead of saying anything back, I reach out and wrap my arms around her. I hug her so tightly that I can feel more tears being squeezed out of her body.

"We're going to be okay, River Boy," Eve says, and hugs me back.

And even as we stand in the park, hugging and crying, I know that she is right.

A NOTE FROM JAMES BIRD

* * * * * * * * * * * * * *

Dear Reader: Boozhoo! (Hello in Ojibwe.) If you're anything like me, you have probably been told how different you are. You learn differently. You speak or think differently. And those words may have made you feel like an outsider, or someone who doesn't belong. I heard it all many times growing up. And you know what? They were right. I am different. I used to think that was a bad thing, but as I grew up, I realized it was actually the best compliment anyone can ever give you. Being different is awesome. Being just like everyone else is boring. Thinking outside the box rocks! Embrace your uniqueness. As you get older, all those people who did everything the same way and never colored outside the lines are going to wish they did things differently. They are going to wish they listened and paid attention to the "weirdo" deep inside them that they were always too scared to let out. But you and I, we did it. We wore our weirdness. We did the different. We flew that flag. We danced to the rhythm of our own beat. And as long as you stay true to yourself and be who you are, even when feeling different is difficult, you will, as I did, see why you were created to be different. My brain led me to storytelling. And I love every moment of it. Who knows where your brain will lead you? One thing is for sure—it won't lead you down the path that everyone else is heading down. Your adventure will be different. And like I said, being different is awesome.

So next time someone calls you weird, odd, awkward, or strange . . . say thank you. Because that will just be a little reminder for you that you are well on your way toward a path of greatness. And remember, the opposite of weird is normal, and what I've learned most in my life is that the last thing I'd ever want to be in this exciting world is normal. Normal is bland. Normal is boring. The world needs us weirdos. We are the artists. We are the ones who invent things, sing songs, paint, write books, act in movies, design clothes, dance onstage, and bring happiness to people. We are the people who keep the world spinning. So let's spin it together! Your brain is a train. Get on board and enjoy the ride. Miigwech! (Thank you in Ojibwe.)

A BRIDGE OVER SILENCE

KAREN JIALU BAO

Content Note: This story references sexual assault, post-traumatic stress disorder, depression, and suicidal ideation.

Everywhere I go, I carry the dead weight of an instrument I no longer play. A hollow in my chest, a silence in my throat, and a stillness in the wind tunnel through which melodies once soared before they left my body.

Speaking doesn't count. It's like tapping the lid of a grand piano without touching the keys.

So when I hear the blond girl humming while studying across from me fail to hit the high E of a Joni Mitchell song because she doesn't know how to pull the note out from deep in her belly, I take it as a sign to leave the library and finish the rest of my history notes at my house. I avoid reminders of a past life when I sang. Studying will be easier at home, where the only distraction will be Mom bringing me a bowl of sliced papaya or disemboweled pomelo or whatever other fruit she bought from the Chinese supermarket over the weekend.

The girl's a ninth grader, judging by appearances. Sweet face, eyes that dart everywhere as if she knows she's being watched. Wired earbuds. Lip gloss like an oil slick, skinny legs, shirt a size too large, pants a size too small.

I wish some senior had stopped me when I was that age and told me, *Shut up, you literal child. Stop belting just because you can. Stop attracting so much attention.*

I'm embarrassed that I'm still taking my senior spring finals so seriously. It's not that Columbia would rescind my admission now, unless I pulled straight Cs. It's that every A I've gotten for all of high school has felt like a breath of air into a deflating life raft. Routine and perfection provide safety. The As are power-ups for my future, if I ever decide to start caring about it again.

I've enrolled in an EMT crash course over the summer to pad the résumé and rein in my ricocheting thoughts, even though I have no intention of becoming a premed. I'll go to bed at ten every night so I can work out in the morning (running, yoga, or Pilates) before reporting to the classroom, and I'm going to get top marks on everything, even though grading is pass/fail. I enjoy achieving a stranglehold on the things I can control to make up for all the things I can't.

I throw my shit into my backpack and leave the library, then take the long path out of the school building to avoid the music wing.

The sweet vibrato of an acoustic guitar draws my eye to a lanky black-haired figure sitting under a tree, her fingers scuttling across the strings like so many ant legs. Fucking Joanna Lim, making it all up as she goes along. You can tell by the way the tempo quickens and slows down as she thinks of ideas and then executes them. She used to improv for me like this, naming chords as they came and went. I hear them now: E major 7(9), she keeps coming back to that one. Some licks pose a question and the next one answers them. She's having a full conversation with herself, one that makes sense. It's nothing like the thumping and twisting that goes on in my own head.

Only when she looks up and the music stops do I realize I've been walking toward her.

Long fingers tuck a sheet of shoulder-length black hair behind one ear. "Ray," Joanna says, using my nickname where everyone else just calls me Rachel—or in the case of substitute teachers, "Rachel duh" instead of "doo," the way Du should be pronounced.

"I didn't mean to interrupt your practicing," I say.

Joanna laughs. "First, I wasn't practicing," she says, putting the guitar back in its case but not closing it. "Second, I was getting bored listening to myself." Her voice has gotten lower over the past three years—it's a solid contralto now. Mine has remained a mezzo-soprano. Maybe hers has leveled up, like how the rest of her shape-shifted from an awkward girl in miniskirts to this . . . this almost-boy in black cargo shorts. She looks like stage crew mixed with a hint of ninja.

I watch her silently. I've been procrastinating on the task of talking to her again before we both leave this school, letting the senior trip to Disneyland and even prom pass by without exchanging more than a superficial greeting. But now that we're here, alone, I don't know where to start. Maybe I was hoping she'd say something to me, return the pieces of me I hope she's been safeguarding since we were fourteen. Why would she have kept anything of mine, though, considering the way everything ended?

"Can I help you?" Joanna's face is serious now.

"I guess I don't know what I walked up to you for."

"You can at least sit down." This is funny coming from Joanna because she famously disrespects every chair she sits in—putting one leg up, sitting with her legs far apart, or, if the chair has arms, dangling one leg over the arm.

I sit cross-legged across from her on the grass. "When are you moving to Boston?"

Joanna shrugs. "Sometime before the semester starts. To pick up gigs ASAP. I'm going to room with the gayest people I've met in the accepted students' group. A lesbian music student colony. Naturally, no one has any idea yet where we're going to live, but we already know which houseplants we'll buy."

"Isn't that stressful?"

"Isn't it stressful having to know everything you're going to do months before it happens?" Joanna smirks. "Though it seems like you don't need any life advice, Miss Columbia."

Actually, I do. New York is going to swallow me. I'll fall into a mouth lined with skyscraper teeth and get chewed up by all that metal. I used to have music, which tied me to something solid so tightly I never felt adrift in the world. Then I learned that music was like a fishing lure that reeled in more evil than good. Now all I have is studying, which I do to distract myself from the feeling that I never want to be connected to anything again.

I want to steal Joanna's ease. Even though she's a (talented) slacker who definitely smokes weed with the jazz band's rhythm section after every rehearsal, she acts like the whole world is her home, or at least, the small corner of it I've watched her occupy. How did she become so . . . chill? She was awkward and off-tempo when she was high femme and still studying hard to please her mother and too tall for her clothes. Then, somehow, she became an androgynous supermodel music ninja, and—can I say it?—hot.

"You think we could've stayed friends if that whole thing had never happened?" I venture.

Joanna stares at me. She rubs her fingers together as if rolling a joint. She probably would smoke one if we weren't on school property in broad daylight. "I don't know. Who do you think you'd be if you'd never met Hernandez?"

The words form a rope in midair, which loops around my neck, constricts my throat, and steals my speaking voice.

This man has the loveliest hands in the world, *I think as Mr. Hernandez auditions about half the girls in the school to be the band's vocalist. When my turn comes, I step closer and take him in. He wears glasses with rectangular black frames that he's constantly pushing up the bridge of his nose and has plenty of soft brown hair and light skin that looks tanned from the summer sun.*

His fingers coax the opening bars of Ella Fitzgerald's "I Said No" from the keys, lazily, because he's played the song a hundred times in the last two hours. But I come in, laughter in my voice because the song is about a woman who rejects a magazine salesman until she caves and ends up subscribing to Playboy. Hernandez's fingers perk up; a smile paints his face bright. The linoleum-floored band room transforms into a smoke-filled jazz club in a basement in Harlem. I can almost feel the lights dim; I register a hint of shock on the onlookers' faces that these sounds are coming out of a small Asian girl, before they all blur into the background.

Too soon, it's over.

"You're it," he whispers to me over the sporadic applause. "You'd better free up your schedule."

What follows are 4:00 p.m. rehearsals to get me "caught up"— which turn into conversations that meander like a wandering stream until my parents pick me up at six. He insists I call him Fer when we are alone. He's only twenty-four, fresh out of a famous music school, and travels into the city some nights to perform. He's going to be a star, I know, and I'll be singing next to him when it happens.

In band class, other girls look at him the same way I do—one trumpeter, one flautist, two who play alto sax, a pianist—and I want to outdo them. I sing love songs to him, looking him dead in the eye in front of everyone. The exhilaration feels like jumping off a swing and soaring, not knowing if I'll stick the landing. But I also don't care. What's a skinned knee or a broken bone to a girl who's finally found love?

"He's part of me," I say to Jo. "I can't separate him from the rest of who I am." It stuns me that I say it out loud without flinching. What he did filtered out the gritty essence of my personality. I've let go of everything else.

"At least you're being honest," Jo says.

"You knew how fucked it was, Jo. But then I couldn't get ahold of you."

What I mean to say: *Why didn't you try harder to stop me?*

"You were so in love with our child molester band teacher that *you* stopped talking to *me*." Joanna's voice is full of slow-cooked anger. "Remember the LA trip? The band competition where you won Best Soloist? You just sat with him on the bus, leaving me to deal with Tory Roberts testing whether I was actually gay, thinking he could convince me I wasn't."

"I thought you'd be fine," I retort. "You were so intimidating, the best musician in the band by a mile. He was an ass, but I never dreamed he'd bother *you*."

"Flattering," Joanna says. "But it didn't help me then. You were too busy chasing our sociopath band teacher."

I hang my head, unable to deny it. "Were you jealous of—of Hernandez?"

Tears leak from Jo's pretty black eyes. "I thought you knew better than to go for a washed-up pianist who hits on teenagers . . . especially when I was around, fully available."

A tangle of thoughts forms in my mind. I can't give voice to any of them. *I was fourteen. I just wanted him to hear me! He was supposed to be an example for us. How was I supposed to know that he was hitting on me?*

Joanna angrily flips her hair back. "Anyway, you weren't the only one who got busy on that trip to LA," she says darkly.

"What?" I'm shocked that there was anything I didn't know about Joanna during that year we were inseparable. But I'd been rather self-absorbed.

"Tory and the worse senior drummer—Matt, wasn't it? I was hanging out with them in their hotel room, and somehow things got to second base with Tory, and I hated every minute of it, but with Matt there I couldn't say no, otherwise I thought they'd get violent.

Or go off and tell everyone I was gay, because what girl on earth would reject them? At the time, I still really wanted to be someone who liked guys. I felt like I had to prove it. There were already so many dyke rumors about me because I couldn't handle myself when I was with you."

Now I'm crying, too. "Why didn't you tell me?"

"I didn't want to tell anyone. They were all talking about your situation. Yours was so much worse than mine, and I had no evidence." Joanna angrily wipes her nose with the back of her hand.

I offer her a tissue from the pocket pack I always carry around. She blows a snot rocket into it. I scan the lawn, hoping no one is witnessing this Oscar-worthy drama, and notice a couple of figures far enough away that they don't seem to be eavesdropping. Meanwhile, Jo cranks up the volume on the sniffling and nose-blowing. She doesn't seem to care who sees.

"I'm sorry, Jo," I say helplessly.

Jo tosses the tissue into her open guitar case.

"When I was with him, I felt like I was possessed," I say. "Like without him I'd be nothing, so I couldn't say no to anything he wanted. He said some horrifying things, and I took them as fact!"

"I'm sure he said some real shit about me," Joanna says. "Guy *hated* me. Slapped a C on my report card for two quarters in a row. He didn't give me a solo for the rest of the time he was band director. Not even a crappy eight-bar slot."

I don't care to repeat what Hernandez said, so I remain silent. It's a blessing to spare her the details. But the details are what have stuck with me the longest.

The second night in LA, after we win the jazz band A division category and I take home Best Soloist, Fer invites me to his room for a toast. He opens warm beer that tastes like piss, but I chug a can to make him see me as more than some ninth grader with nice pipes.

"You don't have to prove anything to me," he says. "Every time you sing, it makes me want to have sex with you."

A kiss turns into a hand up my shirt, which then careens into my clothes on the floor and the feeling that I am being split open. Lips on lips was as far as my fantasies had taken me. It hurts so bad I stop feeling. From that point on, I am on autopilot. While my throat makes noises I've heard women make in movies when they were enjoying sex with a man, my mind is off remembering the first time I stood on the Great Wall of China with my parents. I wish I were there again, alone. I imagine jumping off the tallest guard tower, freely falling in midair, not thinking about the impending crash and crunching of bones.

When we return home, there's the unexpected feeling of incompleteness, like we've started playing and left off in the middle of the song. I want to show him, and myself, that what happened in LA was intentional. I was not a puppet but the mastermind.

So when his girlfriend, a five-foot-tall Korean violinist, travels for work, I go to his studio apartment and do it all again.

Notice me. Love me. *When his eyes meet mine, which happens rarely, I silently beg him to read that I need to be noticed and loved. To feel like somebody in a sea of ninth-grade girls, even though I'm not white enough to be a beauty queen or old enough to have accomplished anything notable.*

One Friday afternoon, *I fail to show up at Hernandez's apartment. My mother had come home early from work; the school nurse had called her because I freaked out about needing STD and pregnancy tests. It doesn't take her long to guess who the man is.* "How could this happen?" *she cries in Mandarin.* "We did everything! We tried so hard to give you a good life here . . . This wasn't supposed to happen."

Instead of confessing that my parents are onto us, I tell him the next day before morning bell, my hair still dripping from the shower, that I was with Joanna. He says, "I don't want you hanging out with that girl. She wants to turn you into one of them."

"One of what?"

"A feminist lesbian. Even Asian girls are falling for that shit now. Feminists have nothing to complain about. All that shouting when women are already equal to men . . . I can't stand it. Your voice is better used for other things, Rachel."

He means singing the songs that he feeds to me, winning awards, impressing his superiors. The sound waves turn him on while sucking the light out of me. My voice changes. Every time I sing, it's like I've been punched in the ribs.

It's not long before he texts me that he can't see me anymore, and that's when I know my parents have told the school. He writes, **I need to extract myself from this situation with you. Don't come to the band room or my place anymore.**

I read the text once; it cuts me open. Then I read it again, to rub the salt in. Why does he sound like I was holding him hostage in this "situation"? Before I go cross-eyed from wondering, I delete the text and everything else he ever sent me.

I stop singing with the band, even after the school hires a new director. Then I stop singing at all, just in case his spirit is still lurking in a corner, listening, with one hand on its cock.

"The best thing he did for this school was quit," Joanna says. "But who knows what he's been doing at his new one?"

"Are you implying I should've gone to court?" My voice stretches thin and tight; thank God I don't sing anymore because I'd probably hurt myself if I tried while my body's this tense. I regret not having the strength to put Hernandez on trial while the DNA evidence was inside me. But I was still in love with him, still bleeding from when he'd broken it off. The hatred only arrived later, after I realized he'd done things to me against my will simply because he could, and that

Rachel as a person meant nothing to him. My parents knew that my grades, and thereafter, my college applications, would go to hell if I got caught up dealing with character assassination, which inevitably happens to every victim who sets foot in court. These days, I'm guiltily glad I didn't try to put that man in prison.

"I used to think you were wrong not to put him on trial, given how much he could hurt other girls. But I read Chanel Miller's book, and I couldn't believe what she went through just to put her rapist in jail for a few weeks—now I know that you'd have been hurt so much worse if you *went* to trial. Shit, I hope Hernandez hasn't repeated his whole act with some other ninth grader by now."

"If he has, she's probably . . ." I make a circular gesture toward my own face.

Joanna repeats the motion with her hand and smirks. "Asian? Yeah, he's got the kind of yellow fever that I wish killed people. Typical entitled white guy behavior."

"He's Cuban, Jo."

"He's a piece of shit and he stank and I'm glad he's gone. Mr. Andros is way better. He makes us play Pat Metheny pieces with wacky time signatures. He's always asked me when you were going to sing with us, and I said not to bet on it."

Joanna pauses, then says, "I wonder what would've happened if I'd told you straight up that I wanted to kiss you. Before we went to LA."

I gasp, replaying her words in my head. *She wanted to kiss me.*

"I would've said yes."

"And we would've had so much more fun in our hotel room," Joanna says. She smiles, but it's more of a wince, like she's sucking on the pit of a sour cherry.

Joanna's mom works investment banking hours, so we're left alone in her house all afternoon and past the sunset. She rushes through her homework and picks up her instrument while I pore over my books, hacking through trigonometry. She puts on Miles

Davis, then Metallica, then Ariana Grande and layers her guitar's voice over each song.

"I'm playing this cheesy stuff ironically," she says, strumming absent-mindedly to John Mayer. I can't concentrate on trig, anyway, so I put the pencil down and swivel the chair to face Jo. I sing about love on the weekend and her body being a wonderland. My breath spins air molecules into song. The wind moves into my lungs and leaves them, warmed up, and I feel so connected to Joanna. To the whole universe.

*When we're done, her head rests heavily on my shoulder. I could turn my head and take my first kiss from her lips, but I stop myself, thinking—*What if I read this wrong? What if she doesn't want me, or any girl?

One of the first lessons we were taught as little girls was to keep our hands off what isn't ours.

All of it had been an invitation, and I hadn't opened the envelope, let alone RSVP'd. But I didn't know then that girls liked girls in the real world, not just on some TV shows or in Pride parades. That it was allowed, and even encouraged, in certain sectors of the student population. And besides, it was *Joanna.* I wanted to be her so badly I never thought I could be *with* her.

In another universe, Joanna and I would have dated and gotten a kick out of making passersby clutch their pearls and fought with our parents over our queerness, and mourned that being gay or bi was even up for debate. But in this universe, I got raped. So instead of telling Mom how unstraight I am, I had to listen to her lectures on protecting myself and never going to a man's apartment and, yaaaaa, maybe I should learn self-defense. I don't know if there'll ever be room for that other conversation. Because we're definitely not done processing Hernandez.

"We could've saved each other," I say. I want to cry again.

Or do I? Do I *really* wish it had never happened? Having been raped makes me feel like I know more than other people. That I'm superior for having seen how the world really is at the age of fourteen: bleak, hopeless, terrifying. Everyone else is living in an illusion.

"Sure, okay, both of us would've been spared for ninth grade," Joanna says. "But eventually, dudes would come for us. Like the Grim Reaper. Everyone's gotta die at some point."

Hernandez quits his job and changes schools after my parents tell the principal. The principal refers to me as an "underage woman." No one has the stomach to call me what I am—a girl. Dad can't look me in the eye; whether out of disappointment in me or shame in his inability to protect me, I can't be sure. But in my interest (or Hernandez's, more likely), the school keeps our secret on lock, though that can't prevent rumors from flying around the creative quadrant of the ninth-grade class. The only other person who knows exactly what happened? Joanna, because I told her I was in love with him beforehand. Maybe that was the moment "we" split into "she" and "I."

The hopelessness and brutality of existing in this body convinces me, junior year, to tip sixteen of Mom's ten-milligram white zolpidem sleeping pills into my hand. I swallow only three before Dad catches me, and in a fit of shouted Mandarin, he drives me to the hospital to get my stomach pumped. It's my first time going there, my first time letting strangers touch my body after what happened.

Dad is shaking so hard he almost crashes the car, and his angry silence is only punctuated by the question "How could you let this happen to you?" The thought passes through my head that I'd be outraged at the victim-blaming if I weren't falling unconscious. Then I forgive him. If I could've somehow prevented it from happening, I'd still have some agency in the situation, and that's what Dad is hoping for. He wants to believe that I retained a little bit of control in a world where so much is

out of your control. Especially if you're a fourteen-year-old girl
with golden skin and monolid eyes.

I'm out for the stomach pumping, thank God, due to the pills
and anesthesia. That hospital's going to make bank off my parents
and their so-called insane, depressed daughter.

So far, I haven't tried again. It would be too much of a
headache if I got caught or it didn't work, at least while I'm living
at home. But I know the world has betrayed me and I constantly
remind myself of it, in case I ever start forgetting. I've read
the campus rape stories, plowed through articles about UVA,
Stanford, Swarthmore, Harvard, St. Andrews, Boston College,
Baylor, Michigan State, College of Charleston, USC, UNC, Rice,
U Minnesota, Vanderbilt, Cornell—and, yes, Columbia—et cetera,
et cetera. I am addicted to every nugget of information that
confirms that the world is not safe and never will be. Even if I
didn't get raped again on campus, I'd go to internships and face
leering bosses and the weird dual expectation that I'd be good
at my entry-level desk job because I'm Chinese but also bad
at it because I'm female. Eventually, everyone gets assaulted,
physically or verbally, to varying degrees. You're even more of
a target if you're Asian, like me and Jo and Hernandez's then-
girlfriend and his ex from college. Every car honk and catcall
directed at me, every "Ni hao" and "Konnichiwa," every dickhead
on the sidewalk who looks at me as if he's about to order me
for dinner like General Tso's chicken (which people don't eat in
China), reminds me of these facts and knocks me flat on my back
on that hotel mattress in LA.

"So if we've both already died," I say, "where do we go from here?
We're stuck on earth, but it feels like Hades. All because of one band
trip."

Joanna stares into the sound hole of her guitar as if the cavern
inside her instrument has the answer. Then she looks into my haggard

face. "Ray, one day you've got to realize that it was something that happened to you and not who you are. It happened in the world, but it's not the whole world."

I give her a look that says, *You're shitting me.* What he did to me subsumed every waking moment and every dream, when I did manage to sleep.

"I'm not an expert . . . but I think you have to try on bits of your old self like falling-apart clothes and see what might still be wearable. Some of it's going to feel like trash and some of it's going to feel great. Femininity and pretending to be straight felt like trash for me, so I dumped them in the garbage. Music? That still slapped. I held tight to that."

"Are we trying on each other now?" I say.

"I guess so." Joanna smiles through her drying tears.

"You feel like . . . a soft oversized flannel that's been washed too many times."

"Um, that's a lesbian stereotype, but okay, I'll take it."

"Would you rather be a pair of low-rise skinny jeans with no stretch?"

"God, no!"

And we burst out laughing.

My own tears stop. There's a spark in my heart, the tiniest, slowest-burning of baby lantern flames. Joanna Lim figured out a way forward. This is how she walks through the world like the whole thing is her home, even if she's faking it sometimes.

If she can do it, I can, too. It feels so good not to be alone.

"Are you telling me I should be singing?" I say.

"I'm not going to tell you what to do," Jo says. "But yes, I think singing might feel good."

"I'm not singing. My larynx has been used only for talking since ninth grade."

Jo shrugs. "I never said you had to do it now."

"I'm gonna sound like shit."

"All right, you're gonna sound like shit, and I'm one of those giant lizards in the Galápagos. Three years later I still haven't heard anyone I like better than you. Don't give me excuses about not practicing. I didn't play the entire summer after the LA trip—I just couldn't—and then it took me just a couple weeks to get my fingers back. Your body remembers." Jo tosses her magnificent hair back over her shoulder. "I wish you'd sing for me now. I miss your voice. But I won't push."

I could hold her close to me right now, this girl who feels like the only one in the world who understands me. Not in a romantic way— okay, maybe in a romantic way.

Joanna picks up her guitar again and starts tuning it.

"Your A's flat," I say, remembering fondly how I used to annoy her with my perfect pitch.

She rolls her eyes but brings the A up until I signal to stop. It's a pleasing, bright 110 hertz.

"I'm gonna go now," I say. The urge to get back to the day I planned for myself is too strong to ignore. "Gotta do a last edit on that essay for English."

Jo sighs at the mere suggestion of caring about school three days before graduation. "Did I give you what you were looking for?"

I think for a moment. She hasn't exactly given me a gift—it's more like she provided directions to long-lost treasure. "It was hiding in me the whole time," I say. "Thanks for drawing it out."

"Bu xie," Jo says. *Don't thank me.* "Now, please get out of my face, Ray. I want to cry alone this time."

After dinner with the parents, I go upstairs and shut the door to my room. Put in my earbuds, put on that Joni Mitchell song that the girl in the library hummed with such love. Who cares about her technique? Maybe, if I were still a singer, I would've taught her how to align her spine and reach into her belly to find the top of her vocal range. Maybe I still have a chance before I graduate. How does the world have room enough for a child molester band teacher and a smiling ninth grader wearing lip gloss who knows Joni songs by heart? I hope the world has room for me, too. I'd like to think I'm in the beautiful part of things. And that beautiful things make up more than half the world.

By the second verse, I'm humming, and by the second chorus, I'm singing softly, pulling the lyrics out from dust-covered vaults in my brain.

The bridge arrives, daring me to bare my heart, and I run across it naked. I do so on my tiptoes, embracing the high E before touching down on the opposite shore.

A NOTE FROM KAREN JIALU BAO

✳ ✳ ✳ ✳ ✳ ✳ ✳ ✳ ✳ ✳ ✳ ✳ ✳ ✳ ✳

I was sexually assaulted by an authority figure in my teens. For the next decade, PTSD muted everything I'd previously enjoyed about life and robbed me of the will to play my violin, which had been my absolute favorite activity since I was four. When I was twenty-six, friends, music, and a good therapist helped me acknowledge and mourn my trauma while moving on with the expansive, wild adventure that is now my life. "A Bridge over Silence" is about how it feels to start feeling again.

ALMOST BEAUTIFUL

MARCELLA PIXLEY

Content Note: This story references obsessive-compulsive disorder and severe anxiety.

Apocalypse. Armageddon. Cataclysm. Catastrophe. Pandemonium. Pandemic.

The *Oxford English Dictionary* has entirely too many Latinate, multisyllabic words that mean the end of the world. If you say them out loud, one after another, the explosive consonants sound like sharp things falling from the sky. They are an auditory concussion. Fire and brimstone. Even though I am drawn to recite them backward and forward and in reverse alphabetical order, they do nothing to soothe my horrible worries even for a fraction of a second or allow me to take a break from my dismal thinking to enjoy this momentous almost-beauty, which just might be my very last pleasant experience before the human race succumbs to plague and we all die in a wheezing, coughing, infectious cloud of sin.

Big deep breath. Hold it. Let it out.

Sunday is always a hard day, but I have everything I need to stay calm spread out on the kitchen table. Cell phone. Cornflakes. Coffee. Little yellow sticky note with Mom's hospital number. Watercolors. Precut squares of journal paper. My favorite purple pen. I am doing the only thing I know how to do these days when I sink into despair, which is cover my journal page with blue and purple watery swirls.

It feels good, my hand on the thin brush, curving slowly across the page as the new morning sunlight shines through my favorite half-gallon jug of hand sanitizer and onto the kitchen table, where a perfect prism of diffuse, viscous light is cast across my journal page, a veritable gift from God.

The sunlight shining through the bottle of hand sanitizer is almost, but not quite, beautiful. Still, *almost* is pretty good for me these days. As I swirl my colors together, I realize that I should try to stop obsessing for a minute and appreciate the sunlight. Dr. Sokol says it would be good if I could learn how to find the beauty in ordinary moments. Practice gratitude, he says. It might help things feel more bearable.

Besides my sister, Sophia, and my mom, Dr. Sokol is probably the one person on this earth who knows me best, so I try to take his advice. I close my eyes, and in the smog of my tortured mind, I say thank you for this almost-beautiful moment, brought to you by the letter Q for quarantine. "Thank you," I whisper out loud into the empty kitchen. All at once, I realize the irony. Seventeen-year-old girl, recovering from COVID-19 at home while mother struggles to breathe in hospital, finally learns power of optimism just before demise of entire human race.

Ha ha, says God. *That's a good one.*

I take an imaginary bow.

Lights out. Curtain. Unenthusiastic applause.

It probably won't surprise you to learn that having constant terrifying thoughts makes it very difficult to practice gratitude, so I settle for almost-gratitude while I paint my journal page blue and purple, drink my tasteless coffee (#SideEffects), and try with all my might to simply recognize the potential for a nice moment on this strange spring morning in quarantine while my mother struggles to breathe in the hospital and sunlight streams through my favorite bottle of hand sanitizer, casting a perfect prism onto my journal page, as though God himself decided to take a short break from his very important demolition of humanity to write a little story in sunlight about me.

Once upon a time, writes God in whispered strands of silken sunlight, *there was a girl named Claudia who called herself Claude because she liked making people wonder. Claude had always been kind of a loner. I should know. I made her that way. Introverts amuse me. Then I waved my magic God wand and made a whole bunch of really bad things happen to her all at once. I gave her sister, Sophia, an internship downtown, just a little too far away for their weekly cup of café mocha. I made COVID-19. I made quarantine. I stoked Claude's desperation for café mocha and lured her to the supermarket. I made Claude catch the virus. And then, just when she was about to get better, I made her pass it to her mom. Then I sent her mom away in an ambulance to a hospital that does not allow visitors. I'm twisted that way. I like to see how much people can take before they crumble. But don't worry, Claude. There will always be the almost-beauty of small moments. And the blessing of hairless cats. And if that's not proof of my bizarre sense of humor, you are not paying enough attention.*

Just look at this one.

His name is Turnip, and I made him smell like feet.

Turnip leaps onto the kitchen table and makes the quintessential *prrt* of feline inquiry. *What are you doing already awake and downstairs and sitting at the kitchen table on a Sunday morning when the motherly person who usually feeds us isn't anywhere to be seen, not dancing around the kitchen in her colorful bohemian nightgown, not singing the Grateful Dead at the top of her lungs, not doing any of the weird middle-aged nerdy adorkable things she usually does, because she is not here. She is not here. She is in the hospital having fever dreams, with tubes blowing oxygen into her nose.*

Turnip walks past his empty food dish. He twitches his bony tail. Then he walks across my journal pages and sticks his naked cat butt in my face. I scratch the base of his tail and along his dry, wrinkly back to the top of his scaly head, which I pet and pet. Turnip closes his eyes and curls up like a gargoyle in the patch of sunlight. Before long, he is asleep and purring. Apparently the naked cat knows how to appreciate the beauty of small moments while the human is utterly incapable of gratitude. Another piece of irony.

See what I did there? says God. *I made the human beings foolish, but I gave wisdom to the cat. That's what you call satire. Especially because the cat looks almost human, not unlike a wrinkly old man. The whole thing is hilarious. Don't you think?*

I do. And I laugh out loud to prove it.

Turnip raises his head and looks at me like I'm crazy. Which, I guess, I sort of am.

Don't say crazy, says God. *It's derogatory. Say complicated. You are complicated, dearest Claudia, because I made you that way. I gave you a mind that loops and echoes and reflects itself and spins on its axis. I made you a mind that skates in circles. I gave you the ability to look inward so deeply you can lose yourself in yourself. Isn't that exciting? Every day is an adventure. A dungeon. A labyrinth. You will never be bored for as long as you live. No. No. Don't thank me. Just adore me and sing my praises. In Hebrew please. I have always liked Hebrew.*

God knows I am not the kind of person to sing any kind of praises. He and I are more like buddies. We are on a first-name basis. God and Claude. We rhyme. The last time I prayed in Hebrew was my Bat Mitzvah, and the truth is, I can get pretty dismal these days. Especially on the weekend, when there is no school to take my mind off Armageddon. On the weekend, I actually miss the utter awkwardness of Zoom school, the teachers' glitchy, remote voices trying in vain to connect with us through cyberspace while we slump, muted before our screens.

The first weeks of the pandemic, teachers tried so hard to be interesting online, the exertion made their faces sweat. They were like circus clowns doing anything to get our attention. Their expressions were so extreme, they looked like caricatures of human beings. They used their hands as punctuation marks. They hopped back and forth from one foot to the other. They wore funny hats, did cartwheels, cracked dad jokes, performed silly pet tricks, introduced us to their spouses and their babies, demonstrated baking and bubble-blowing and tap dancing. But now, after a month, they have become almost as flat and expressionless as we are. The pandemic has beaten them down. Still, I feel lost without them. During the week, there are class discussions and questions to answer and assignments to complete, and there are all those satisfying little Zoom squares to contain and organize this baffling world. On the weekend, it is just me and God and Turnip and my blue and purple swirls. And my phone. Thank God for my phone, which fairy-twinkles right on cue.

It's Sophia. It is always Sophia. Ever since Mom left for the hospital, Sophia has been FaceTiming me three or four times a day just to make sure I am okay, which is both aggressively sweet and also a little annoying, because of course I'm not okay. After all, the world is ending. Our mother is deteriorating. The human race is doomed. What does she expect? Exuberance? My phone fairy-twinkles again and again. Turnip gets up, stretches, and then stalks away on tiptoes, annoyed. Then, when it twinkles a fourth time, I answer it.

Sophia likes to hold the phone so that the camera catches her image at a three-quarters profile from just a little bit above her left eye so you can see her forehead and then down the beaky nose that reminds everyone so much of Mom, whose profile has always been hawkish. Sophia thinks this angle makes her look thinner and younger, which is really irritating because she is plenty thin and young already, and besides, why would someone who just graduated from college need to look younger than they are? The pretentious angle thing just makes her seem vain. Especially under the circumstances. Sophia in her own apartment. Me alone in our empty house. Mom in the hospital with oxygen up her nose. And the whole world falling apart around us. Who cares if the camera catches your cheekbones at the perfect angle? Pretty soon we all will be six feet under.

Ah, mortality, says God. *It really knocks the wind out of you.*

"The hospital called," says Sophia, her voice tight with worry. "She still isn't breathing well. And it's getting worse. They think our best bet is moving her to the ICU and putting her on a ventilator until she gets stronger. Mom wants to do this, Claude. It's a tube down her throat. Intubation. She won't be able to talk to us for as long as she is on the machine. You need to call her. Right now."

I feel cold and my fingers tingle. My heart starts beating hard. I dip my paintbrush in water and swirl blue and purple paint across my journal. It doesn't work.

Apocalypse. Armageddon. Cataclysm. Catastrophe. Pandemonium.

"Do you hear me, Claude? They're doing it this morning. You need to call her and tell her you love her just in case."

I want to ask, *Just in case what?* But I already know the answer to this question, and I don't want to hear Sophia say the terrible words, so instead I ask, "How do they get the tube down her throat?"

"What?" asks Sophia, exasperated.

"How do they get the tube down? Do they just shove it in? Do they make her swallow it? Mom is a tiny person. How could such a tiny person possibly swallow a tube without the gag reflex pushing it out again? Can you tell me that?"

My voice sounds unhinged. I can hear it echo in the room. High and hysterical.

"What is wrong with you?" says Sophia. "I have no idea how they get it down her throat. It's a medical procedure. They give her anesthesia. And they insert it somehow. The nurse said the machine is going to breathe for her until she gets stronger. But it could take her a while to get stronger, Claude. And some of them don't make it. So you need to call Mom right now before they intubate her and tell her you love her."

"She is going to be in pain."

"What?"

"Having a tube down her throat. Pushing air in and out. Breathing for her. Not being able to talk. Not being able to swallow. That's not going to feel good at all."

"They will sedate her so she won't even remember any pain."

"Not remember being on a ventilator? I highly doubt that." I begin googling "what I remember about being on a ventilator" and something like three million results come up. "I don't know where you are getting your facts. But all these people remembered. This guy from Fresno said it was the most pain he ever felt in his life. I don't think you got enough information when you said it wasn't going to hurt. I think you're confused, Sophia. I really think you're confused."

"Fine," says Sophia. "I'm confused. You got me. But listen, Claude. We don't have much time. In about twenty-five minutes they are going to put Mom on a ventilator. And we can't visit her because of COVID. So please, Claude. Get yourself together for a minute. Give her a call and tell her you love her. And then call me so I can make sure you're okay."

"I'm not going to be okay," I say, feeling the tears well up.

"Call her," says Sophia. "Call her right now. Then call me back."

The screen goes blank.

My hands are shaking.

I dial the number as fast as I can with trembling fingers.

The nurse answers it. "Hello? Carolyn Bergman's room."

My voice comes tumbling out of my mouth like children falling down stairs. "Hello. This is Claude Bergman. I'm Carolyn Bergman's younger daughter. I heard she's being moved to the ICU to go on a ventilator. I wanted to call before she left."

"Perfect timing," says the nurse. "We were just about to wheel her down." I can hear him place his hand over the receiver while my mother coughs. A strangled, desperate sound. "Carolyn, it's your daughter Claude on the phone. Are you up for trying to talk a minute?" And then back to me. "She wants to try. But listen, honey, she's having a lot of trouble breathing right now. And we've given her a sedative to get her ready for the intubation, so she's already a little groggy and her voice might sound different than you're used to. But she can talk to you for a minute."

"Okay," I say.

The nurse hands over the phone to my mom.

"Claudia," says Mom.

Hearing her say my full name breaks me open.

"Mom," I say. "Mommy. I am so sorry."

"Don't be sorry," she rasps.

Her voice is low and slurred. I can tell it is taking every ounce of her energy to speak. The rattle of her breath brings me to my knees.

"It is all my fault," I sob.

"It's not your fault. It's just what happened. No matter how this all goes, I don't want you to think it's your fault."

"I wish I could be with you."

"I know," rasps Mom. "I wish you could be with me, too."

She begins coughing again.

I hear the nurse's voice in the background telling Mom that it's time to go.

But I can't let her go. Not yet.

"I'm going to be okay," says Mom. "This is going to help me. Try not to worry."

We are both silent a heartbeat, knowing that for me, trying not to worry is like trying not to breathe. I can hold it for a little while, but eventually something's got to give and I'm going to start gulping air hard and fast, even with my coffee and my journal pages and the almost-beauty of sunlight through the hand sanitizer (dimming now as the sun rises higher), and even with Turnip sitting under the table like a challah and God by my side telling bad jokes, and even with Sophia calling me every couple of hours to make sure I am okay when I am obviously not okay. I can feel the panic rising like a riptide, threatening to consume me, and I know that no matter what I do next, I am going to drown in it.

"I love you, Claudia," Mom gasps.

Her breath is the sound of claws slashing through velvet.

"I love you, too."

The nurse takes the phone from her. "Okay, honey. We need to get this going," he says. "Call this afternoon and we'll give you an update."

"Okay," I whisper.

Mom coughs in the background.

And then the nurse hangs up.

I am alone again.

I clutch my phone.

I know I should call Sophia, but for some reason I can't get myself to do it. The sound of her voice is going to break me, and I will crumble right there on the spot. I draft a text to her. I type, **I'm not okay.** But I can't get myself to send it.

Maybe I should call Dr. Sokol. Maybe he has time for an appointment. But then I remember. It's Sunday. He won't call back until the office opens on Monday. That means I will be drowning for twenty-four hours. No one takes twenty-four hours to drown. They sink to the bottom like a stone. Even very small stones sink fairly quickly. And that's the end of it.

I'm not okay, I whisper to Dr. Sokol in my mind, imagining that I am in his office, looking at his listening face. *I am really, really not okay.*

I go to the window and try to find something beautiful to notice.

The world is empty.

Everyone hides in their houses, burrowed beneath the ground like moles, wrapped in their own solitude. They are smart. Smarter than I was when I stood in line at the supermarket behind that grumpy old maskless guy who kept sniffling. I glared at him, hoping in vain that my fury would inspire him to step back. He met my eyes totally unfazed and almost smiling. And then of course the guy coughed. And sneezed. And rubbed his honker with those grubby hands, because we all should be free to do whatever the heck we want, even if what we want is going to lead to the destruction of humanity.

I should have run away right then. I should have left my pathetic plastic container of café mocha mix right there on the conveyor belt, gotten out of line, and run back home to Mom and Turnip and God. But no. I just had to have my coffee. With Sophia in her own apartment downtown and all the coffee shops closed, I just had to have my fix. So I stayed in that line. And I got sneezed on by the creep, and I put my café mocha on the humid conveyor belt, and I caught the bleeping virus, and even though I sanitized on my way out and washed my hands with antibacterial soap as soon as I came home, and even though I showered and changed my clothes before dinner and turned my face away when Mom tried to kiss me, I still gave it to her, like a really terrible Chanukah gift that no one wants.

Apocalypse. Armageddon. Cataclysm. Catastrophe. Pandemonium.

I think my lungs are failing.

Maybe I need a ventilator, too.

Outside the window, the streets are still. Just closed doors. Everyone hiding while the apocalypse puts an end to human arrogance, our gluttonous, selfish, shortsighted misuse of this planet. The whole godforsaken human race spreading its ravenous population across the trembling landscape, a scourge on the face of the earth. Festering, even more insatiable than the virus. Greed. Consumerism. Deforestation. Pollution. No wonder God is putting an end to us. We don't deserve to live. We messed it up. And now we are paying for our sins. Millions of jerks standing in line for their fix when they should have stayed home.

Sophia is trying to FaceTime me. I want to slam my twinkling phone to pieces on the windowsill, but somehow, even in the midst of my own unraveling, I know that destroying the phone would probably be a poor choice. Without my phone I won't be able to call the hospital. I won't be able to order food from Grubhub. And I won't ever be able to talk to Sophia again. So I decline her call and put my phone in my pocket, where it buzzes against my butt, which is incredibly irritating and also kind of weirdly sexy in my state of existential panic, and so I scream and throw my phone across the room, and it almost hits Turnip, who is sitting inside the sink like a salamander, catching drops of water from the faucet with his tongue.

The phone clatters into an empty spaghetti pot. Turnip hisses and leaps from the sink. The phone buzzes against the sides of the pot. It is the sound of the human race trembling on the verge of destruction.

You need to calm down, says God. *You are totally losing your shit.*

God is right. I am totally losing my shit.

I lurch to the sink and fish my phone out of the spaghetti pot.

It is oily, and it smells like garlic and Parmesan, but after I wipe it against my jeans, it turns on fine. My screen is festering with texts from Sophia. Little bubbles of sisterly panic. I crawl under the kitchen table because under the table is the best place to lose my shit. I bring my knees up to my chest and scroll through my phone, trying hard to make out the words despite my tears and despite the phone quivering as my fingers shake.

S (9:03): What's going on? Call me.

S (9:04): Did u talk to mom?

S (9:07): Why aren't you answering?

S (9:10): I am kinda freaking out that u aren't answering.

S (9:11): At least text me and tell me u r reading this.

S (9:12): I am getting worried now.

S (9:13): Pls call. I won't say anything. I'll just listen. I promise.

This last one is a ridiculous proposition. Sophia never just listens. She always has something to say. When I was worried that Turnip had feline leukemia, she told me I was being melodramatic. When I was worried that the freckle on Mom's nose was cancer, she suggested that I drink some chamomile tea. When I was worried that an asteroid was catapulting toward Earth, she suggested that I watch *Family Guy* because *Family Guy* makes me laugh and laughter releases serotonin and serotonin makes human beings feel tranquil, and for most people, feeling tranquil is preferable to panicking. None of it is bad advice per se. Any of these things might make a normal person feel better. And sometimes some of them even work for me, at least for a moment or two. If they didn't, I wouldn't have a journal filled with a hundred pages of blue and purple swirls. What Sophia doesn't understand is that it is a matter of degrees. My worry is exponential. It multiplies. It feeds on itself. It is its own cheerleader. Once I'm at a certain critical point, no amount of chamomile tea is going to work, and no amount of good advice from a well-meaning sister will help me unless it is paired with a couple months of therapy and an additional twenty milligrams of Prozac each day. You've got to love those green-and-white capsules. So I appreciate your offer, dear sister, but even though you just might be my last remaining family member alive on earth, I do not think I will be calling you back anytime soon because the mortal coil that just barely tethers me to this failing planet is already frayed and ready to break at any moment.

Apocalypse. Armageddon. Cataclysm. Catastrophe. Pandemonium.

I can't breathe.

I find Dr. Sokol's name in my contacts.

"Hello. You have reached Doctor Samuel Sokol. I am either on the phone or away from my desk. If you have reached me after hours and need to speak to someone before the next working day, feel free to call Doctor . . ."

I hang up and call again so I can hear his voice for longer.

"Hello. You have reached . . ."

"Hello. You have reached Doctor Samuel Sokol. I am . . ."

"Hello. You have reached Doctor Samuel Sokol. I am either on the phone or away from my desk. If you have reached me after hours and need to speak to someone before the next working day, feel free to call Doctor Elise Chandra at 617-555-2958 or dial 911 if it is an emergency. If you want to leave me a message, please speak after the beep and I will call you back as soon as I can."

"Hi, Doctor Sokol. This is Claude. Bergman? But I guess you know my voice by now, and you probably have caller ID, so you know I've called a whole bunch of times. And I didn't really have to announce myself. But there you are. Claude. Bergman. Me. So. Anyway. I'm calling. I'm calling and calling, actually. Because I am really not doing so well right now. I mean. I'm really. Not. Doing well. I am under the table, actually. And I don't know what to do, Doctor Sokol, because they're putting Mom on a ventilator and now I won't be able to talk to her until this is all over, except maybe I won't be able to ever talk to her because maybe she's not going to make it."

Turnip tiptoes under the table. He does not seem surprised to find me sitting here. He circles four times before he curls up like a bagel in my lap. I pet his skin absently. The blessing of a hairless cat.

"The worst part is, I can't stop thinking about the world coming to an end. And I can't stop thinking that somehow this is my fault. Even though Mom says, and I know it's true, that it's not my fault. Technically. It's just what's going on in the world. I mean, how could I have known that guy was going to sneeze on me. Right?

"Anyway. I've been doing everything you said. To keep myself almost okay. I've been trying to find the beauty in small moments. Like earlier. There was sunlight coming through the hand sanitizer. And it was almost beautiful. And I've been writing and painting in my journal, and that kind of helps. And I have been trying to practice gratitude in the mornings and at night before I go to bed. Like thank you for the springtime. And thank you for the earth hanging in there with me. But right now, I have to admit, it's really getting hard to find things to be grateful for. Because every time I turn on the news it seems worse. And for as long as I can remember, it has always been me and Mom and Sophia. Just the three of us. And now it's just me. And the world is coming to an end and I'm all alone and I don't think I can do this on my own."

I can't help it. I start sobbing.

Loud, ugly sobbing.

God's comedic timing is impeccable.

It is at precisely this moment that Dr. Sokol's answering machine runs out of time, and I am left sobbing into a busy signal.

"You've got to be kidding me," I mutter.

Nope! says God. *Not kidding! You are totally on your own now.*

"I could call him back," I say, seething. Gotcha, God. Technology wins.

He'll think you're crazy.

"Don't say crazy. It's derogatory. Say complicated. Blessed art Thou, Lord our God, Ruler of the Universe, who has made me complicated and has given me fingers steady enough to call back my therapist even though he is not there. Amen. There you are. Gratitude."

Nice, says God.

I dial Dr. Sokol again.

"Hello. You have reached Doctor Samuel Sokol. I am either on the phone or away from my desk. If you have reached me after hours and need to speak to someone before the next working day, feel free to call Doctor Elise Chandra at 617-555-2958 or dial 911 if it is an emergency. If you want to leave me a message, please speak after the beep and I will call you back as soon as I can."

"It's me again. The machine cut me off. But I am calling back because I wasn't totally finished. So I guess what I want to say is please call me back when you can. I'm going to try to do all the things you taught me how to do. And I'm going to try not to think about the end of the world, even though we both know how this works. The more I try not to think about it, the more I think about it and the worse it gets. But you're right. You're right. Finding the beauty helps. Like the hand sanitizer. That was really nice. And maybe if I look for it, there will be something else today. To remind me. That maybe it's not too late for me and human beings and the world and my mom to be okay. All right. So. I'm hanging up now. And I'm going to go outside and look one more time. Maybe there will be something out there. Thank you for listening. Call me when you can."

I push Turnip off my lap, gather up my pen and my journal pages and a mask from the kitchen table, and walk to the back door like a person just emerging from a cave. The world outside the window is fragile in its brand-new springtime. It is shivering April, just before the weather turns warm. The first buds on the trees glow like green filigree. I turn the doorknob and walk out on the porch in my bare feet.

The air feels different. Cleaner. Maybe it is because I've been crying. Maybe it's because I've been spending so much time indoors that I've gotten used to it. Or maybe it's because the entire human race has been hiding inside their houses for a month and no one is driving cars anymore. No one is traveling. There are no airplanes in the sky. I wonder how long it would take for the earth to heal itself. What would happen if we had to quarantine for a year. What if all of us stopped wasting our time acquiring a million plastic containers of café mocha and spent more time crying over the people we loved, talking to God, standing barefoot on our porches, and noticing suddenly that somehow, despite everything that's gone wrong, somehow it's springtime again and springtime is always good because it gives us a chance to start over even when we don't deserve it.

There is a rustle in the woodpile by the old shed, and all at once a red fox steps onto the new green grass in her black slippers, completely unafraid, looking proud, as though she knows she owns this space and any human being she might encounter along the way is completely inconsequential. She steps past the firepit and up the hill into our fallow vegetable garden, where she sits among the dried tomato stalks and stares at me. One by one her kits follow from their den under the shed, loping up to the garden where the sun is shining, tumbling over one another, pouncing on blades of grass and each other's tails. They gather around their mother. Batting at her ears. Reaching up with their snouts to nuzzle at her.

They are beautiful.

I write it down in my journal as quickly as I can. I don't want to miss a moment of this. The mother and her kits. The new sun shining. The writer, forgetting her panic for a moment to stand still and watch and not be afraid.

Until the sound of an engine inserts itself like an exclamation point.

A car door.

The mother fox and her kits freeze and then race back down the hill to dive beneath the shed. I stop writing. Sophia gets out of her beat-up old car and starts walking toward me. She is tiny and furious. I can see it in her face even beneath the mask as she storms from the driveway toward the porch, my older sister who looks so much like Mom, skinny as a rail with her torrent of black hair.

"Why didn't you call me back?" she says. "Why aren't you answering my texts? I've been worrying about you all morning." She starts up the porch steps, but I back away.

"Wait," I say. "Stay there. I know it's been almost two weeks, but I might still be contagious. And I would never forgive myself if you got sick. So just please. Stay where you are. Okay? We can talk from here." I take my mask out of my pocket and put it on.

Sophia looks up at me. Her own masked face looks older than it did when I last saw her in person, just over a month ago. There are shadows around her eyes. Her brow is furrowed. It is amazing what you can see in a face even when most of it is covered. The texture of the skin. The intensity of the eyes.

"You were supposed to call me back after you talked to Mom," says Sophia.

"I'm sorry," I say. "I've been in really bad shape."

"I knew you would be. That's why I said to call."

"I just needed to be alone."

My words sound like a lie because they are. How can I tell her that I couldn't muster the strength to answer the phone, to hear her voice, to hear her not listen, to steady my voice so I sounded okay when I wasn't okay at all. How can I tell her that sometimes it's all I can do to keep on going when my thoughts are so dark and so deep and I can't find a ladder to climb out of them and back into a world where sisters answer phone calls.

"You're too young to be alone during something like this."

"What are you going to do, move back in?"

"Maybe," says Sophia. "For a while. Just until Mom comes home."

I like how that sounds. *Until* Mom comes home. *Until* sounds so certain. There isn't even an implication of *if.* No doubts of recovery. Just healing, implied in the grammar. And suddenly I am imagining my tiny horrible empty kitchen filled with my sister's enormous presence and her voice, and I am imagining meals with her across the table, and I am imagining me and Sophia together calling up the hospital later this afternoon and finding out that Mom is going to be okay. The ventilator is doing what it needs to be doing, and she is going to come home soon.

"What about your internship?" I ask Sophia.

"What about it?" She smiles. "Everything's virtual anyway. I can work from here just as well as I can work from my apartment. We can keep each other company. It'll be like the old days. Besides, I miss Turnip. I need to scratch his scaly little face. Is he still as ugly as he was when I left?"

"Even uglier," I say.

"Good," says Sophia.

We stand there for a while staring at each other. Me on the porch and Sophia on the steps.

"I wish I could hug you," I say.

"How about an air hug?" says Sophia.

She throws her arms around herself. And I throw my arms around myself. And we hug and hug so hard we practically hug the air out of our lungs. We rock and hug and close our eyes and pretend the heat we feel comes from our sister and not ourselves. It is almost as good as a real hug.

When it's over, Sophia looks up at me, and I can tell she is smiling even though I can see only her forehead and her eyes.

"So," she says, in a voice that sounds so much like our mother's I can barely believe it. "Are you going to let me come up, or am I going to have to sleep out here in the vegetable garden? I promise I'll keep my mask on, Claude. I'll keep my distance. I'll wash my hands. I'll eat on paper plates. Just please. Let me stay here with you until Mom comes home. I don't want you to be alone."

"I don't want to be alone," I whisper.

"Let's start with the porch. Is that okay?"

"Yes," I say. "That's okay."

I back up so Sophia can climb the steps of the porch and still have her distance.

Sophia sits down in one white rocking chair near the steps, and I sit down on the other by the door, and we stay like that a long time. Two sisters wearing masks. Not speaking. Just rocking together despite the distance. Sometimes we find each other's eyes. Sometimes we just watch the wind move the fragile spiderwebs of branches and the new, lacy green buds on the trees, and the thin brown maple leaves turning to earth in the fallow garden.

Sophia inhales quickly. I know there is something she wants me to see.

The mother fox and her kits are back. They step out again from beneath the shed by the woodpile, this time more cautious. They jog up the hill to the garden, where the mother fox sits back down in her patch of sunlight, her red coat gleaming. She knows we are here. She can see us slow and then stop our rocking chairs, and she can smell what makes us human. All our imperfections. Our quivering, clumsy, uncertain breath, filtered through cloth masks. We stumble, we stammer, we blather like fools. She turns her head and looks at us. Her eyes are bright and almost apologetic. *I am so sorry you are human.* The kits look at us, too, their eyes gleaming like coal. They are still for a moment. We are all still. Looking at one another and wondering. Me and Sophia on the porch. The foxes in the fallow garden. The sun shining down. A moment of recognition. A wonderful, glorious moment full of the possibility that perhaps there really is room on this earth for something as imperfect and uncertain and almost beautiful as a human being like me, Claude Bergman, precious as springtime and perfect as a breath of fresh air.

A NOTE FROM MARCELLA PIXLEY

* * * * * * * * * * * * * * * *

Although I have lived with obsessive-compulsive disorder for as long as I can remember, it was not until I turned fifty and published Trowbridge Road *that I ever admitted in public that OCD is a challenging, exhausting, and often very frightening part of my life. My obsessions have always been internal, linked to the fear of death, illness, and catastrophe, so Claude's worries in "Almost Beautiful," set early in the pandemic, mirror my own experience closely. Like Claude, I practice strategies that help me tolerate my fears during this challenging time, including therapy, journaling, getting outdoors as much as possible, and most important, reaching out to people I love rather than holding my fears inside. Like Claude, I have learned that even when we are in crisis, there is enough beauty in this imperfect world to give us light and strength. Please don't wait as long as I did to tell people when you are not okay. Despite our own imperfections (or maybe because of them), human beings really are brave, creative, and beautiful. I am here for any reader who needs to be reminded that they are not alone.*

THE CALL: A ONE-ACT PLAY

FRANCISCO X. STORK

Content Note: This story references depression and suicidal ideation.

On the stage are two separate rooms divided by a shared wall. One room is dark. There is a night-light by the bed and light coming through a window. In the room we see a single bed with someone sleeping, a night table with a digital clock and a lamp, a desk with an open laptop, a bookcase, and an easy chair with a teddy bear. On top of the desk is a bulletin board overflowing with pictures and announcements. Behind the bed is a print of a ballet performance at Lincoln Center with a ballerina suspended in midflight.

The other room is brightly lit and bare. There is no furniture, no paintings on the walls, no windows. A young woman in sweatpants and a hoodie sits on the floor cross-legged, staring at the cell phone in her hand as if deciding whether to make a call. Next to her is a bottle of tequila, almost full, and a plastic vial for prescription medication. The young woman puts the phone on the floor and lies down. A few moments later, she sits up, picks up the phone, and taps a number. A cell phone rings on the night table in the other room. A hand reaches out from under the covers, fumbles with the phone. A young woman about the same age as the caller sits up in bed and turns on the lamp next to her.

ELLIE: Hello?

LIZA: Hi. You probably don't remember me. It's Liza.

ELLIE: Liza? I think you have the wrong—

LIZA: Isabel Salgado. That's my full name. I was in your English lit class two years ago. With Mrs. Welch.

ELLIE: I know Mrs. Welch but . . .

LIZA: I sat in the very back until Mrs. Welch made us make a circle with our desks. Remember? So we could be each other's teachers.

ELLIE: What time is it?

LIZA: You have no idea how I hated that circle.

ELLIE: *[Looks at the digital clock on the bedside table and sighs.]* It's four thirty a.m. I don't understand . . .

LIZA: One day after we made the circle, I ended up sitting next to you. Mrs. Welch made everyone exchange phone numbers with the person next to us so we could discuss the book we were reading.

ELLIE: I'm sorry. I don't . . .

LIZA: *Franny and Zooey* by J. D. Salinger. That was the book we were supposed to discuss.

ELLIE: *[Long pause.]* Oh. Yeah. *Franny and Zooey.* You're the girl who never called.

LIZA: That's me.

ELLIE: *[Rubbing her eyes.]* And when I called you, you didn't answer.

LIZA: I know.

ELLIE: I ended up having to discuss the book with Bobby Vertolino.

LIZA: Bobby Vertolino. Big eyelashes. Itty-bitty brain.

ELLIE: *[Starts to laugh and then stops herself.]* Why are you calling me?

LIZA: *[Speaks haltingly, as if out of breath.]* I still remember something you said in class. We were having this discussion . . . about James Joyce's *Portrait of the Artist as a Young Man.* Whether James Joyce's style was original. *[Pause.]* You said that originality did not consist of doing something new or different . . . that originality was more of a shedding. James Joyce simply divested himself of stuff that was not him. I remember being kind of shocked when you said that. I didn't see that kind of answer coming from you.

ELLIE: I said that? *[Sits up in bed, silently exhales, all hope of returning to sleep gone.]*

LIZA: I had you pegged as shallow. You were pretty, popular, into gathering likes. But that answer . . . I was wrong. You were smart, thoughtful. Dissonant.

ELLIE: Dissonant?

LIZA: Someone who doesn't fit in with the group.

ELLIE: *[Silent, reflecting.]* What happened to you? Where did you go? I never saw you again.

LIZA: *[Inhales and exhales deeply.]* I took a very long break from school . . . and things.

ELLIE: Are you drunk, stoned? You sound . . .

LIZA: No. I had a couple of swallows of tequila, but my thoughts are solid and clear tonight . . . like pebbles in a stream.

ELLIE: *[Gets out of bed and walks over to the window.]* It's snowing. It's May and it's snowing. *[Sits on the floor, facing the audience, her back to the bed.]* I have a physics test tomorrow morning . . . later this morning. *[There is no resentment in Ellie's voice. She is merely pointing something out to herself.]*

LIZA: I'm sorry. I scrolled through all my contacts. I must have two hundred names in there. I stared at some of them and had no clue who they were. None. Others, so many others, just wouldn't do. When I came to your name . . . it was like . . . I remembered you from Mrs. Welch's class. I knew it would be all right to call you. Isn't that weird? To have that kind of certainty about a person you know only by something they said in a silly class two years ago?

ELLIE: *[Places the cell phone on her forehead. Lowers her head, thinking.]*

LIZA: *[Stands up, paces.]* Physics. I was right, you are smart. College? You must be going to college in the fall?

ELLIE: *[Serious.]* You didn't just call me to chitchat.

LIZA: No, no. That's true. There are others I could have called for that.

ELLIE: Go on, then.

LIZA: *[Faces a wall so that her back is to the audience. She touches the wall with her palm as she speaks.]* I don't know. I don't know how to say it. I don't have the words for it. All I know is that I had a feeling you would understand what I don't know how to say. I know that sounds so cheesy . . . *[Strikes the wall a few times gently with her closed fist.]*

ELLIE: *[Stares at the cell phone, considering. One small movement of her thumb and she could end this call.]*

LIZA: *[Turns to the audience.]* It's okay. You can hang up on me. I know I'm heavy. My words are heavy. I've seen people deflate before my eyes when I talk to them. Whatever is holding them up shrivels when I speak.

ELLIE: What is it that I would understand?

LIZA: *[Sits on the floor again. Wipes her eyes.]* What?

ELLIE: Try to explain it.

LIZA: It's hard. Words sound so phony . . . like I'm reading from a script. Without the right understanding, without the right perspective, what I say could sound like I'm an ungrateful and spoiled brat, like I can't see anything that is good in this world. And that's not correct, there's a lot that's good. Don't get me wrong. *[Wipes her runny nose on the sleeve of her hoodie.]* I know there is. I'm just not able to see it sometimes. And even worse, what I say may sound as if I'm asking for sympathy, which is not it, not it at all. That would be the worst thing you could think I'm doing here.

ELLIE: *[Gets up, sits on the desk chair, and runs her hand over her hair.]*

LIZA: *[Stands again, paces from side to side.]*

ELLIE: Maybe we should chitchat a little.

LIZA: *[Wipes her cheek with her wrist.]* Okay, but I'm not very good at it.

ELLIE: That's something that I'm good at. I need to be if I'm into gathering likes.

LIZA: I didn't mean . . .

ELLIE: But it's true. About ninety percent of what I do is so that people will like me. Except this call, by the way. If I stay on the phone, it's not because I want you to like me.

LIZA: I promise. I promise I won't like you.

ELLIE: Good.

LIZA: Good.

ELLIE: So . . . chitchat. Let me see. Oh, I just remembered something about Mrs. Welch's class.

LIZA: Yes?

ELLIE: Yeah. When the class met again and I told Mrs. Welch we had not connected, she paired me with Bobby Vertolino, who had been absent the day of the assignment. Anyway, I agreed to meet him after school in the library. He hadn't read the book, of course, and when I told him that the story was about a young woman who had a mental and emotional meltdown, he began to tell me about how quote, unquote, "irrational" his girlfriend got during her period.

LIZA: Sounds like Bobby.

ELLIE: You know, I think I silently cussed you out at that moment. I didn't know anything about you, but whoever you were, you left me stranded with Bobby Vertolino.

LIZA: You did? You thought of me?

ELLIE: Not in a nice way. Do you like Franny? As a character I mean.

LIZA: *[Long pause.]* Franny was . . . I understand Franny.

ELLIE: I really like Franny. And I like her brother Zooey. Did you like Zooey?

LIZA: Yes. You're right when you say that Franny's meltdown was mental and emotional. It was mental because her mind wasn't working the way it should, but it was emotional because she felt alone . . . dissonant. Do you know what that's like? That kind of meltdown?

ELLIE: *[Thinking.]* Not really. Not the kind where all you can do is repeat a prayer.

LIZA: *[Places her hand on top of her head and shuts her eyes.]* It's like my mind's eating itself. Unstoppable, ugly, slimy thoughts devouring anything inside me that is good or hopeful. Eventually all I have left is the unbreathable smell of self-disgust.

ELLIE: *[Stands. Walks around the room in silence. Finally, she stops in front of the bookcase and begins to look through the shelves.]* I think I have the book somewhere around here. I remember underlining the heck out of that book. But there was something that Franny said that made me put three stars next to it.

LIZA: I do that, too—put three stars.

ELLIE: I used a purple marker, and when the ink dried, I couldn't read some of the words. I can't find it. Miriam must still have it.

LIZA: Miriam?

ELLIE: My little sister. She's a sophomore now, taking Mrs. Welch's class, no less. Anyway, I think the line that I underlined and triple-starred is when Franny says something like: I'm sick of everyone that wants to be interesting and go places. Everyone that wants to be somebody.

LIZA: I liked that, too. My favorite one is when she tells Zooey that she's sick of not having the courage to be an absolute nobody.

ELLIE: Hmm. That reminds me of something Miriam wrote in a paper for Mrs. Welch. She got an A-plus, which is probably the first A-plus Mrs. Welch ever gave out. Miriam is too modest to show her work to anyone, even me, but I read it one day when I went into her room looking for printer paper.

LIZA: *[With a shaky voice.]* Can you share with me what Miriam said in her paper? I won't tell anyone else.

ELLIE: Knowing Miriam, I don't think she would mind at all if I shared it with you. You know how Zooey tells Franny that it's okay to want to be somebody? In fact, it's not only okay, it's her duty?

LIZA: *[Silence.]*

ELLIE: Miriam said that inside us there was a Franny who wants to be nobody and a Zooey who wants to be somebody.

LIZA: And the meltdown is when Franny wins?

ELLIE: Or when Zooey wins. Miriam thinks we need Franny and Zooey to be in harmony.

LIZA: *[Laughs softly.]* I think your sister might be onto something.

ELLIE: Right? She should be a college professor or a brilliant writer. Instead she wants to go to nursing school like me.

LIZA: *[Exhales and straightens her back as if a weight has been removed from her shoulders.]* You're going to nursing school?

ELLIE: That's the idea. Assuming I pass the physics exam I'm going to take in approximately four hours.

LIZA: Oh, no. I feel so bad.

ELLIE: *[Walks over to the bed, arranges the pillows, and sits with the pillows behind her.]* Nah, don't feel bad. Mr. Deeves has never flunked anyone who halfway tries. *[Takes a deep breath.]* You should have called me back then. Why didn't you?

LIZA: Oh, I don't know. That was the beginning of a long slide. I had a feeling that . . . Please don't take this the wrong way, but I had a feeling that maybe if we met and talked about the book, we might end up becoming friends. I was afraid of us being friends.

ELLIE: And that's a bad thing because . . . ?

LIZA: No, no, that would have been a good thing.

ELLIE: Okay. Wait. I don't get it.

LIZA: You are healthy, Ellie. Your mind is healthy. Your Franny and Zooey are pals. But when you're sliding like I was, a good thing can be terrifying. I know that's hard for a healthy mind to understand.

ELLIE: No, I think I understand. But . . . you called me today.

LIZA: Not because I want us to be friends.

ELLIE: Are you still sliding?

LIZA: *[Lies down on the floor.]* I stopped sliding. No more sliding. I dropped out of school. Then came drugs, abusive relationships, the dragging of my family through hell, psychiatrists, hospitalizations, therapies, total isolation, and then finally I arrived at the place of no return. That's where I am now—the place of no return.

ELLIE: *[Rubs her temples. Looks up at the ceiling. What can she possibly say?]* What's that place like?

LIZA: Oh, gosh. How can I describe it? Well, the hungry monsters in my head are finally fully fed and satisfied. They've devoured everything. But . . .

ELLIE: But . . .

LIZA: It's different now—it's like I went on a journey with others to a distant star, and the star turned out to be made of ice, extremely cold and dark, and we landed, and I went off exploring by myself, and when it was time to get back to the spaceship, I discovered they left without me. Either they forgot about me or they didn't want me with them.

ELLIE: *[After a few moments of reflection.]* I've never been to the place of no return, but it seems to me you're not there yet, not entirely, if you called me. There is that mysterious something you want me to understand or something else you want to hear from me.

LIZA: No, no. I don't want anything from you. I no longer want anything from anybody. If you had hung up on me, I would have been okay.

ELLIE: You would have known for sure that the world and everyone in it sucks. Is that what you want? Confirmation that it all sucks?

LIZA: *[Sitting up.]* The world and people are not bad. Not completely. I'm deflating you now, I can tell.

ELLIE: Stop it! You're not *deflating* me. I'm not some basketball full of hot air. Believe it or not, it's interesting . . . talking to you. In a strange, serious way. But I'm the kind of person who likes to figure out the reason for things, and I'm having trouble figuring out what you need right now, what I should say to you.

LIZA: You're right. You're right. It's not as if I just wanted to hear any voice. I'm fooling myself thinking I don't want anything from this call.

ELLIE: Yes! There you go. Now at least you're being honest.

LIZA: I'm *trying* very hard to be honest.

ELLIE: If you want something from another person, if you're still looking for something, then you're not in the place of no return.

LIZA: What if instead of wanting something for myself, I called to give *you* something? I can be in the place of no return and still give, no?

ELLIE: *[Long pause.]* But don't you see that wanting to give is the same as wanting to live? There's a Zooey inside you that still wants you to be somebody. Somebody who gives. *[Remembering.]* What exactly did you want to give me?

LIZA: *[Sighs.]* I wish I had called you two years ago.

ELLIE: Forget two years ago. You called today. *[Looks out the window.]* The sun's coming out. What will you do now?

LIZA: Now? *[Picks up the plastic vial of pills, looks at it, puts it down.]* I'm tired. I wasn't expecting my brain to work so hard. I wasn't expecting it to work at all. You and your *figuring things out* got my weird brain totally exhausted. I'm sleepy all of a sudden.

ELLIE: Yeah?

LIZA: You know, some things can't be figured out.

ELLIE: I don't believe that. And I still don't know what you wanted to give me.

LIZA: *[Starts to say something and then stops, speaks with kindness in her voice.]* You'll have to figure it out.

ELLIE: *[Laughs.]* Hey, Mr. Deeves grades exams the same day. I'll call you tonight and let you know how I did. If I get anything below a C, I will not be my pleasant self. Fair warning.

LIZA: You'll call me?

ELLIE: Yeah, and you better pick up this time.

LIZA: *[Silence.]*

ELLIE: Tell me you're going to answer my call. I want to hear you say it.

LIZA: *[Softly yet firm.]* I'll answer.

ELLIE: Good. Now get some sleep. Rest that weird brain of yours.

LIZA: Okay.

ELLIE: See you.

Ellie and Liza lie down on their sides, facing each other. Ellie on her bed and Liza on the floor. They close their eyes at the same time.

A NOTE FROM FRANCISCO X. STORK

✶ ✶ ✶ ✶ ✶ ✶ ✶ ✶ ✶ ✶ ✶ ✶ ✶ ✶ ✶ ✶

My first experience with the illness we call depression came when I was fourteen, a year after my adoptive father died instantaneously in an automobile accident. I didn't call what I was going through depression. I don't think I had even heard of the word back then. What I felt was an extreme loneliness created by external circumstances but also self-inflicted. The thought of telling someone what I was feeling did not occur to me. Who was there who could possibly understand?

One of the reasons I write books and short stories about mental health struggles is that a book can break open the impenetrable isolation of mental health struggles. A book can bring to us the presence of another heart, of another being who understands what we are thinking and feeling. I hope that the stories in this anthology can give hope to someone who feels that there is no one out there who cares. There is always someone who cares. At the same time, I hope this book encourages us to respond to the call for love, when it comes.

ABOUT THE CONTRIBUTORS

* * * * * * * * * * * * * * *

Mercedes Ángel Acosta (he/him and she/her) is a mixed Cuban comic artist, storyteller, and street medic. Rumors that he can walk up walls are unconfirmed. His debut graphic novel, *Cabaret Macabre*, is coming out in 2025.

Karen Jialu Bao (she/her) does science in the lab, then goes home and writes about it. A PhD candidate at Harvard University, she studies mosquito brains by blasting them with an electron beam. She has eight ear piercings for no reason. Her favorite activities include cooking, tending her plants, singing, and playing her violin. She is the author of the sci-fi novels *Pangu's Shadow*, *Dove Arising*, *Dove Exiled*, and *Dove Alight* and is a writer for the Realm series *Renegade Moon*.

James Bird (he/him) is an award-winning Native American (Ojibwe) author and filmmaker. His films include *From Above*, *Eat Spirit Eat*, *Honeyglue*, *We Are Boats*, and *WifeLike*. His middle-grade books are *The Brave*, *The Second Chance of Benjamin Waterfalls*, and *No Place Like Home*. When he's not writing books or directing films, he is rescuing animals and playing with his greatest creation of all, his son, Wolf. He lives on the North Shore of Massachusetts.

Rocky Callen (she/her), daughter of an Ecuadorian immigrant, is a former behavioral coach and the author of the young adult novel *A Breath Too Late*, which was named a *Kirkus Reviews* Best Young Adult Book of the Year and a Chicago Public Library Best of the Best selection of 2020. It was also featured on the Mujerista's list of Ten Best YA Books by Latinx Authors in 2020. The novel grapples with suicide, depression, and domestic violence and was inspired by her own experiences. Rocky Callen founded the HoldOn2Hope Project, an initiative that unites creatives in suicide prevention and mental health awareness.

Nora Shalaway Carpenter (she/her) is the author of *The Edge of Anything* (named a Bank Street College Best Children's Book of the Year, a *Kirkus Reviews* Best Young Adult Book of 2020, A Mighty Girl Book of the Year, a Discover Great Places Through Reading selection, and a Cybils Award finalist). She edited and contributed to *Rural Voices: 15 Authors Challenge Assumptions About Small-Town America* (an NPR Best Book of the Year, a YALSA Best Fiction for Young Adults nominee, winner of two Nautilus Book Awards, a Junior Library Guild selection, and a *Country Living* Front Porch Book Club selection). Her next novel, *Fault Lines*, is forthcoming in 2023.

Alechia Dow (she/her) is a former pastry chef, librarian, and author of *The Sound of Stars, The Kindred, Just a Pinch of Magic*, and more. When she's not writing, you can find her having epic dance parties with her daughter, baking, reading, or traveling.

Patrick Downes (he/him) has written three novels for young adults, and he's at work on a fourth. He's also written a picture book. Patrick Downes is finishing up a degree at divinity school and exploring hospital chaplaincy.

Anna Drury (she/her) is an all-around book geek. She believes that stories—written, oral, visual, musical, and more—are what make us human. When she's not bookishly involved with reading and writing or working as a high school librarian, Anna Drury enjoys traveling, listening to all kinds of music, cooking for friends and family, hexing the patriarchy, celebrating Jewish joy, and defending the Oxford comma. She holds an MFA in writing for children and young adults from Vermont College of Fine Arts, as well as an MEd in library media studies from Salem State University. She lives in central Massachusetts.

Nikki Grimes (she/her) is a *New York Times* best-selling author and the recipient of a Coretta Scott King–Virginia Hamilton Award for Lifetime Achievement, an ALAN Award for Outstanding Contributions to Young Adult Literature, a Children's Literature Legacy Award, a Virginia Hamilton Literary Award, and a National Council of Teachers of English Award for Excellence in Poetry for Children. She is the author of the Coretta Scott King Author Award winner *Bronx Masquerade*; the YALSA Best Fiction for Young Adults title *Between the Lines*; the National Council of Teachers of English Notable Children's Book in the Language Arts *Words with Wings*; the Lee Bennett Hopkins Poetry Award Honor book *Garvey's Choice*; the *Boston Globe–Horn Book* Honor title *One Last Word*; the Michael L. Printz Honor and Robert F. Sibert Honor memoir in verse *Ordinary Hazards*; *Legacy: Women Poets of the Harlem Renaissance*; the American Library Association Notable Children's Book *Southwest Sunrise*; the *Kirkus Reviews* Best Picture Book of the Year *Bedtime for Sweet Creatures*; and the NAACP Image Award nominee *Kamala Harris: Rooted in Justice*. Nikki Grimes lives in Corona, California.

Val Howlett (she/they) is a folktale lover, curious researcher, and plant enthusiast. A recipient of the Katherine Paterson Prize for Literature for Young Adults and Children, Val Howlett has published fiction in *Lunch Ticket* and *Hunger Mountain*.

Jonathan Lenore Kastin (he/they) is a queer, trans poet with an MFA in writing for children and young adults from Vermont

College of Fine Arts. His poems can be found in *Mythic Delirium*, *Goblin Fruit*, *Liminality*, and *Abyss & Apex*. His other short stories can be found in *Cosmic Roots and Eldritch Shores*, as well as a forthcoming issue of *On Spec* and the forthcoming anthology *Transmogrify!* He lives with two mischievous cats, more books than he could ever read, and a frightening number of skulls. He is trying to write a novel. Pray for him.

Sonia Patel (she/her) is a first-generation Indian American born in New York and raised in Hawai'i. Her experience was lushly and brilliantly explored in her debut novel, *Rani Patel in Full Effect*, which was a finalist for the William C. Morris Debut Award, received four starred reviews, and was a YALSA Best Fiction for Young Adults selection and a *Kirkus Reviews* Best Teen Book of 2016. Her subsequent YA novels, *Jaya and Rasa: A Love Story* and *Bloody Seoul*, both received Library Services for Youth in Custody In the Margins Book Awards. Her fourth YA novel, *Gita Desai Is Not Here to Shut Up*, is forthcoming in 2023. She was a jury member for the renowned NSK Neustadt Prize for Children's Literature in 2021. As a child and adolescent psychiatrist trained at Stanford University and the University of Hawai'i, Patel has spent more than twenty years providing psychotherapy to young people and their families. She lives in Honolulu with her husband, teen, and dog, and misses her older teen, who's attending college on the mainland.

Marcella Pixley (she/her) is the author of four acclaimed books for children. Her most recent novel, *Trowbridge Road*, was a National Book Award Long List selection, a Junior Library Guild selection, a Bank Street College Best Children's Book of 2021, and a best book of 2020 by *Shelf Awareness*, Amazon, *Reading Group Choices*, and A Mighty Girl. It was also a finalist for the Massachusetts Book Award, the Vermont Golden Dome Book Award, and the Julia Ward Howe Young Readers Award. All of Marcella Pixley's novels, including *Ready to Fall, Without Tess*,

and *Freak*, explore mental health and the dynamics of complicated families. She teaches eighth-grade language arts in Massachusetts, where she lives with her husband, her two sons, and
a huge, ridiculous, shaggy dog named Mango.

Isabel Quintero (she/her) is an award-winning writer and the
daughter of Mexican immigrants. She proudly lives and writes
in the Inland Empire of Southern California. She is the author
of *Gabi, A Girl in Pieces*, the chapter books *Ugly Cat & Pablo* and
Ugly Cat & Pablo and the Missing Brother, the graphic novel
Photographic: The Life of Graciela Iturbide, and *My Papi Has a
Motorcycle*. Her books have garnered many starred reviews and
have appeared on NPR's yearly Book Concierge list, the New
York Public Library's best-of list, and the *New York Times* Best
Books list. When she's not writing, she enjoys hiking, laughing,
and cooking with her partner and beautiful child.

Ebony Stewart (she/her), also known as the Gully Princess, is
an award-winning, top-touring international poet, spoken-word
artist, writer, performer, and observer of the life she's living. She
has a bachelor's in English and communication studies and a
master's in clinical social work; she hopes to one day provide
affordable therapy to artists. She also aims to validate the human
experience and provide a layered perspective of mental wellness through poetry, storytelling, and reflection. Ebony Stewart's
work has been studied at secondary schools and institutions of
higher education. Ebony Stewart also developed a curriculum
based on her poetry collection *Home.Girl.Hood.* Her work has
been featured in *AfroPunk*, Button Poetry, For Harriet, the *Texas
Observer*, Write About Now, and more. For more information,
visit EbPoetry.com.

Francisco X. Stork (he/him) emigrated from Mexico at the age
of nine with his mother and his adoptive father. He is the author
of nine novels, including *Marcelo in the Real World*, winner of

a Schneider Family Book Award; *The Last Summer of the Death Warriors,* which received the Amelia Elizabeth Walden Award; *The Memory of Light,* recipient of the Tomás Rivera Award; *Disappeared,* a Texas Institute of Letters Best Young Adult Book and a Walter Dean Myers Award Honor Book; and *Illegal,* a Library Services for Youth in Custody In the Margins Book Award winner, a Texas Institute of Letters Best Young Adult Book, and an International Latino Book Award winner. His recent novel *On the Hook* received the 2022 International Latino Book Award for Best Young Adult Latino Focused Book.

RESOURCES

* * * * * * *

IF YOU ARE IN CRISIS

Crisis Text Line
Free 24/7 mental health support via text message
Text HOME to 741741
www.crisistextline.org

NAMI (National Alliance on Mental Illness)
1-800-950-NAMI (6264), available Monday through Friday,
10:00 a.m. to 10:00 p.m. ET, or info@nami.org

National Suicide Prevention Lifeline
1-800-273-8255
Note: 988 is the three-digit dialing code that will route callers
to the National Suicide Prevention Lifeline.

FOR LGBTQIA+ YOUTH

The Trevor Project
Text START to 678-678 or visit thetrevorproject.org/get-help

GENERAL RESOURCES

Born This Way Foundation
Cofounded and led by Lady Gaga and her mother, Cynthia

Germanotta, this foundation supports the mental health of young people and works with them to build a kinder and braver world. Through high-impact programming, youth-led conversations, and strategic, cross-sectoral partnerships, the foundation aims to make kindness cool, validate the emotions of young people, and eliminate the stigma surrounding mental health.
https://bornthisway.foundation/
https://bekind.findahelpline.com/

CDC (Centers for Disease Control and Prevention)

The CDC is the nation's leading science-based, data-driven service organization that protects the public's health. For more than seventy years, they've put science into action to help children stay healthy so they can grow and learn; to help families, businesses, and communities fight disease and stay strong; and to protect the public's health.
https://www.cdc.gov/mentalhealth/index.htm

The Mighty

The Mighty is a safe, supportive community for people facing health challenges and the people who care for them.
themighty.com

NAMI (National Alliance on Mental Illness)

NAMI is the nation's largest grassroots mental health organization dedicated to building better lives for the millions of Americans affected by mental illness. It started as a small group of families in 1979 and has blossomed into the nation's leading voice on mental health. Today NAMI is an alliance of more than six hundred local affiliates and forty-eight state organizations that work to raise awareness and provide support and education that was not previously available to those in need.
https://nami.org

Finding Help

www.nami.org/Your-Journey/Kids-Teens-and-Young-Adults/Teens/Finding-Help

HelpLine

The NAMI HelpLine is a free, nationwide peer-support service that provides information, resource referrals, and support to people living with mental health conditions, their family members and caregivers, mental health providers, and the public. HelpLine staff and volunteers are experienced, well trained, and able to provide guidance.
1-800-950-NAMI (6264), available Monday through Friday, 10:00 a.m. to 10:00 p.m. ET, or info@nami.org
www.nami.org/help

How to Talk to Your Friends
www.nami.org/Your-Journey/Kids-Teens-and-Young-Adults/Teens/How-to-Talk-to-My-Friends

How to Talk to Your Parents or Guardian
www.nami.org/Your-Journey/Kids-Teens-and-Young-Adults/Teens/How-to-Talk-to-My-Parents-or-Guardian

Social Media and Mental Health
www.nami.org/Your-Journey/Kids-Teens-and-Young-Adults/Teens/Social-Media-and-Mental-Health

Support Groups
www.nami.org/Support-Education/Support-Groups

Video Resource Section
www.nami.org/Support-Education/Video-Resource-Library

Your Mental Health and School
www.nami.org/Your-Journey/Kids-Teens-and-Young-Adults/Teens/Your-Mental-Health-and-School-en

SAMHSA (Substance Abuse and Mental Health Services Administration)

SAMHSA's National Helpline is a free, confidential, 24/7 treatment referral and information service (in English and Spanish)

for individuals and families facing mental and/or substance use disorders.
www.samhsa.gov/find-help/national-helpline

UT Austin Boot Camp: Digital Resources for Mental Health at All Ages

With approximately 4.7 billion internet users across the globe, more people than ever have direct access to digitally available mental health resources. This page includes a comprehensive, age-segmented overview of some of these resources focusing on various aspects of mental health, including a variety of top-rated apps selected for their effectiveness and popularity.
https://techbootcamps.utexas.edu/blog/digital-resources -for-mental-health-at-all-ages/

WHO (World Health Organization)

Founded in 1948, the WHO is the United Nations agency that connects nations, partners, and people to promote health, keep the world safe, and serve the vulnerable—so everyone everywhere can attain the highest level of health.
www.who.int/news-room/feature-stories/mental-well-being -resources-for-the-public

FOR THE LGBTQIA+ COMMUNITY

The Trevor Project

The Trevor Project is the world's largest suicide prevention and crisis intervention organization for lesbian, gay, bisexual, transgender, queer, and questioning young people.
www.thetrevorproject.org/resources/category/mental-health/

FOR THE BIPOC COMMUNITY

Live Another Day

Live Another Day was created as a response to the unprecedented increase in substance abuse, mental illness, and deaths

resulting from the COVID-19 pandemic. Per the organization's website, "People of color have long been left out of the conversation on mental health. We've compiled culturally competent resources that address the specific needs and available means of support to help ensure no one is left out."
https://liveanotherday.org/bipoc/

The Summit Wellness Group
This Georgia-based rehab center has curated a list of the top resources that support the mental health of the BIPOC community.
https://thesummitwellnessgroup.com/resources/bipoc-resources/

HOW TO FIND LOCAL ORGANIZATIONS WITH MENTAL HEALTH EXPERTISE

MentalHealth.gov
This database includes organizations that can help coordinate community events, locate speakers who have expertise in mental health, offer peer and family support, and provide general information on mental health as well as treatment and available services for mental health issues.
www.mentalhealth.gov/talk/community-conversation/services

HOW TO TALK WITH A FRIEND ABOUT MENTAL HEALTH

Seize the Awkward
Having a conversation about mental health might be uncomfortable, but it can make all the difference. Check out Seize the Awkward for tools—from conversation guides to tips—that can help you help those in need.
https://seizetheawkward.org/

ADHD

alie ward
Science journalist Alie Ward interviews scientists and health experts on her podcast *Ologies*. She discusses ADHD with Dr. Russell Barkley in the episode "Part 1: Attention-Deficit Neuropsychology (ADHD) with Russell Barkley."
www.alieward.com/ologies/adhd

ADDitude *magazine*
"How ADHD Ignites Rejection Sensitive Dysphoria"
www.additudemag.com/rejection-sensitive-dysphoria-and-adhd/

YouTube
How to ADHD
Videos offer tips, tricks, and insights into the ADHD brain.
https://youtube.com/c/HowtoADHD/

BIPOLAR DISORDER

Anxiety and Depression Association of America (ADAA)
https://adaa.org/understanding-anxiety/co-occurring
-disorders/bipolar-disorder

DEPRESSION

Anxiety and Depression Association of America (ADAA)
https://adaa.org/understanding-anxiety/depression

Child Mind Institute
childmind.org/topics/depression-mood-disorders/

GRIEF

Modern Loss
modernloss.com

What's Your Grief?
This website promotes grief education, exploration, and expression in both practical and creative ways.
whatsyourgrief.com

OBSESSIVE-COMPULSIVE DISORDER

International OCD Foundation
The mission of this foundation is to help those affected by obsessive-compulsive disorder (OCD) and related disorders to live full and productive lives. Its aim is to increase access to effective treatment through research and training, foster a hopeful and supportive community for those affected by OCD and the professionals who treat them, and fight stigma surrounding mental health issues.
https://iocdf.org

How Do I Get Help for My OCD? (OCD in Kids)
https://kids.iocdf.org/for-kids/how-do-i-get-help/

National Institute of Mental Health
www.nimh.nih.gov/health/topics/obsessive-compulsive
-disorder-ocd

The OCD Stories Podcast
The host of this podcast, Stuart Ralph, interviews some of the best minds in OCD treatment and recovery to share their advice and to both entertain and educate listeners toward a healthier

life. The podcast was created in 2015 and its episodes have been downloaded more than four million times globally. Episode #230 features contributing editor Nora Shalaway Carpenter.
https://theocdstories.com

PMS AND PMDD

MGH Center for Women's Mental Health
The Center for Women's Mental Health at Massachusetts General Hospital provides state-of-the-art evaluation and treatment of psychiatric disorders associated with female reproductive function, including premenstrual dysphoric disorder (PMDD), pregnancy-associated mood disturbance, postpartum psychiatric illness, and peri- and postmenopausal depression. Clinical care is complemented by research ranging from studies of treatments for women who suffer from PMDD, postpartum depression, and depression in menopause to studies for women who suffer from mood disorders during pregnancy.
https://womensmentalhealth.org/resource/patient-support
-services/teen-pms-and-pmdd-guide/

PTSD

Anxiety and Depression Association of America (ADAA)
https://adaa.org/understanding-anxiety/posttraumatic
-stress-disorder-ptsd/resources

National Institute of Mental Health
www.nimh.nih.gov/health/topics/post-traumatic-stress
-disorder-ptsd

SEXUAL ASSAULT

RAINN (Rape, Abuse & Incest National Network)
RAINN is the nation's largest anti-sexual-violence organization.

RAINN created and operates the National Sexual Assault Hotline in partnership with more than a thousand local sexual assault service providers across the country and operates DoD Safe Helpline for the Department of Defense. RAINN also carries out programs to prevent sexual violence, help survivors, and ensure that perpetrators are brought to justice.

1-800-656-HOPE (4673)

www.rainn.org (English)

rainn.org/es (español)

STRESS MANAGEMENT

SuperBetter

This free app gamifies stress management to build resilience, achieve goals, and tackle challenges including anxiety, depression, stress, chronic pain, concussion recovery, and more.

App Store: https://apps.apple.com/us/app/superbetter /id536634968

Google Play: https://play.google.com/store/apps/details?id=com .superbetter.paid&hl=en

SUICIDE PREVENTION AND CRISIS COUNSELING

Crisis Text Line

Crisis Text Line provides free 24/7 mental health support via text message.

Text HOME to 741741

www.crisistextline.org

The Jed Foundation (JED)

The Jed Foundation is a nonprofit that protects emotional health and prevents suicide for teens and young adults, giving them the skills and support they need to thrive.

https://jedfoundation.org/

Live Through This

Established in 2010, Live Through This is a collection of portraits and true stories of suicide attempt survivors across the United States.
https://livethroughthis.org/about/

The National Suicide Prevention Lifeline

The National Suicide Prevention Lifeline is a network of local crisis centers that provide free and confidential emotional support to people in suicidal crisis or emotional distress 24/7 in the United States. The Lifeline is committed to improving crisis services and advancing suicide prevention by empowering individuals, advancing professional best practices, and building awareness.

1-800-273-8255

Note: 988 is the new three-digit dialing code that will route callers to the National Suicide Prevention Lifeline.
https://suicidepreventionlifeline.org

ACKNOWLEDGMENTS

✳ ✳ ✳ ✳ ✳ ✳ ✳

NORA SHALAWAY CARPENTER

Huge thanks to Rocky Callen, coeditor extraordinaire. I'm so very glad you said yes. You have made this massive project as vibrant and affirming as I dreamed it would be. Thank you to Victoria Wells Arms for believing in this project from the moment I mentioned it, and to Kaylan Adair for championing the book passionately and continuing to be such a joy to work with. Big thank you to Matt Roeser for the gorgeous cover, Stephanie Pando for all the promo, and the entire Candlewick team for recognizing the immense need for this book to exist in the world.

Thanks to all the therapists and doctors who devote their lives to mental health advocacy and education. And thank you to the educators and librarians who want to learn more, who are brave enough to acknowledge their students' suffering, and who understand that speaking about mental health may very well be what saves a student's life. I hope this book and its resources help better prepare you for the very real mental health crisis that exists in schools all across the United States.

There have been many people who have helped me on my own journey with mental health, but a few pulled me along when I needed it the most. First, my partner in life, Josh Carpenter. There is a reason every story in this book features a supportive relationship that enables the protagonist to heal and grow. Thank you to my cousin, Matt Leight, and my aunt Dawn Leight. Thanks to my friends Hillary Harris, Monique Buckley, and Joanna Mulligan.

Thank you to Chloe Pearson and my parents, Linda and Scott Shalaway, who took care of my kids so I could finish this project, and to all my neighbors who helped in ways big and small. It truly takes a village.

Thanks to Tirzah Price and Anna Drury for beta reading the first draft of "Spidey Sense." Thank you, contributors, for saying yes and for delivering pieces that exceeded my wildest hopes. Someone will keep going because of you.

ROCKY CALLEN

Thank you, Nora, for bringing me on to coedit this anthology. We came to this project with fierce passion and devotion, and it has been an honor to work alongside you.

Thank you to each phenomenal contributor—you have made this collection extraordinary. Your art and heart shine bright in these stories, and I am awestruck by what you have put onto the page.

Thank you to the champions and advocates of mental health access and education. This is important and necessary work, and you are on the front lines.

Thank you to every person who has paved the way to make this anthology possible. Nora, Victoria, Holly, Kaylan, Stephanie, Matt, and the whole Candlewick team—you are powerhouses, and this book is so lucky to have all of you.

Thank you to the people who have supported and inspired me over the years. Jese, my husband, thank you for seeing me. Martina and Erin, thank you for dreaming with me. George and Lori, thank you for believing in me. Carissa, thank you for holding space for me. And for this book, I also want to send big love to my dear friend Mollie Zwiebel. You are a fighter. An inspiration. You deserve applause and standing ovations. You'll have to settle for mine for now.

Thank you to every reader who picks up this book and shares it. This collection is the heartbeat of my own mission in the world. I hope it finds those who need it the most.